Karen grew up in a small country town in north-eastern Victoria, Australia. She spent her childhood riding horses through beautiful scenery of eucalypts, lakes, and snow-capped mountains and her love of landscape deeply affects her writing. She worked in a range of educational settings and holds a Ph.D. and M.Ed. (Hons) in the areas of fantasy. She is particularly interested in the power of the hero's inner journey which she explores through Deep Fantasy. Karen has travelled extensively overseas but enjoys nothing more than camping in the Australian Outback. She lives in Melbourne and now writes full-time. You can find out more about Karen and her books on her website.

Connect with K. S. Nikakis

Amazon: https://www.amazon.com/author/ksnikakis
Twitter: https://twitter.com/KSNikakis
Facebook: www.facebook.com/ksnikakis
Goodreads: www.goodreads.com
Website: www.ksnikakis.com
Email: author@ksnikakis.com

i

WORKS BY K S NIKAKIS

Non Fiction

Journey: Seeking the Sacred, Spirit and Soul in the
Australian Wilderness

Fantasy Novels
Series

Angel Caste series:
Angel Blood
Angel Breath
Angel Bone
Angel Bound
Angel Blessed
Angel Caste – Complete 5 Book Series

The Kira Chronicles trilogy:*
The Whisper of Leaves
The Song of the Silvercades
The Cry of the Marwing
remnant hard copies only

The Kira Chronicles series:
The Whisper of Leaves
The Silence of Stone
The Secrets of Stars
The Thunder of Hoofs
The Crying of Birds
The Music of Home
The Kira Chronicles – Complete 6 Book Series

Fantasy Novels

The Emerald Serpent
Heart Hunter
The Third Moon
Messenger
I Heard the Wolf Call My Name – *Finalist - Best YA
Novel Aurealis Awards, 2019*

Fantasy Short Stories

The Gift
The Tale of Prince Anura
Dragon Sprite
Glass-Heart – *Finalist – Best YA
Short Story Aurealis Awards, 2019*

THE THUNDER OF HOOFS

K.S. NIKAKIS

First published by SOV CONSULTING LLC - SOV Media Australia 2018
Amazon: www.amazon.com.au

The Thunder of Hoofs Book 4 The Kira Chronicles Series
© copyright by KS Nikakis 2018

Publisher: SOV CONSULTING LLC - SOV Media Melbourne, Australia.

Cover by AS Nikakis: http://asnikakis.com
Shutterstock.com/nutriaaa

National Library of Australia
Cataloguing-in-Publication entry:
Nikakis, Karen Simpson
The Thunder of Hoofs Book 4 The Kira Chronicles Series
ISBN 978-0-6489797-0-8

For my second cousin and birthday twin on the other side of the world: Jessica Pomfret

THE THUNDER OF HOOFS

MAP OF NORTHERN LANDS

The Tremen

Of the Bough – Tremen heart of healing
Maxen (dec) – Kashclan - Tremen Leader
Fasarini (dec) – Sarclan – bondmate of Maxen
Merek (dec) – eldest son of Maxen
Lern (dec) – second eldest son of Maxen
Kiraon (Kira) – Tremen Leader - daughter of Maxen
Kandor (dec) – youngest son of Maxen
Sendra (dec) (helper) – Sarclan

Kashclan – descended from Kasheron
Miken – Clanleader
Tenerini – Barclan – bondmate of Miken
Tresen – son of Miken
Mikini – daughter of Miken
Brem – experienced Healer and Protector
Arlen – learner Healer and Protector
Paterek – learner Healer and Protector
Werem – learner Healer and Protector
Kertash – Protector Leader

Sarclan – descended from Sarkash
Berendash – Clanleader

Tarclan – descended from Taren
Farish – (dec) Clanleader
Kemrick - Clanleader
Sarkash – (dec) Protector Commander

Morclan – descended from Mormesh
Marren – Clanleader
Kest – Protector Commander
Kesilini – sister of Kest
Feseren – (dec) Protector
Misilini – Barclan – bondmate of Feseren
Penedrin – Protector

Renclan – descended from Renen
Sanden – Clanleader
Pekrash – Protector Leader
Sanaken – (dec) Protector

Kenclan – descended from Kentash
Tenedren – Clanleader
Senden – Protector Leader

Barclan – descended from Baren
Ketten – Clanleader

Sherclan – descended from Sheren
Dakresh – Clanleader
Sener – elder son of Dakresh
Bern – (dec) younger son of Dakresh
Bendrash – Protector Leader

Tallien
Caledon e Saridon e Talliel – Placidien
Roshai – sister of Caledon
Pisa – youngest daughter of Roshai
Mechtlin – husband of Roshai

Tain
Beris – King
Adris – Prince, son of Beris

King's Guard
Remas – Guard Leader
Ather – Second Leader
Belzen
Archorn

Troopsmen
Dorchen – Commander
Selvet – Troop Leader
Somer
Tardich
Derz

Physicks
Dumer – Physick General
Aranz – Major Physick
Speri – lesser physick

Gatherer
Jaitich

Terak Kirillian
Rulership
Tierken – Feailner
Laryia – sister of Tierken
Darid (dec) – last Feailner, uncle of Tierken
Merench (dec) father to Tierken and Laryia
Lyess (dec) mother to Tierken and Laryia
Poerin – military trainer of Tierken

Marken

Rosham – father of Farid

Milsin

Borsten

Gelf

Domain

Farid – Keeper of the Domain

Ryn – Horse Master

Mouras – Room Master

Niria – server, wife to Marin

Domain Guard

Tharin – Guard Leader

Daril – Guard Second

Patrolmen

Marin – Patrol Commander

Jonred – Patrol Leader

Slivkash

Anvorn

Nordrin

Arnil

Barid

Ralin

Sarim

Serden

Derkash

Ayled

Shird

Vardrin

Jarvid

Wirinkash
Farian
Kanil

Kessomi
Eris – Darid and Merench's mother; grandmother to Tierken and Laryia
Thalli – childhood friend of Laryia
Leos – husband of Thalli
Jafiel – brother of Leos
Kira – baby daughter of Thalli
Robrin – stable master

The Shargh
Cashgar

Erboran – (dec) Chief
Arkendrin – younger brother of Erboran
Ergardrin (dec) – father of Erboran and Arkendrin
Tarkenda – join-wife of Ergardrin - mother of Erboran and Arkendrin
Palansa – join-wife of Erboran – Chief-wife – guardian of next Chief
Ersalan – baby son of Erboran and Palansa – next Chief

Loyal to Erboran
Erdosin
Irsulalin
Ormadon
Erlken – Ormadon's son
Irmakin
and their blood-ties

Loyal to Arkendrin
Irason
Ermashin
Urpalin
Orthaken
Irdodun
Urgundin (dec)
and their blood-ties

Weshargh
Orbdargan – Chief
Orfedren

Soushargh
Yrshin – Chief

Ashmiri
Uthlin - Chief

Founders of the Four Shargh Peoples
The Cashgar Shargh – Artmenton
The Soushargh – Urchelen
The Weshargh – Irkardin
The Ashmiri - Ashmiridin

The Thunder of Hoofs

Thus spoke the Last of the Shargh Tellers:

If Healer sees a setting sun
and gold meets gold, two halves are one,
then Westerner with silver tongue
will love and lose the golden one,
but bind a friendship slow begun.
If horses graze in forests deep
where trees their summer greening keep
then fire will be the flatswords' bane
and bring the dead to life again.
Deeds long past will hunt the Shargh
and funeral smoke consume the stars
until the thing that draws no breath,
devours the dark that feeds on death.

1

Tierken grimaced as Kira disappeared over the ridgeline but he held Kalos steady. His men had witnessed the *gold-eyed woman* hurl insults at him before striding off and waited to see how the *Feailner* would react. 'I'll join you at Cover-cape Crest with our *guest*,' he said to Marin, ensuring his words carried to the patrol.

'It would be wise not to delay too long, Feailner. The Kirs say the Sarsalin will gift us storms before the day's out.'

Tierken glanced up at the clear sky and nodded. The Kirs were known for their weather-wisdom, and the Sarsalin for its sudden and dramatic changes of mood. He nodded to Marin and turned Kalos south again. Kira had reached the third ridge but he made no effort to shorten the distance between them, just followed several lengths behind. She refused to acknowledge his presence, and it was not until the fifth ridge that she finally swung around to face him.

Her color was high from the speed of her travel and her hair glinted like spun gold in the new sun, but it was her eyes that held him. They pulsed between gold and green which told him she was both angry *and* fearful.

'Why do you follow me south?' she demanded. 'Your stinking stone city's many days to the north.'

He dismounted but did not approach. He was taking her to Sarnia, but he did not want it to be as a prisoner, despite the accusation she had flung at him earlier. 'Five days by horse, to be precise,' he said evenly, 'but at least eight on foot. Whereas Maraschin's two days by horse and almost four on foot. But you're not from Maraschin are you? How far is it to your lands, Kira?'

'By horse or foot?' she asked sarcastically.

'You are on foot.'

'From Maraschin it's fourteen to the edge of the forests, and another four to my kin.'

'Eighteen days. That is a long way when you barely have any food.'

'I'll get some in Maraschin,' she snapped.

'Which is almost four days away on foot,' he replied calmly. Kira said nothing. 'You haven't had any breakfast either and neither have I. We can eat here, it's a pleasant enough place.' He slipped off his pack pulled out his patrol kit. 'Maizen bread, cheese and russetnuts,' he said. He settled on a stone near her, relieved she did not stride off. 'I know you eat maizen bread and russetnuts, but do you eat cheese?' he asked conversationally.

'No.'

He smiled. 'Is that prasach too?'

She winced and looked away. 'We keep no animals, so it's not eaten.'

Something had distressed her but had no idea what, nor time to find out, not with the Sarsalin's weather. He broke the small loaf and set half on the stone for her then glanced around the ridge. 'I can see why you wanted to gather,' he said. 'Icemint, annin, bluemint and bruise-ease.'

'You know of herbs?'

She had taken the bread and her eyes had softened, telling him her anger and fear had ebbed. 'My grandmother Eris is a Healer in Kessom. We'll visit her after we reach Sarnia *if* you wish. I know Healers like to exchange their knowing.'

'They do,' she said. 'Slivkash told me Kessom is in the Silvercades.'

'Yes. A day's ride from Sarnia.' He wanted to stretch the time away from the gaze of his men, to keep her eyes free from fear, but the air had freshened. 'The wind's changed,' he said briskly, and packed away the food. Then he mounted Kalos. 'Come,' he said, and offered his hand but she did not move.

'No one travels the Sarsalin alone, Kira. If you were a Kir herder, or an Illian, or a Terak, or even an Ashmiri, I'd take you with me. There are fanchon and wolves, and storms that kill, even in summer, and you've only seen the pleasant face of the plain so far. There's also the matter of *obligation*.

'When Marin took you from the Shargh, you came under Terak Kirillian protection. I'm *bound* to take you to a place of safety. You can come willingly, or unwillingly, but you *will* come.'

Kira considered her options. The Terak Feailner switched from bullying to charming back to bullying with ease, but everything about his hard gaze, and the way he held his massive horse barely in check, confirmed her only choice was whether she *took* his proffered hand, or was *seized* by it. And whatever her feelings about him, her task remained to reach the Northern king and gain aid for the Tremen.

She placed her hand in his and he pulled her up behind him but she had barely settled before they galloped at full tilt down the ridge. She clamped her eyes shut, fearing the horse would crash and fling them to their deaths, but it reached the bottom safely, and its powerful haunches drove it up the next ridge. They sped down the other side again, terrifyingly fast and she wondered whether the Feailner punished her for the trouble she caused him.

The rest of the ridges followed and they reached the flatter ground and the horse stretched out in a hard gallop. They pounded over the plain, the grasses pale gold, the blue-black clouds boiling above them. She had run before the storm on the Dendora but Tierken did not run before *this* storm, he ran *towards* it. He crouched low over his horse's neck and she crouched low behind him.

Squalls whipped grit into their faces and then the rain began, as hard as stones. Thunder cracked and as lightning slashed the sky, Tierken swerved into a shallow run of land and sped towards a tunnel-like opening. They plunged into darkness and he leapt off, taking Kira with him, and hauled her and the horse deeper into the tunnel.

Kira slumped against the wall as she dragged in breath, and the horse snorted and blew, the smell of its hot sweat filling the small space. Beyond the tunnel mouth, garish lightning lit a murky sky.

'What . . . is this . . . place?' she panted.

'A storm-safe. Herders built them over countless seasons. I thought we would beat the storm here but the Sarsalin had other plans.' It must have been a massive task, thought Kira, as she peered about. The walls were lined with blocks of stone. 'You should change into dry clothes,' said Tierken, pulling off his sodden jacket and shirt, and taking dry ones from his pack.

The lightning revealed a crisscross of scars and Kira gasped in horror. 'Your back!'

He turned. 'Do you think I expect my men to bear what I haven't?'

'It's barbaric!'

The skin of his chest and torso was golden, with dark hair that curled across it. 'Pain is a powerful teacher,' he said, pulling on the shirt. 'Do the Tremen train their men to fight?'

'To *protect*.'

'And when they are disobedient, or careless, or learn their lesson's poorly, how are they taught to remember?'

Kira's hands clenched. 'Not by beating!'

'Which explains why you ended up in Shargh hands.'

'The fault wasn't theirs!' she cried. 'They would have sacrificed everyone, down to the last man, to protect me!'

Tierken's eyes flashed. 'Then why didn't they?'

'Do you think I *want* people to die on my behalf? To have them so badly slashed it takes half the night to stitch them up? To have my family—' she choked to a stop.

'*Properly* trained men prevent such things.'

'They *are* properly trained men,' said Kira furiously. 'But we live by Healing, not by killing, not like the stinking Terak Kutan!'

Tierken froze. 'What did you call us?'

'The Terak Kutan,' said Kira in a small voice, recalling too late Slivkash's reaction to the term.

Tierken's eyes burned with fury and he wrenched her close. 'Be *grateful* the Terak *Kirillian* do not raise their hands to women,' he gritted. 'Don't *ever* use that phrase in my hearing again!' He shoved her away from him, strode to the tunnel entrance and stood staring out at the rain.

Kira slid down the tunnel wall until she was sitting on the ground and rubbed her bruised arms. Part of her argued she could expect nothing better from a brutish Terak *Kutan*, but a bigger part felt shamed. Her task was to beg help from the Terak king, not alienate his men by spitting insults the Tremen had used since the Sundering.

She just wished she were in the north, not stuck here with a patrolman who had Kandor's face *and* smile.

The thunder slowly rumbled away and the rain eased. 'Time to go,' he said coldly, and Kira followed him out. The ground was sodden, but the sky had cleared to a washed-out gold that mirrored the sweep of the plain. Tierken mounted and wordlessly held out his hand, and while Kira could not bring herself to apologize, she resolved not to cause him further trouble.

They went on at a gentler pace but she knew he was still angry. At least his silence gave her plenty of time to think about Caledon, what might be happening in Allogrenia, and what she must say to the Northern king when she reached Sarnia.

It was close to dusk before they reached the patrol's camp. Fires had been set between two rises and shelters erected, probably because of the storm, she guessed. The shelters looked like sleeping-sheets strung over ropes between poles and Tierken stopped at one and set her down. 'This is your *gifan*,' he said.

'Do you—' she began, but he rode off and was soon in conversation with Marin. She heard the word *Ashmiri* float back and then they were out of ear-shot.

The men ate at the other fires and her belly rumbled, but she could see no sign of Jonred, who was *in charge* of her, and she did not want him to be punished like Slivkash if she wandered off in search of him. Anger at Slivkash's beating surged again. They might not call themselves the Terak *Kutan*, but they were just as violent.

She ducked inside the gifan, surprised to see a sleeping-sheet set ready, pulled off her boots and crawled into it. She was hungry but she was desperate to shut out the day's events, and she curled into a ball and slept.

14

2

Tierken had not expected to share Cover-cape Crest with the Ashmiri but as Marin delivered his report, he realized that passing on *Terak greetings* provided an opportunity to remind them of Ashmiridin's oath. It also provided an opportunity to discover if the Ashmiri now *dishonored* their ancestor's oath.

Tierken's eyes narrowed. Kira's captors had ridden Ashmiri horses but if things were about to turn ill, Cover-cape Crest provided his men with good protection. It was too steep for the mounted fighting the Ashmiri preferred and the storm-slicked slope would hamper the Ashmiri's descent. The waxing moon aided the patrol too; its light preventing any surprise attack.

'You chose a good camp site,' he said sardonically, and Marin nodded. 'How many sorchas?' There could be half a dozen Ashmiri herders and their kin-links spread out between the Silver- and Azurcades at any given time, including the Ashmiri chief.

'Five sorchas and about three hundred ebis,' said Marin.

'It could be Uthlin,' said Tierken thoughtfully. Ashmiri wealth was measured by ebis and a large number of herd animals with few sorchas, meant wealth *and* influence. Tierken rubbed his stubbly jaw. Perhaps the storm had granted him more than a hard ride and a violent argument with his *guest*. 'Get the horses saddled and the men prepared,' he said abruptly. 'Anvorn's in charge of Kira if we come under attack.'

'You plan to visit them?'

'The Ashmiri will know I'm here. It would be an insult not to present my compliments. But we will go on foot: me, you, Jonred, Drinen and Shird.'

'*On foot*, Feailner? Do you think that's wise?'

'Are you suggesting our Ashmiri oath-swearers are *oath-breakers*?' he asked sourly.

'The Shargh ride Ashmiri horses.'

'Not something I've forgotten. And nor should we forgot, Marin, that it's unwise to force men to choose between blood and words. It's far better to remind them of honor and for the Ashmiri, it's stronger than both.'

'And are we to go weaponless as well, Feailner?' asked Marin, not placated.

'Of course not, and nor would they expect it. We'll take knives in case we must fight up close, and swords to maintain *our* honor, and we'll take arrows to fire over our shoulders in case we must run,' he added dryly.

'Meros grant it doesn't come to that,' grumbled Marin.

As soon as the camp was prepared, Tierken led his small party up the crest. Its summit revealed the sorchas and cropping ebis, silver under the waxing moon. The Ashmiri set watchers and as expected, Tierken's party was met some distance from the sorchas. The Ashmiri watcher gave a brief bow and Tierken and Marin exchanged glances. The usual Ashmiri gesture of respect was a brow palm so either the man had adopted the Terak custom out of respect for them, or he denied them the Ashmiri gesture of respect.

They went on through the ebis up a gentle slope to the highest sorcha. The man indicated they were to wait, and as soon as he disappeared inside, Tierken signaled Shird, Jonred and Drinen into defensive positions. He heard speech from inside, the language sounding harsh to his ears, but so had Kir and Illian before he mastered them.

Apart from Marin who was Illian, Tierken had chosen Terak for his party. They had a bent for thoughtful action, unlike Kirs, who were all dash. It was a difference forcibly brought home to him by Poerin, who had thrashed Tierken's Kir tendencies out of him over the long hard seasons of training.

The man reappeared, palmed his forehead, and waved them in. Tierken's mind raced. Either the more usual gesture of respect was a good sign, or a trap. It was warm in the sorcha and luxurious compared to the patrol's conditions of travel. The floor was covered with wolfskins, and lamps hung from the roof struts, their intricate metal-work and stained glass throwing patterns onto the hide walls. A fire burned beneath the smoke vent, and metal pans and pots gleamed on the coals.

Uthlin sat on the fire's far side, the single black dots tattooed onto his cheekbones making him easy to identify. Warriors sat to his sides, their cheeks tattooed with single dots in white, green, red, blue or yellow. They wore flatswords and daggers in their belts and their spears lay on the skins behind them.

Tierken bowed. Despite being *invited* to enter, he must lower his head first, Ashmiri customs something else Poerin's *gentle* guidance had drummed into him. Uthlin palmed his forehead and gestured Tierken to sit. Marin settled at Tierken's right hand, Jonred at his left, Shird and Drinen to either side of them. Tierken's men would not be introduced or acknowledged, except by their status which, like the Ashmiri's, was determined by their position in relation to him. Nor would Uthlin's warriors palm their foreheads to him; their presence at the meeting introduction enough.

Even without his gold eyes, Uthlin would know who he was. Some called the Ashmiri *dwinhir*, for their ability to see what moved on the plain, but others called them *skinhovers*, after the plain's scavenger birds.

'The Ashmiri greet the Feailner of the Terak, Kirs and Illians. May your time be blessed with rich pastures and many sons,' said Uthlin, in good Onespeak.

'The Feailner of the Terak, Kirs and Illians thanks you and is honored to sit in the sorcha of a people whose friendship has endured from the time of Terak himself,' replied Tierken.

Uthlin's eyes glittered as he inclined his head and Tierken wondered if he had been pre-emptive in reminding Uthlin of his forebear's oath. There was a tension about the Ashmiri chief and his warriors that did not augur well. Uthlin filled an ornate metal cup from the pan on the fire and had it passed to Tierken. 'The Sky Chiefs send their storms early,' he said.

The offer of drink, in this case spiced sherat, and the small talk, suggested Uthlin had taken no offence, but the Ashmiri chief was definitely on edge. Tierken brought the cup to his lips, as he was obliged to, but was careful to just sip. Only fools dulled their reflexes when they sat with the Shargh's kin.

'The Sarsalin has many moods,' he replied politely, as the sherat burned through him.

'We know the Sarsalin well,' responded Uthlin tersely.

Tierken gazed down at the sherat, as if he considered its merits, but he let the silence stretch. Poerin had taught him that, with the Ashmiri, silence spoke louder than words, and he was soon rewarded for his patience.

'But there's a place where the wind and rain might enter even the best set sorcha,' added Uthlin. It was the Ashmiri way of saying they had suffered misfortune. Tierken was relieved the tension did not stem from him, but he remained silent and again it was Uthlin who spoke. 'The storm has burned a warrior and we wait to see if the Sky Chiefs call him home.'

Tierken nodded but his thoughts raced. The Ashmiri were free to set camp wherever and whenever they chose and even if one of their warriors were struck by lightning, they would not necessarily pitch sorchas, the giving and taking of life the Sky Chiefs' prerogative. Yet Uthlin had pitched sorchas and the tension inside was palpable. It could only mean the injured man was important, even of Uthlin's line. And in revealing the accident, Uthlin had sought help.

Tierken's thoughts swung from Marin, a skilled bone-setter, to Kira, a Healer who loved herbs as his grandmother did. If Kira *could* aid the man, it would generate goodwill, and if the Shargh's murderous inclinations continued, he was going to need all the Ashmiri goodwill he could muster. But if Kira caused more suffering, the result would be the opposite. 'A Healer travels with us—' he began.

'Our Hals are skilled,' interrupted Uthlin.

Tierken paused. Uthlin's breach of protocol was a sign of his distress and suggested the injured man *was* of his line. 'The Healer isn't Terak, Kir or Illian,' said Tierken carefully. 'Nor is she of the Kessomi people, but of a people in the far south, beyond the Azurcades.' *The Healer is a stranger to us both. If she fails, the failure will not be Terak, nor the debt for her efforts, Ashmiri.*

Uthlin nodded briefly and Tierken gestured to Shird, who rose and left. Kira did not know Shird, but Tierken could not send his *senior warriors* Marin or Jonred on an *errand*. Nor did he want to be left without his best fighters.

'How grow the pastures south of the ridgelands?' asked Uthlin, topping up his own cup as he moved on to more mundane matters.

Tierken described the grasses, soil moisture and spring levels of the lands they had passed, an exchange of information expected amongst grazing peoples, and Uthlin's tension seemed to ease. In contrast, Tierken's ratcheted up as he considered how little he actually knew of Kira. It was possible he had just made the worst mistake of his life.

Kira gave a cry as she was jerked from her sleep. For a moment she thought the Shargh still had her but it was a Terak patrolman who crouched over her in the gifan. 'The Feailner says you are to come.'

Kira's throat tightened. 'He's handing me back to the Shargh?'

The patrolman shook his head impatiently. 'You are to come. And bring your pack.'

Kira numbly pulled on her boots but she scarcely had time to grab her pack before the patrolman hauled her outside. The night was freezing and the moon big, its light showing the horses were saddled and ready to leave. They only delayed to rid themselves of her, she realized in horror and started to shake.

'Put your jacket on,' ordered the patrolman, and barely waited for her to comply before he hauled her away from the camp and up the ridge at the back. The view from the top showed hundreds of herd animals and a series of strange round shelters.

The patrolman kept hold of her arm making escape impossible, but there was nowhere to run to anyway. Maybe if she fell to her knees and begged the Feailner forgiveness for insulting him, he would let her live, but she doubted it. A Shargh loomed from the darkness and Kira shrank back, but he did not kill her on the spot, just provided escort to one of the shelters. The patrolman stopped and their escort disappeared inside.

Tierken broke off his description of the western springs as their Ashmiri escort reappeared. He presumed Shird waited with Kira outside and hoped Shird had reassured her the Ashmiri *were not* the Shargh and she had been summoned because of her healing skills. The escort spoke to Uthlin, and Uthlin murmured something to the warrior beside him, who rose and left. Tierken's heart raced and he whispered to Marin to go too, and Marin followed the Ashmiri out.

Uthlin continued his questions about the western springs, but Tierken found it almost impossible to concentrate. Uthlin had sent out the warrior to his *right*, presumably to oversee Kira's healing, and that meant the injured man's blood-tie must be very close indeed.

Kira half expected the Shargh who appeared with the escort to be the one who had seized her at the Thanaval, but he was a stranger. His black eyes swept over her and sweat oozed down her back. Then Marin appeared. 'Shird told you why you're here?' he whispered, as they followed the Shargh past other huts.

'You're handing me back to the Shargh,' she choked out.

Marin glared at the patrolman behind her and lowered his voice. 'These are the *Ashmiri*, not the Shargh,' he hissed. 'They have need of—' but before he could finish, their escort ducked into a hut, and the hard-eyed Shargh behind them ensured they did too.

The first thing Kira noticed was glorious warmth and then agonized groans. Shargh crowded the huts edges, no, *Ashmiri*, she corrected dazedly, though they looked the same, and then she forgot all about them. A young man lay on his side, naked on a sheet, his cheek, shoulder, arm, torso, hip, and thigh blistered. Even the hair on the side of his head had been burned off.

His raw flesh had been covered with a greenish paste that the scent told her was a mix of silversalve, sorren, bruise-ease and honey, as good as salve as any for burns. A young woman held the man on his uninjured side, her cheeks colored with dots, and Kira noticed others in the hut had dots on their faces too.

Kira knelt beside the young man and the hard-eyed Ashmiri knelt beside her, his hand on his dagger. 'He was struck by lightning,' muttered Marin in her ear.

Kira knew from the Protectors that young men hid their pain, but this young man was so consumed by it, deception was impossible. 'Was he on a horse?' she asked in Onespeak to the room and the hard-eyed Ashmiri nodded.

His burns would be painful but Kira sensed something else triggered his groans. If he had been struck while riding, he would have fallen, and the horse too. He might have terrible injuries inside or be bleeding. 'I need him on his back,' she said.

The hard-eyed Ashmiri said something to the young woman, and she clenched her teeth and eased him over. 'Don't let me fall on him,' Kira whispered to Marin, and brought her hands down over the man's heart. She did not need to touch him; the pain was so great she plunged

22

straight into the fiery tunnel, and what she saw was the boiling core of injury in his lower back.

Kira pulled back, nauseous as she always was, and Marin gripped her arm. The injured man no longer groaned but turned his head, his eyes fixed on her, and she saw his unburnt cheek had a black dot marked on it.

The sorcha was absolutely silent. 'I need him on his belly,' she said.

The young woman turned him and Kira crouched over him and ran her hands down his back, carefully flattened her palms against his spine, and pushed. The young man grunted as the bones slipped back into place, then gave a shuddering sigh of relief.

The young woman cried out in joy and as excited chatter erupted in the hut, the hard-eyed Ashmiri hurried out. Kira left more slowly, supported by Marin. 'What did you do?' he whispered, as they followed their escort through the icy air.

'I put his back in,' said Kira, still light-headed.

'No, before that. What did—' Their escort ducked through the door-flap of the sorcha in front and Marin was forced to save his questions for later.

Tierken's heart thundered as Uthlin's right-hand warrior strode across the sorcha and whispered something in Uthlin's ear and Uthlin bowed his head. Uthlin's kin was either cured or killed. The escort appeared next, followed by Kira and Marin. Kira was ashen-faced and Marin lowered her down next to Tierken, inadvertently giving her his position, not something Uthlin missed, his shrewd gaze darting between them.

Then he straightened, his attention on Kira, and Tierken tensed. 'You have cured my son,' he said. 'What would you ask?'

23

Tierken's relief was tempered by a fear Kira would now insult Uthlin by demanding something inappropriate. 'I am a Healer from the Southern Forests,' she said. 'In my lands, it is the custom to give healing.' It was an answer Tierken's grandmother would have been proud of, both generous and nonjudgmental of those who traded or sold their healing skill.

Uthlin's face remained expressionless but his gaze swept the Sorcha. 'Healer of the Southern Forests,' he said solemnly. 'You are a long way from your home and tread a plain unforgiving of the stranger. I, Chief Uthlin of the Ashmiri, grant you the protection of my people.'

Tierken struggled to maintain his composure. Within the next few days, every Ashmiri, no matter where they roamed, would know what Kira looked like and their obligation to protect her. Uthlin's pledge was as binding as Ashmiridin's had been countless seasons ago.

'We eat now,' announced Uthlin, and the tension broke.

'I thank you,' said Kira, but whether she thanked him for food, or protection, was unclear.

Some of the warriors rose as women appeared with steaming platters: *loti*, a spicy sausage; *sahin*, slivers of meat fried; and *misil*, smoked cheese. There was nothing Kira would choose to eat but eat she must, if she were not to offend Uthlin. 'You must eat,' he whispered to her as the platters were passed around. Kira nodded but her pallor increased, as if she were going to be sick just at the sight of it. 'I'll serve you,' he muttered. At least that way, he could keep her portions small.

The bowls and platters were offered to him first, as the most important guest, and Tierken put a small chunk of each of the foods in Kira's bowl. Serving her before himself could be construed as respect for the service she

24

rendered the Terak Feailner in fulfilling his reciprocal obligations to the Ashmiri, or as acknowledgement of her as his mate. Given their physical similarity *and* that she sat at his right hand, Tierken suspected the Ashmiri would see it as the latter.

There was an air of celebration now and the higher voices of the women mixed with those of the men as they ate. Kira winced as she swallowed chunks of food without chewing and Tierken ate his own meal quickly then rose and signaled to Marin to help Kira. She looked on the point of collapse.

The Ashmiri did not expect Tierken to stay late. Courteous words had been exchanged and food shared, and peoples who journeyed all day, did not carouse deep into the night. Tierken bowed. 'I wish you fine weather and fair travel,' he said, reciting the customary farewell of herders.

'To you and yours also,' returned Uthlin.

3

They came back out into the freezing night and set off in silence, Shird and Drinen on the flanks, Marin by his side, and Jonred at the rear with Kira. Tierken sensed Marin's impatience to speak but it was Kira who broke the silence. 'Can they still see us?' she asked thickly.

'They—' began Jonred, but before he could finish, Kira fell to her knees and was violently ill.

Jonred crouched beside her but Tierken ordered him up. 'Jonred, Drinen and Shird, go on ahead and settle the horses for the night. Marin, set a fire near Kira's gifan. I'll bring her when she's ready.' The men marched off but Marin loitered. 'The Ashmiri don't murder those they have just shared meat with,' said Tierken, pre-empting his objections. 'I'll hear your report at camp.'

'Yes, Feailner,' said Marin, and strode off after the others.

Kira's vomiting became dry retching and she sat back on the wet grass, her knees drawn up, her head hanging forward. 'You've a waterskin in your pack?' he asked. She nodded and he slipped the pack off and rummaged around till he found it, then gently washed her face. 'That was the meat?'

'That and an empty belly,' she mumbled, without looking up.

'Didn't you eat with the men?'

'You said to stay with Jonred and he wasn't there.'

'I didn't mean to go hungry, if he were with me,' said Tierken in exasperation. She made no response and he wished he could see her face. The rope burns on her wrists

26

were clear though and he grimaced as he considered his behavior at the storm-safe. Poerin had reminded him of the value of patience more than once, but it was a lesson he still struggled to learn.

She seemed to be thinking about the storm-safe too. 'I need to beg your pardon for insulting you earlier,' she said. 'I . . . I didn't know what *kutan* meant.'

'Is that what they call us in Maraschin?' asked Tierken, wondering whether the Alliance was beyond redemption.

'I didn't hear it in Maraschin. I lived in the Sanctum and the Hea—*physicks* only spoke of gathering, or herbs, or curing. I wasn't in King's Hall with Ad—*Prince Adris* and Caledon.'

'Prince Adris? King Beris's son?' Kira nodded. 'How old is he?'

'Twenty-five, twenty-six seasons.'

'You've met him?'

'Yes.'

There was something in her tone that sharpened his attention. 'You don't like him?'

She raised her head but her gaze was still on the ground. 'It's not Adris's fault he acts like he does. Caledon told me King Beris has been ill for many seasons, and Adris is frustrated because the king doesn't authorize him to counter Shargh attacks. Anything he does, like sending out the King's Guard, must be done without his father's knowledge.'

'I see,' said Tierken. Kira had called the prince, *Adris*, not *Prince Adris*, which implied a greater level of familiarity than he would have expected from a simple Healer working in their Haelen. 'This man *Caledon*. He's a friend of Prince Adris?'

'Yes.'

'He's Tain?'

'He's from Talliel.'

'Talliel?' said Tierken in surprise. 'He's a long way from home.'

'He journeys a great deal,' said Kira softly.

The change in tone again caught his attention. 'Is Caledon in Maraschin now?' he demanded. If there were feeling between them, why in Irid's name had the man allowed her to go gathering?

'I don't know.'

The answer was evasive but Tierken bit back his next question. A Tallien called Caledon might wait for Kira in Maraschin, but this woman who shared his eyes and his face was now under *his* protection and on her way to *his* city. And at this moment, he could not see any reason why she would ever return.

Kira did not wake until the sun penetrated the gifan. It made the small space pleasantly warm and she stretched and yawned as she thought of the burned Ashmiri. Healing always gifted her a sense of well-being and it was no different now, despite the Ashmiri's resemblance to the Shargh. She hauled her pack closer, fished out the comb and dragged it through her knotty hair. Her hands were grubby and her clothes travel-stained, but at least her hair was no longer unkempt, thanks to Speri's gift.

Patrolmen's voices sounded beyond the gifan's walls and her thoughts turned to Tierken. He had been very considerate last night, roasting nuts for her, and brewing metz, or cotzee as the Terak called it. But for all his courtesy, he was of Terak's line and her arms bore the bruises to prove it.

She sighed. Why in the 'green did he have to look like Kandor? And why not have brown eyes like Tresen, or blue eyes like Kest, or even grey eyes like Caledon? Why did his eyes have to be gold? It made being with him horribly disturbing.

'Kira? Come and eat.'

She started then crawled out and straightened. The sun was well up, the sky a brilliant blue with wisps of cloud. Tierken smiled at her, as he had last night, and she struggled with the joy and despair *Kandor's* smile roused. Tierken was happy because, as he had told Marin last night in Terak, her healing had strengthened the Ashmiri treaty.

She settled beside the fire and he passed her a large bowl of roasted nuts. 'I can't eat all those,' she protested.

'If all you eat are nuts, you're going to have to eat more of them,' he said. 'You're little more than bones.'

'I eat other things as well,' she said defensively, as she started on the nuts. They were sweeter than black- and rednuts and very good.

'Such as?'

'Riddleberries, mundleberries, sour-ripe, osken, beggar leaves, scavengerleaf, pitchie seeds, sweet fish, feathergrass tubers, honey,' she listed off.

'They're the foods of the Southern Forests?' Kira nodded. 'It's not much. Are the rest of your people thin too?'

Kira swallowed in a painful gulp. 'No, the forest Shelters us. I just didn't take enough food with me when I left. I thought I would gather on the Dendora Plain, but there was little to be had.'

'The Dendora's Shargh grazing, and even before the long drought, offered only sparse gathering. The Sarsalin's the same. How long were you in Maraschin?'

'About two and a half moons.'

'Obviously, there wasn't enough food there either,' said Tierken acidly.

'There is plenty of everything in Maraschin, including food, *if* you have something to trade,' said Kira, failing to hide her bitterness. 'But I didn't need to trade. I healed in the Sanctum with the Tain physicks, and King Beris provides for the Sanctum's needs.'

'What else does the king do?' asked Tierken, pouring her some cotzee.

'I don't know,' said Kira honestly. 'Most things seem to be at Adris's command.'

She finished eating and wiped her fingers on the grass. 'Kashclan thanks the Terak Kirillian,' she said formally as she passed the remainder of the nuts back. 'Is there somewhere I can wash?'

'You can wash at the grove. I'll take you,' he said. Kira followed him away from the camp towards some trees, aware of the men's gaze. 'After you wash, you can have a riding lesson,' Tierken tossed over his shoulder.

'A riding lesson?'

He waited for her to come level. 'If you are to spend time in the north, you will need to be able to ride. You can start off on Slivkash's mount. Frost is quieter than Kalos.'

'Won't Slivkash mind?' asked Kira, thinking of the beating he had suffered on her behalf.

'The Kirs are horse-people. He won't mind.' The trees thickened and Kira stopped, open-mouthed. 'What is it?' asked Tierken sharply, his hand already on his sword.

'They're alwaysgreens!'

'*Allogrenias*,' he corrected. 'The most southerly stand on the Sarsalin.'

Kira stared at him in bewilderment. '*Allogrenias*?' Had the word turned into *alwaysgreens* in the same way *Kirillian* had turned into *Kutan*? Or had Kasheron changed the tree's name to avoid confusion with his new settlement? It didn't matter. Their spicy scent was the same *and* the deep peace and Shelter of their broad spreading boughs, and Kira embraced the nearest bole with wide-flung arms.

Memories of the Renclan Sentinel stormed back, of burying Kandor's pipe, of turning her back on everything she loved and trudging away alone. She imagined her palms flattened against the warm skin of Nogren, or Esogren, or Enogren and tears slid down her face.

'Kira?' Tierken's voice was gentle.

'I need to wash,' she muttered embarrassed.

'The spring's a little further,' he said, and took her hand.

His hand was warm and she managed to steady as he led her deeper into the trees. The birdsong helped and the dapples of sunlight and leaf-shadows that danced across the litter. The spring was dark and quiet, the water seeping too slowly to ripple and the dense canopy allowing only the occasional spark of sunlight in to glint off its surface.

Kira knelt by the edge and sluiced water over her face and arms but Tierken stripped off his jacket and shirt and laved water over his chest and back. 'I'll turn away if you want to wash more thoroughly,' he said.

But Kira could not tear her gaze from his back and the dapple of sunlight that caught his face deepened her horror that somehow, it had been Kandor who had been brutalized. 'Your back,' she said hoarsely. 'Does it still pain you?'

'No.'

'Can I . . . can I examine it?' The need to reassure herself Kandor did not suffer was overwhelming.

'I've told you there's no pain.'

'I *need* to know.' Tierken shrugged and turned his back. 'No, from the front.'

He turned back and Kira laid her hands over his heart. She had never done this before with someone who was uninjured, and instead of a fire-filled tunnel, she found a place of warmth and safety. And then she was back in the cooler air of the grove but with none of her usual nausea, just an immense sense of peace.

Kira looked up at Tierken in astonishment, and even in the emerald-colored air, she saw his eyes lighten. He brought his arms around her slowly, to give her time to step back, but she remained in his Shelter, and her palms felt his heart quicken as his mouth came to hers. She answered him kiss for kiss, lost in the wonder of his Shelter, and then he pulled away, leaving her bereft. 'You're under my protection,' he said angrily.

'I feel completely safe,' she said, still lost in the languorous dream. 'I thank you.'

'We need to go back,' he said, and strode off. Kira followed and the exquisite sense of peace stayed with her until they reached the plain's bright sunshine again.

4

Tierken went quickly through the trees, incensed he had given into the urge he had felt since Kira had first raised her face to his on the plain. He knew he should have returned her Maraschin, as did Marin, but the woman they had rescued was beautiful, with fine slender hands and a spirit every bit as fiery as Kalos. She had stood toe to toe with him unbowed in her defiance and then healed in the same selfless way as Eris did.

He considered Marin's report on the injured Ashmiri as he came out from under the trees. *I had thought the man was for the next world for sure*, Marin had said. *He was in the sort of agony where death is as sweet as a feather bed but then she puts her hands over his heart, and by Meros, he stops groaning and starts looking around.* If anyone else had said it, Tierken would have dismissed it as fanciful, but Marin was a bone-setter and knew about pain.

He touched his mouth as the sweet sensation oozed through him again. Maybe she had simply sought comfort after being distressed by memories stirred by the allogrenias. As a Healer, she would be concerned about injuries too, whether old or new. The scars on his back were no longer tender and he had humored her by letting her touch him, but her proximity had fired every sense in his body. It had taken all his self-control to give her time to refuse him but she had not, her need as great as his.

His men watched them and he lengthened his stride, so that she fell even further behind. Let them think his *guest*

33

had defied him *again*, rather than he had found a toy to amuse himself with on the homeward journey.

Kira watched Tierken stride off with Marin and turned back to the men. Jonred was part of a circle intent on some sort of game and she settled nearby. She had no idea what they played but there was much laughing and clapping of backs, and then the circle broke and most of the men headed off into the trees. Jonred and one of the patrolman remained. They spoke Terak which told her the man was either Terak or Kessomi.

'I'll wager you ten traders I'll have Mesia by Mid-market Day,' the man boasted.

'You do and I'll wager ten more you'll be married by the next,' replied Jonred.

The man lounged back on the grass. 'I'll not be marrying her,' he said. 'There's other men she's spread her legs for.' Kira's face warmed and she broke off a stalk of grass and stared at it as if she had never seen grass before.

'Her father won't see it like that,' said Jonred. 'You'd be better off spending your traders in the Caru Quarter. Hand them over and take your pleasure with no complications.'

The man laughed. 'I don't waste traders on what I can get for free,' he said, and glanced across at Kira. 'What about the Feailner and our gold-eyed guest? Want to wager he'll have *her* before we reach the city's walls?'

'She's under our protection,' said Jonred curtly. Kira jerked another grass-stalk from the ground and dug her thumbnail into the stem.

'It's been a long time for him and she's *exeal*,' the man said softly. 'Must be tempting.'

'She's under our protection,' repeated Jonred. 'You insult the Feailner.'

'No insult intended,' the man replied easily and got to his feet. 'I'm off for a game of sweep-seven. Coming?'

'I have other duties.'

Kira gazed at the grass-stalk sightlessly. She had no idea what *exeal* meant, but Tierken had broken some sort of rule in kissing her which was why he had been angry with himself afterwards. And yet he *could* kiss her apparently, and do whatever else he wanted, because she was *exeal*.

'Are you recovered from your sickness of last night?' asked Jonred courteously.

'I am well this day. I thank you.' Jonred's eyes narrowed and she looked away, wondering if her face had betrayed her feelings.

He scrambled to his feet and Kira glanced up to see Tierken approach with Slivkash's horse. 'Ready for your first riding lesson?' he asked.

She nodded and brushed the grass from her trousers as she reluctantly followed him up the slope. She did not want to be near the Ashmiri again but when she reached the top of the crest, the plain was empty.

'Do you fear horses?' asked Tierken, his shrewd gaze on her face.

'They are strange to me,' she admitted. 'Before I went to the Tain lands, I had never seen a real horse, only the running horse in the chimes we hang in our windows at home.'

'They like chimes in Kessom too,' said Tierken, busy adjusting the harness, 'more so than in Sarnia. They make them of wood in Kessom and in Sarnia mainly of stone, but you can trade for metal and glass ones at Mid-market.'

'Metal is prasach,' said Kira automatically.

'Ah yes, but it tinkles beautifully,' he said with a smile.

35

He began the lesson in the same way he had been taught: the position of the saddle rug, the parts of the saddle, how to adjust the stirrups, how to ensure the girth was the right tightness, the parts of the bridle, how to put the bridle on, the importance of not injuring the horse's mouth. He made Kira undo the girth, shift the saddle, redo the girth, take the bridle off, put the bridle on. Her slightness made all the tasks difficult. A typical Kessomi, he thought, and caught himself. *Tremen*, he corrected, whatever that was.

At least she did not show any fear and Frost was at ease with her. He snuffed at her face as she struggled with the bridle strap and she laughed. It was the first time he had seen her other than angry or fearful, and his resolve not to pursue her evaporated like cotzee dregs on fire-stones. 'Frost likes you,' he said.

'And I like Frost. He's very beautiful.'

'Not as beautiful as you are,' he said softly.

Her smile disappeared. 'Don't tease me.'

'Tease you?'

She shrugged, her gaze on Frost who now cropped the grass. 'I don't like being called beautiful.'

'Why? Who's called you that?'

'Kest,' said Kira reluctantly.

'And Kest is?'

'Protector Commander Kest of Morclan.'

'He's in charge of the Tremen fighters?'

'The *Protectors*,' said Kira.

'What about the Tallien in Maraschin? Did he call you beautiful?'

'I've been teased by many people.' She pushed the hair from her face and looked up at him, her eyes more green than gold. 'Do you like having gold eyes, Tierken?'

'No,' he said honestly.

'Neither do I. I was never Maxen's daughter or Merek's sister, or a member of Kashclan. It was as if my eyes were more important than me. I was even named for them.'

Tierken's brows drew. 'What? *Kira*?'

'There's a gold-eyed owl in the forests called the mira kiraon. Kira's short for Kiraon.'

Tierken's guts churned. She had his eyes and his face, Kessomi healing skills, and now the same name as the Terak's most revered queen. It was hard to believe it was all simply chance. He could all but hear Poerin's gravelly voice. *Too many chances make up facts, Tierken. Face them or face the consequences. The former is often harder but less deadly*. Harder *and* more complicated, and more complications were the last thing he needed in Sarnia.

'Kiraon was the mother of the man who founded our peoples and was greatly loved,' he said tersely. 'Out of respect for her, the name's not been given again so I suggest you continue to call yourself Kira.'

Kira nodded, keen not to compromise her mission in the north. 'What does the word *exeal* mean?' she asked.

'Exeal?' She had used the Terak word. 'Where did you hear that?'

'One of your men said it while he looked at me.'

'Which one?' demanded Tierken.

'I don't know his name. What does it mean?'

'It means an outsider; someone who isn't kin-linked or treatied. Once all peoples of the north were wanderers, single families or families linked by blood, like the Bishali. Then bloodlines formed into groups, bound by treaty, alliance, and marriage, and these groups formed into what we are today. The Terak, Kessomis, Kirs and Illians came together to make us one people, kin to each other and, as

37

the Terak Kirillian, we're treatied to the Tain and Ashmiri, but we have no obligations to those who are exeal.'

'So, the Terak Kirillian must aid peoples who are kin-linked or who they have a treaty with?'

'Yes, although treaties and alliances vary. Our treaty with the Ashmiri only obliges us to allow them to graze where they wish and for them to refrain from attacking us, whereas our treaty with the Tain obliges us to come to each other's aid if fighting breaks out. Why do you ask?'

'The Tain are under Shargh attack.'

'They haven't requested aid.'

'But if the Tain did request it, or a kin-linked people, would you give aid?'

'We're obliged,' said Tierken. He took a long rein from the saddle-bag and attached it to the bridle. 'Now, time to learn how to mount.'

Getting on and off Frost was a struggle, and Tierken made Kira do it over and over again. Then it was moving in rhythm with Frost's trotting, then cantering, bringing him to a halt, turning him, making him trot and canter again, then walk. Kira felt like she could not do a single thing right. She sat too heavily, jerked Frost's mouth, *which you should never do*, held the reins too loosely, too tightly, unevenly, failed to grip well, almost fell off, and so on.

When Tierken finally called a halt, she slithered off Frost and had to hang onto his neck until her legs supported her. 'Kashclan thanks Frost,' she muttered.

'Doesn't Kashclan thank the Terak Kirillian?' asked Tierken.

'Not until my backside stops hurting.'

He laughed then and his good mood lasted all the way

through the evening meal, when he insisted she eat more nuts and drink cotzee, before he allowed her to crawl into her sleeping-sheet. She slept solidly until Jonred's hand shook her awake and told her they must soon be on their way.

They cleared Cover-cape Crest and picked up speed. Kira was glad Jonred's broad back sheltered her from the freezing wind and thankfully the wind dropped as the light strengthened, but she noticed how often the patrolmen glanced up at the yellow-tinged clouds. 'Snow clouds,' said Jonred over his shoulder. 'We will be fortunate to make the Breshlin before it starts. And still one cursed day to winter,' he muttered in Terak.

Kira thought of what she must do once they reached Sarnia. She must seek an audience with the king as soon as possible, and might have to pretend to the king's advisors she was acquainted with King Beris in order to gain it. She would need to be careful in how she revealed the kin-link too, and tactful in the way she requested him to honor his obligation to her people.

The thought of men like Slivkash being wounded or killed was abhorrent but maybe just the *presence* of the Terak, with their fiercesome reputation, would be enough to turn the Shargh from their murderous path. Caledon sought Tremen volunteers but if she gained Terak help quickly enough, the Tremen might be able to return to Allogrenia without fighting.

Something cold stung her face and Kira looked up in astonishment to see snow swept on the wind. Snow was rare in the forest and when it broke through the canopy, fell in clumps. She had not realized it swirled like lissium blossom and laughed in delight.

'Snow this early isn't funny,' said Jonred dourly.

Tierken's big grey suddenly pounded beside them. 'We detour to Ember Keep,' he said to Jonred.

'Yes, Feailner.'

Tierken turned to her, crystals of snow bright in his dark hair. 'We turn north-west to Ember Keep,' he said in Onespeak. 'There's good shelter there. The snow will delay us a day *unless* the Sarsalin turns it to a storm then it could be several.'

They sped on and the snow thickened until it was hard to tell ground from sky. The men's silver horses appeared and disappeared like wraiths and Jonred eased his mount back to canter, then a trot. Kira still found the snow beautiful, but as the day wore on, her hands tingled where she gripped the saddle-strap.

It was almost dark when a long howl cut the silence. More howls followed and Jonred spat over his mount's shoulder. 'Sarsalin wolves,' he muttered, and half turned his head. 'Snow *and* wolves,' he said in Onespeak. 'Meros *is* in a nasty mood.'

Marin appeared out of the murk, eyebrows stiff with snow. 'The Feailner's taken the Kirs and Illians west. If the pack hunts east of the Finewater, there's likely Kir herders in trouble. You're to go direct to the Keep. Use the east approach. We'll join you there.'

'The *east* approach?'

'You forget our guest,' said Marin.

Jonred slowed to let the patrolman behind them come level. 'Let the men know we're to use The Steps, Vardrin,' he said.

'The Steps? In this weather?'

'The Feailner's orders,' said Jonred.

40

Vardrin's eyes flicked to Kira. 'I'll tell them,' he said, and spurred away.

'The Keep's near, but the way we go is steep,' said Jonred in Onespeak, half turning again so she could hear him. 'You need to hold on tightly and if I tell you to dismount, keep hold of my cape. If we come under wolf attack, do *exactly* as I say. Do you understand?'

'Yes,' said Kira, heart thudding.

The patrolmen pressed closer, their horses' flared nostrils a brilliant crimson against the snow-filled air. The men unslung their bows but the howl of wolves seemed further off, *unless* they were muffled by the snow. Kira shivered as she blinked the snow from her eyes, not risking letting go the saddle-strap to use her hands. The horse's back tilted as it climbed and its sweat hung acrid in the air.

'Beware rocks!' exclaimed Vardrin behind them.

Kira tightened her frozen fingers. She had no idea how Vardrin could see rocks when she could see *nothing* and just hoped Jonred knew the safest way. There was nothing beautiful about the snow now; she just wanted the trek to end.

'Time to walk,' grunted Vardrin.

'Not yet—' began Jonred, and then the snow collapsed under his mount's haunches and there was a violent jolt breaking Kira's numb grip. The horse's back tilted sharply and she slipped backwards, aware of Jonred's desperate lunge to catch her before she landed with a jarring thump on the edge of the path. The snow gave way and then she was falling.

5

Tarkenda gazed out across the Grounds, well pleased with her work at the Speak. The idea that Arkendrin's right to the chiefship depended on leading the Shargh to glory in the north had taken root easily, fed by excitement over the Weshargh Chief's return and news of the Soushargh's willingness to contribute to the coming triumphs. Even those whose allegiances were to the firstborn chiefs had been caught up in it, the babblings of Orsendron's blood-ties, Ertheren and Irsmiron, as shrill as those of Irdodun's cronies.

How short their memories were! How little regard they had for past lessons! The Sky Chiefs had recently gifted them rains and lush pastures, a surfeit of grahen eggs, and plump silverjacks, easy to hunt. The ebis were well-fleshed, their milk creamy, the cheeses ripe and flavorsome. Children shouted at play on the lower slope and people slept without fear in their sorchas, but it was not enough for the Weshargh and Soushargh chiefs, and it certainly wasn't enough for Arkendrin.

Arkendrin must be nearing the Grounds but Tarkenda's fear had lessened. The Shargh warriors' thoughts had turned north, away from the creature of the Last Telling, and such was the prize Orbdargan and Yrshin dangled before them like blackfish bait, they were unlikely to turn back again.

It was deep in the night when Tarkenda was woken by a wailing that set her heart pounding.

'Can it be?' gasped Palansa, sitting up.

Tarkenda shook her head. Her visions had shown fighting and that meant Arkendrin still lived. But *someone* had died and she recalled Ormadon's bald summation that Arkendrin had a gift for losing the lives of those around him.

Footsteps sounded and Tarkenda heaved herself up. The wailing was louder now but confined to the lower slope. 'Chief-mother?'

'Enter Ormadon,' said Palansa, as she pulled a jacket over her shirt.

'What has happened?' demanded Tarkenda.

'Arkendrin and Irdodun have returned.'

'But not Ermashin and Orthaken?'

'And the gold-eyed Healer?' broke in Palansa. 'Did they bring her?'

'No, Chief-mother. They were attacked by Northerners.'

Palansa shut her eyes. 'Praise be to the Sky Chiefs,' she breathed.

'The Northerners killed Ermashin and Orthaken and took the Healer?' asked Tarkenda.

'They killed Ermashin and Orthaken. It's unclear what became of the Healer, but it's likely they took her.'

'What else have you heard?' asked Tarkenda.

'The Soushargh share their southern grazing with the Ashmiri and the Ashmiri roam beyond the Braghans.'

'And?'

'They claim the Northern chief has gold eyes too.'

Tarkenda groaned and collapsed onto a chair. 'What is it?' demanded Palansa, her gaze flicking between Ormadon's blank face and Tarkenda's stricken one.

'Don't you see?' asked Tarkenda hoarsely.

'See what?' demanded Palansa.

'*Gold meets gold, two halves are one.*'

43

'The Last Telling,' whispered Palansa. 'But surely—'
Tarkenda cradled her head in her hands. 'It has begun.'

Kira slid faster and faster, spread-eagled across the slope, her hands gouging the snow as she fought to slow. Then her boots struck something solid and she jagged to a stop. The slope was so steep she was almost upright. Snow had forced its way up under her shirt, scraping her belly and making it burn, but she dare not move, lest she continue her plunge.

The men screamed her name but her chest was hard up against the slope making it hard to scream back. She heard Jonred bellow for quiet and took a deep breath. 'Jonred,' she yelled.

'Kira!'

'I'm all right,' she shouted, despite knowing she was not. 'Something's stopped me.'

'Stay where you are! Don't move! Don't move, Kira!' Jonred's voice was frantic and she guessed the drop below her was very deep. She had no idea whether she balanced on a jut of rock or a log, ready to roll. There was a shrub several lengths to her right and out of reach, but nothing else and she took a shuddering breath.

'I'm coming down,' came Jonred's voice again. '*Don't move*! Just call to me so I can find you.'

'All right,' she yelled back.

Silence descended and the only thing that moved was the soft drift of flakes. She had the terrifying thought the patrol had ridden on and left her and panic threatened. 'Call me, Kira,' boomed Jonred's voice out of the blackness.

'Jonred,' she yelled.

'Keep calling,' he ordered.

Kira could not see or hear anything above her but she yelled his name, paused, then yelled again and after a while, he appeared to her right and clawed his way towards her. 'Don't move,' he instructed. 'I need to get this around you.' He passed a rope under her arms and around her chest, pulled it tight and fastened it to his waist. 'Put your arms round my neck and hook your legs around me,' he ordered.

Kira winced, her hands skinned like her belly, but did as he bid and then Jonred yelled to the men above and they hauled them up. It was a long way back to the top, the darkness like a bottomless pit below them, and a cheer erupted as they were finally heaved back onto the path. Jonred undid the rope and stowed it in his pack but he did not let go of her. Vardrin took his mount, and Jonred took her, and the whole party continued on foot.

'It's not much further,' he said reassuringly, 'then we'll get the fires going and some hot food into you. Meros must have favored you. If you had kept going . . .' He coughed to clear his throat. 'It was my mistake for not having walked earlier.'

'It wasn't *your* mistake,' said Kira quickly. 'It was *my* mistake for not holding on properly. You *told* me to hold on tight and I didn't. It was *my* mistake,' she repeated, thinking of Slivkash. Jonred said nothing, his grip firm on Kira's arm as they walked. 'In any case, there's no harm done,' she said. 'There's no need to discuss it further.'

A deeper darkness yawned ahead and, as they climbed up to it, she saw it was the lip of a massive cave. The front of the roof had fallen in but the back provided a large area of good shelter. Jonred explained that the eastern part of the Keep, where they were now, was harder to reach than the western part. The eastern end had sheer rock on *all*

45

sides, except for *the steps* they used, and while the dark and snow had made the climb hard for them, it made it hard for everything else too.

The men set fires along the front of the cavern using wood from windfall stacked against the back wall, and Kira guessed the fires were as much for protection as warmth and cooking. Jonred ordered she remain at the most easterly of the fires, then went off with the men to settle the horses and prepare food.

She needed to salve the raw flesh of her belly and hands, but needed to wash first and had no idea if the Keep had water. Nor could she leave the fire to find out in case Jonred was punished. He brought her a bowl of roasted nuts and a mug of cotzee but did not stay. The men ate at the other fires, to give her privacy, she supposed, but it mainly gifted her loneliness.

The cave's entrance was filled with a flickering curtain of falling snow and she watched it as she ate. The men's reactions told her she had been fortunate to survive the fall and she shivered. She craved the comfort of Caledon's arms or Tresen's, or Miken's but all three might be long dead, and Tierken too, killed by wolves or some mischance out in the frozen darkness.

She pulled her knees up and rested her head on her arms, keeping her skinned palms clear of her trousers and the next thing she was aware of was a hand on her arm. She started violently. For a moment she had no idea where she was.

'You should be in your sleeping-sheet,' said Tierken, his voice thickened by exhaustion as he hefted more wood on the fire. 'Sitting up is no way to rest.' He settled beside her and Kira rubbed her stiff neck with the back of her hand. The other fires showed the silhouettes of sleeping men but the cave was filled with a cacophony like a thousand tippets.

'What's that noise?' she asked.

'The goats in the west Keep. We've brought in what's left of them. Wolves took a dozen, one way or another, which is a lot to a Kir herder.'

'Do they attack herds often?'

'They're opportunistic and the snow is unseasonal. The herders were caught out from shelter.' He grimaced. 'A bad combination. How did you find the journey?'

'Very cold. I've never seen snow like this before.'

'Nothing else?'

She kept her gaze on the fire. 'No. Just cold.'

'Jonred reports you fell and only survived by Meros's grace.' His fingers gripped her chin and turned her face to his. 'Don't lie to me, Kira. I won't tolerate deceit.'

Kira jerked her face free. 'I don't want Jonred beaten for something that was my fault.'

'He told me it was his lack of judgment that caused the fall.'

'It was *my* fault! He told me to hold on tight and I didn't. Beat me if you need someone to beat!'

'Jonred also told me you escaped injury,' he said, ignoring her outburst.

'I did mainly. I've just got some grazes. I can salve them but I need to wash first.'

'Come, then.' His exhaustion was plain as he got to his feet and held out his hand, then his face hardened as she made no move to take it.

'It's not you,' she said hurriedly, and showed him her skinned palm.

'By Irid! Are the rest as bad?'

'They're just grazes.'

He gripped her elbow and lifted her upright, then pulled a flaming branch from the fire. 'It's dark in the tunnelway,' he said. There was a door-sized hole in the stone at the cavern's back, closed off with a sturdy wooden gate. 'To stop wolves or fanchon coming up from the west Keep,' he said briefly, as he wrenched it open. She followed him down a short tunnel and the smell of wet stone gave way to the smell of wet animals and a storm of bleatings. Beyond the goats, the herders clustered around a fire, the firelight showing a craggy-faced older man, three younger men, several women, one of whom nursed a child, and the smaller shapes of sleeping children.

A white horse loomed from the darkness and Kira stared in surprise. 'It would have taken too long to bring Kalos around to The Steps,' said Tierken wearily, as he led her on past. 'Here's the water.'

A seep in the rockface fed a shallow pool and Kira struggled with her raw palms to unbutton her jacket. 'Let me,' said Tierken, and propped the burning branch against the cave-back. His nearness destroyed all thought and she concentrated on the fire-gilded water. 'It was a mistake to send my men by The Steps,' he said softly, and brought the backs of his fingers gently down her cheek. 'I thought it would be safer.'

'There's no harm done,' she said quickly.

'Someone as young as you shouldn't be so far from home,' he said angrily.

'I'm not young, I'm seventeen. In my lands, I—'

'*Seventeen*!? Are the Tremen so uncaring?'

'Of course not! In my lands, I—'

'Are you injured back or front?' he demanded.

'Front.'

'Let's see.'

48

Kira hesitated but Tierken impatiently pushed her shirt up over her belly. 'By Irid! They're as bad as your hands.'

He lathed water over the scrapes and she winced at the sting. Beyond the goats, one of the Kir children coughed and Kira's head swiveled. 'I need to see to that child,' she said.

'Herders' children always cough,' he said dismissively, as he reclaimed the branch. 'Time for sleep.' She turned towards the herders but he caught her arm and tightened his grip as she tried to pull away. 'Leave it,' he hissed.

'I'm a Healer!' she said, anger kindling.

'That has nothing to do with—'

'I'm a *Healer*, Tierken. If you understand *nothing* else about me, understand that!'

He made no reply, just marched her back up the tunnel to the east Keep and stood over her while she applied the salve and crawled into her sleeping-sheet. She hoped he would take his sheet back to the men, as he always did, but he left it beside her.

He seemed to slip into sleep quickly but she wondered if she rose whether he would spring up to bully her again. The Kir child continued to cough, a wet cough, in need of soothing, and it was a long time before sleep came.

It stopped snowing sometime in the night and as Kira stood on the cavern's lip the next morning, the sparkling, pristine blanket of white was as astonishing as her first glimpse of the Dendora. That terrible moment of turning her back on Allogrenia's Shelter seemed a long time ago. She had seen horses *and* ridden them, lived in an immense city, and worked with Healers whose ways were strange.

She glanced up at the sky, almost as white as the snow. She had donned her spare shirt, her jacket, *and* her cape but still shivered. How much colder would it be in Sarnia? Each dawn took her closer to the day she must bend her knee to the Terak king and beg aid and, given what Tierken said, she knew it would be granted. But she was still anxious about inadvertently insulting the king, remembering all too well how awkward she had been at her first Clancouncil.

Tierken came to her side. 'The first day of winter and a full moon,' he said.

Kira gazed up at it too. 'The Shargh attacked at the full moon,' she said slowly.

'How many attacks did the Tremen suffer?'

'Five.'

'Over how long?'

'Five moons.'

'Starting when?'

'Spring.'

'And before then?' he asked.

'Nothing. Season upon season of peace.' How little she had appreciated it; how much she had taken for granted. Now each day was a gift, to be taken with no expectation of another.

Jonred appeared with the metal box of coals, presented it with a bow and the customary words but Tierken stopped her as she went to follow him. 'You ride with me for a while.'

As she followed Tierken back down the tunnel, she wondered if Jonred had been punished for *failing in his duties*. The Kir herders were ready to leave, heavy packs on their backs, the children carrying small bundles. They kept up a shouted conversation with Slivkash and some of the other Kir patrolmen from the lip of the eastern cavern while Tierken readied Kalos.

The Kir child still coughed and Kira strode off through the goats, their strange white and blue barred eyes staring at her as they gave her passage. 'Kira!' Tierken's voice was full of irritation, but she reached the herders and raked about in her pack for the pouch of annin leaves.

'We don't have time for this,' he hissed, appearing at her side.

'Tell the mother to break the leaves up and mix them with boiling water and honey,' she told him, as she handed some over. 'The child should sip the mixture several times a day.'

Tierken translated and there was much bowing and smiling from the group but Tierken's hand on her elbow already propelled her back to Kalos. 'I *told* you last night to leave it be,' he said, as he mounted, and offered his hand.

'And I told you I was a Healer.'

'Your wrist, not your hand,' he said impatiently. 'You don't want to do yourself even more damage. We've a long day ahead, *too* long for unnecessary delays.'

Kira settled behind him. 'Curing a child's cough is *not* an unnecessary delay,' she retorted. 'Would the Terak king deny his people healing?'

'I've told you before we have *feailners*.'

'Well, would the Terak *feailner* deny his people healing?'

'He would if it delayed his patrol's return,' snapped Tierken, turning Kalos down the snowy slope.

'Then I'm glad I'm not Terak,' said Kira incensed.

'No, you're exeal.'

They reached the bottom of the slope and Tierken brought Kalos around the front of the Keep in a broad loop, the silence between them as icy as the ground. The caverns looked like gigantic eyes while below them, the land fell away in a massive blue fold of snow.

Tierken halted Kalos well south of it, while he waited for the patrol to finish their careful descent. 'Ember Chasm is probably another collapsed cave like those of the Keep,' he said. 'It's thought to be about a hundred lengths deep, but no one really knows. It claims goats and I've seen wolves go over it when they are pack-hunting and unaware. Men have died in it too. You're the first person I've known to survive it,' he said and gently touched her leg. It was a peace offering but Kira did not respond, still angry at his willingness to deny healing.

The air warmed as they rode and Kira would have enjoyed the journey had her hands not been so sore. Tierken kept Kalos at a steady pace, despite his ill temper at their delay, and it was close to midday before they reached the end of the snow, its edge as sharp as a knife-cut.

'If you're going to get early snow, it will be between Cover-crest and Breshlin,' he said over his shoulder.

'Is that snow ahead too?' asked Kira, peering at a gleaming strip of silver in the distance.

'That's the Silvercades. They're snowy in all seasons.'

Another name from the map! And nestled at the Silvercades' feet, was the Terak's stone city. 'How much further to Sarnia?' she asked, her heart starting an uneven thud.

'Two days from the Breshlin Ford which we reach at dusk. Whether we set camp there or go on depends.'

Two days! Soon she would be standing before the Terak king, no, the Terak *feailner*. She faltered. Tierken and the Terak ruler both bore the title of feailner so perhaps the Terak ruler had something more to his title that set him apart. Allogrenia had *Clan*leaders, *Protector* Leaders and the *Tremen* Leader, although in her case, she was also called *Feailner* in recognition of her ability to take pain. Perhaps Tierken's title of *Feailner* recognized his special role as the *taker of fire*.

The northern titles might be complicated but what worried her most was Tierken's complete ignorance of the Tremen. He out-ranked Marin, the Patrol Commander, so was highly placed, and if he had never heard of the Tremen, perhaps the Northern Ruler had not either. Her mouth dried as she recalled the Tain had known nothing of them and nor had Caledon, who journeyed widely. Her task was going to be doubly difficult if she must convince the Northern Ruler of the Tremen's existence *before* she begged his aid.

Tierken half turned. 'What distresses you?'

'Nothing,' muttered Kira, avoiding his eyes.

'I can feel your agitation. Are you in pain?'

'My hands hurt.' Tierken eyed her shrewdly but she could think of nothing to say that was both acceptable *and* true.

'We'll be at the Breshlin soon and you can tell me then,' he said.

6

The Breshlin River appeared with its usual suddenness, for its breadth and shallowness allowed it to merge into the plain. The rushing icy water was straight off the Silvercades and Tierken peered up its shining flow as Kalos splashed through the ford. The patrols always filled their waterskins here, and for Tierken, the tang of the Kessomi forests gave the water the sweetest taste of all the water in his lands.

He lowered Kira to the ground and rode on to where Marin had halted the patrol. It was a long time since breakfast at the Keep but the Breshlin offered little shelter. Ges Grove or The Ials would make better camps but The Ials were further east than he wanted. 'Stay here or go on to Ges?' he asked Marin.

Marin scowled up at the sky. 'I don't think Meros is going to send another snow-dump but the night will be cold. The shelter at the Ges is probably better, Feailner.'

Tierken glanced back to Kira who wandered up and down near the river. It meant a lot of travel in the dark, which was riskier to both horse and rider, despite the full moon. It also meant they would reach Sarnia in daylight, which had advantages *and* disadvantages.

'A quick meal, Marin, and then onto Ges.'

'Yes, Feailner.'

Marin barked orders and Tierken extricated his waterskin from his pack and, leaving Kalos to graze, went back to the river. Kira's eyes were like sunlight on metal and he wondered what had upset her. The last thing he wanted was another argument, especially so close to

Sarnia, and he filled his waterskin before he approached her. 'What troubles you?' he asked quietly.

'It's something you said before about feailners, that I don't understand.'

'What don't you understand?' he asked, unable to recall anything that could have distressed her.

'You said the Terak have *feailners*, not kings. Do the Terak use the word *feailner* for leaders of patrols as well as for the Terak ruler?'

'No. There's only one feailner.'

She stared at him in shock, her eyes brighter than the sun. 'But . . . you don't know anything about the Tremen,' she exclaimed *in Terak*.

By Meros! She knew Terak! It meant she had listened into *every* one of the patrol's conversations! 'You speak Terak. Of all the deceitful—' he began furiously, and then aware his men approached to water their horses, caught her arm and hauled her away out of earshot and released her with a savage shake. 'What are you? A spy?' he demanded. His blood roared at the implications but he could think of no one she could be spying for. '*Who-are-you*?'he demanded.

Her chin was up and her defiance added to his fury. 'I've told you who I am!' she retorted. 'And I don't speak Terak, I speak Tremen.'

'Don't add even *more* lies to those you've told me!'

'I've told you no lies!'

'Who are you spying for? The Tain?'

'I'm not spying for anyone! Tremen and Terak are the same language.'

'Similar they might be, the same they are not!' he spat, but the lilt of her words was stark. It was how Eris spoke, how *all* the old of Kessom spoke. Poerin's acid advice echoed in his head: *face uncomfortable facts, Tierken, or you will rue that you didn't* but he was in no mood to even be in her company let alone decipher her motives. '*Who* and *what* you are, I will discover in Sarnia,' he said coldly. 'Until then, you will *not* leave Jonred's side. Is that understood?' She nodded and he strode off.

The patrol consumed their meal of maizen bread and cotzee quickly, then the fires were doused and they were on their way. Tierken's guts roiled and it took him till nightfall to think dispassionately again. All that had really happened, he assured himself, was he had taken a patrol to the edge of the Tain lands, his men had rescued a woman from the Shargh, and given his obligation of protection *and* his need to be back in Sarnia for the Feailmark, he had brought her north with him. Fortuitously, she had healing skills that had garnered him goodwill from the Ashmiri.

Not only had he demonstrated sound leadership skills but sound strategic ones too in strengthening the Ashmiri treaty. It had been another successful patrol *except* he had lost the ability to differentiate lies from truth, had broken the tenets of protection by kissing the woman and, despite her lies, could think of no explanation for her eyes, her face and her use of Terak with a Kessomi lilt.

Yet she *could not* be Terak or Kessomi because she could not have grown to adulthood and remained unknown. Which left what? He dismissed the possibility she was Tain, given her Kessomi lilt, and forced himself to apply the logic Poerin had drummed into him. *If* she came from the Southern Forests as she claimed, her similarity to him probably resulted from their lines having originated in the same wandering families.

Her line had remained exeal and, like the Bishali, probably small in number, while his had become the Kessomis, then the Terak, and now the Terak Kirillian. The fact her similarity to him remained undiscovered supported her claim she came from the Southern Forests. It told him *what* she was, but none of it told him *why* the Shargh had taken her and *why* she had hidden her understanding of Terak.

He could dismiss the odd chance of them coming together on the Sarsalin as Meros in one of his more mischievous moods, but he was determined to have the answers to the rest of his questions *before* he returned to Sarnia's complications.

Kira listened to the patrol speak openly of the Feailner's clash with *their guest* as they rode, but they kept their voices low so their exchanges did not reach the Feailner at the head of the patrol. Jonred showed no sign of hearing the men's gossip either and when he spoke to Kira, he did so courteously and in Onespeak, and Kira responded in Onespeak.

She gazed at her surroundings calmly but she was in turmoil. She could not have made a worse start to gaining Terak aid. She understood Tierken's anger but by the time she was confident his men were *not* going to kill her, it had been too late to reveal her understanding of their tongue. It would have raised too many questions too, the answers to which were for the Northern Ruler's ears alone, Tierken's, as it turned out.

Despite Tierken's antagonism, she could not abandon her quest for Terak aid. He might believe her to be a liar and a spy but it did not alter the kin-link nor his obligation to honor it. But his ignorance of the Tremen's existence remained a daunting obstacle, and if Tierken had not heard of the Tremen, it was likely no one else in Sarnia had either.

Her thoughts turned to Caledon and the Tremen he would bring to Maraschin. Caledon did not believe the Terak would aid the Tremen or probably even the Tain, and the way things were turning, he might be right. In fact, it might be pointless going any further north and yet she had come so far, and was reluctant to abandon her quest. The Tremen *were* kin, whether Tierken knew it or not, and he *did* owe them aid.

She knew nothing about how the Northern lands were governed but if they had something like a Clancouncil, its members might include men like Clanleader Kemrick, whose passion was not just for his land's histories, but for the truth.

Kira smelled the familiar spicy scent of alwaysgreens well before the patrol reached Ges Grove and closed her eyes in relief. After the day's tumultuous events, knowing they were to camp within their Shelter, was like the sweetest of healing balms. Jonred passed her *care* to Marin, and went off with the horses, but her status as a prisoner was clear now which she sourly supposed was the fate of *liars* and *spies*.

Marin was kind, as he always was, and roasted nuts for her, but her churning stomach made it impossible to eat. The men ate at the other fires with the Feailner and, despite Marin's quietness, she craved solitude.

'I enjoyed climbing trees in my lands, Commander Marin, and would like to climb that one,' she said in Onespeak, and gestured to the one that sheltered them.

Marin nodded and she went to it, swung herself up into its branches and, as the tree's deep silence washed over her, forgot the complications on the ground. It was easy to imagine she climbed Nogren or Essogren, that the Bough still stood, that Kandor still lived.

She concentrated on finding the next branch and, as she neared the crown, searched for one to perch on that faced south. She did not break a hole in the leaves to look out of; she already knew she was a long way from home. She just shut her eyes, inhaled the alwaysgreen's spice, and let its deep Shelter hold her enclosed.

Tierken was in no hurry to confront the *woman* and it was late and the moon small before he made his way to Marin's fire, but Marin was alone. There was a bowl of un-eaten nuts near the woman's gifan, and a cup of cotzee, cold no doubt, and he frowned. 'Our *guest* sleeps?' he asked tersely, as Marin passed him some cotzee.

'Up that tree,' said Marin, pointing above them.

Tierken stared at him in astonishment. 'You *let* her climb the allogrenia?'

'If she's from a forest, she'll know trees.'

Tierken's hands came to his hips. 'It's not safe,' he said. 'She's under our protection.'

'It didn't look like it at the Breshlin.'

Tierken took a swig of cotzee. 'She speaks Terak.'

Marin's bushy brows rose. 'Have you asked her how it's so?'

'She says it's not Terak, it's Tremen.'

'They're the same tongue?'

'So she claims.'

'She has your eyes and face, Feailner, and now she speaks your tongue,' said Marin. 'It would be wise to find out why.' He tossed his cotzee dregs into the fire and rose. 'The Sarsalin stops at Sarnia gate,' he said, and moved off to the other fires.

It was a patrolmen's saying that alluded to the Sarsalin's freedoms being very different to Sarnia's intrigues. Marin warned Tierken Sarnia could use Kira against him, not that Tierken needed any warning; not after three seasons of dealing with the Marken.

He went to the tree and peered up through the branches. The darkness did not help but the tree was silent too. 'Kira?' Nothing. After their exchange at the Breshlin, he wondered if he was going to have to climb up and haul her down. 'Kira?' He called more loudly this time. 'Come down. We need to speak.'

'Yes, Feailner.' Her voice was faint which suggested she was a long way up. He went back to the fire to order his thoughts but it was hard to focus with her so many lengths above the ground. The foliage rustled and then she plummeted from the branches, curled her shoulder into a roll, and came back up onto her feet.

'By Irid! I thought you'd fallen!' he exclaimed, fear he had lost her at odds with his antagonism.

'Why would I fall, Feailner?' Her tone was faintly sarcastic and she used Onespeak, despite his use of Terak.

'I have questions I require answers to,' he said, and gestured to the fire. She came back with him but did not sit, standing with her feet apart, as if she braced herself against him. 'I'll make you some fresh cotzee,' he said, managing to keep his tone even.

'I thank you, Feailner, but I do not *require* any.'

Tierken grimaced. 'Tell me of your family,' he said, deciding to start with the easy things.

'My father was Maxen of Kashclan, my mother was Fasarini of Sarclan, my brothers were Merek, Lern and Kandor of Kashclan,' she clipped out.

Her use of *was* told him he had started with things that were far from *easy* but he forced himself on. 'Your family was killed by the Shargh?' He did not want to open old wounds but their deaths would explain why she had left the forest. She did not answer and even in the fire's small light, he saw her eyes darken. 'Speak Terak,' he said more gently. 'It will easier.'

'I don't speak *Terak*.'

Tierken's breath sifted through his teeth. It was going to be a long night unless one of them gave ground. 'Speak Tremen then,' he said tersely. 'And I'm waiting for the answer to my question.'

'The Shargh murdered my family, apart from my mother, who died when I was young.'

By Irid! The language *was* the same! 'I know you're Kashclan; what are the other clans called?'

'Sarclan, Tarclan, Morclan, Renclan, Kenclan, Barclan, Sherclan.'

Only eight, which confirmed his guess the Tremen were small in number, but the clan names meant nothing to him despite the shared language. 'Does each clan have their own lands?'

'The longhouses are set a day's walk apart and each clan has gathering rights within a fixed boundary around them. Allogrenia is like the spokes of a wheel. The longhouses and their octads fan out from the Bough in the centre.'

Tierken's eyes narrowed. 'Your settlement is called *allogrenia*? Like these trees?'

'Yes.'

Her line *had* to have originated from the same families that had given rise to the Kessomis. Longhouses, allogrenias, her appearance and language: there were too many similarities for any other explanation. 'What is *the Bough*?' he asked distractedly.

'It was the most beautiful building in Allogrenia, as befits a place of healing,' she said. 'Kasheron built it.' Tierken stared at her, thinking he had misheard. 'Kasheron and his followers created a place of healing in the Southern Forests, after they left the brutal ways of the north behind.'

Of all the things Tierken thought she might say, the claim was so bizarre he threw back his head and laughed. 'Kasheron took his cowardly skin and those of his followers north, over the Oskinas,' he said. 'He deserted Terak *and* their comrades at a time when they fought for their very existence. If it weren't for Terak's bravery *and* that of *his* people, *and* the loyalty of the Kirs and Illians who fought with them, the Shargh would be doing to the Terak Kirillian, what they've already done to the Tremen!'

She was rigid, her gaze unwavering. 'As the Terak Feailner, I call upon you to honor the blood-link to your kin the Tremen and aid us against the Shargh attacks.'

'There *is* no blood-link! Kasheron and his fellow traitors fled over the Oskinas seas.'

Her eyes were brighter than fire-flames. 'You *refuse* to honor your obligations to your kin?'

Tierken quelled a surge of anger at the insult. It was clear she believed what she said and that meant the Tremen, like the Bishali, had concocted tales of grand ancestors to compensate for their unimportant and often precarious lives. 'I've already explained what *exeal* means,' he said evenly. 'You, and presumably the Tremen, share many things with us, but *not* our history.

'Your people probably came from the same families as the Kessomis did, at a time when they all roamed in small groups. Some of these families gave rise to the Kessomis, who in turn gave rise to the Terak, and the Terak later joined with the Illians and Kirs, who together with the Kessomis, now form *my* people. Others of these families obviously went to the Southern Forests to become the Tremen. There *is* no kin-link to honor.'

'So, you not only deny *us* but our histories too!'

'*If* your histories say you are of Kasheron's line, they are false,' he said bluntly. 'The Terak Kirillian's histories are well known, as is Kasheron's desertion. Now, as it is late, Kira, I suggest you sleep. We have another long day tomorrow.'

8

Kira was too angry to sleep and the Terak *Kutan's* insult of Kasheron added to her fume. Kasheron and his followers had sacrificed *everything* to carve out the healing community of Allogrenia when it would have been *so* much easier to stay in the north's luxury, like the Terak Kutan's forebears had!

She shouldn't be surprised at the leader of the Terak Kutan's behavior, she concluded savagely, but while Caledon had warned her the north wouldn't aid the Tremen, he had not warned her they would deny the Tremen's histories altogether! It didn't seem to have occurred to the *mighty* Terak Kutan leader, that his *mighty* histories of the *mighty* Terak *Kirillian,* might be false!

It was also very convenient! If the Tremen were the descendants of *exeal* families, the *mighty* Terak Kutan leader could *dishonor* the kin-link without *dishonoring* himself! She was so churned up she crawled back out of her gifan and was surprised to see Marin sitting by the fire. 'Jonred's on guard duty,' he said. 'Do you need time alone?'

'No,' she snapped, and took a deep breath. 'I thank you,' she added, and settled beside him.

'Dawn is close,' said Marin, and shifted a pan of water onto the coals to heat.

Kira stared at the flames but her thoughts were on the Tain and the Tremen *volunteers*. If the fighting lasted for moons, the volunteers might all be killed protecting Maraschin, and the Tain were under no obligation to protect the longhouses. 'Do you know how a treaty is made, Commander?' she asked.

'Treaties or alliances are pledges of aid exchanged by leaders of different peoples,' he said, as he stirred spices into the water. 'They usually spring from friendships of many seasons but they can also be used to *stop* fighting between enemies, as they were with the Ashmiri.'

Kira's thoughts swung to Kasheron again. He had severed *all* friendships at the Sundering, and the forest's isolation had sustained the breach. She had never seen the Sundering in this light before. It was as if she were on the outside of the trees looking in, rather than on the inside looking out.

'One more night and we'll be in Sarnia,' said Marin cheerfully. Kira swallowed dryly. Everything she knew of Sarnia involved metal and dead stone. 'There's nothing to fear in Sarnia,' he said, as he poured the cotzee into cups.

Kira liked Marin, not just because he had rescued her from the Shargh, but because he was kind. He was also Illian rather than Terak Kutan. 'You have a bondmate in Sarnia?' she asked curiously.

'A *wife*,' corrected Marin, and smiled. 'I do indeed, and a daughter about your age and a son of thirteen seasons. Tisia is soon to be married but Stinian insists on following in my footsteps, despite me warning him he'd be better to work wood or metal,' said Marin, his pride plain. 'Now, as Jonred's busy, you will have to put up with my cooking. We travel all day, so you'll need something to stick to those ribs of yours.'

'I'm not hungry.'

'You look hungry though I'm not sure for what,' he said and handed her the cotzee. Kira felt her face warm but Marin's gaze had shifted to a point over her shoulder, and he poured another cup, set it next to the fire and moved away.

'You're up early,' said Tierken in Terak, as he sat beside her.

'So are you,' she said in Onespeak, keeping her gaze on the fire.

She sensed his displeasure but his tone remained determinedly light. 'I must have spread my sleeping-sheet on a root,' he said. 'Not conducive to a good night's sleep.' Neither is being told you are not kin, your histories are lies, and your ancestor was a treacherous coward, thought Kira bitterly.

'We have one more night on the Sarsalin,' he went on. 'I've sent scouts ahead to inform the Domain of your arrival. Laryia will prepare rooms for you, clean clothing, and anything else you need.'

'Is Laryia your wife?'

'Do you think I would have kissed you had I been married?'

He *was* angry now but she still refused to look at him. 'Your men brag of the women they trick to their beds and how they hide their deceit from their wives.'

'There are faithless men and women in most lands,' said Tierken, 'even in the forests, I suspect. Aren't there?'

Kira shrugged and it was Tierken who finally broke the silence. 'I understand why you're upset, Kira,' he said gently. 'When we get to Sarnia, and you've had a chance to rest, and eat properly, and feel safe, we will talk again. Then you will understand.'

Kira kept her gaze on the fire until his footstep thumped away. She already *understood*; he had made things abundantly clear last night. And he seemed to have planned out her life to his liking in Sarnia too! She paced around the fire and then stopped and looked up at the alwaysgreen.

The more she thought about it, the less reason she had to go to Sarnia at all. She needed to be in Maraschin with Caledon and her people not stuck in the north with a man who not only denied her people aid, but kinship as well.

The patrol was on the move again by dawn. Kira kept her gaze on the Silvercades as she rode behind Jonred and listened to the men discuss wagering, alehouses, the women of the Caru Quarter, and everything else they planned to enjoy once they were back.

The sun had westered before Marin shouted orders and the patrol wheeled east. A scattering of trees emerged from a dip, their growth too sparse to be a grove and, as they drew nearer, Kira saw a series of shallow pools. The patrol halted and Jonred set her down and rode off.

Kira stayed where she was. The men collected windfall, set fires and pitched gifans, a sure sign the night was going to get colder. They spoke together as they worked and laughed at some joke or other. They were one people, but not *her* people, as far as their leader was concerned.

Kira hugged herself as she stared at the trees but they were alien too. There were no groves of ashaels and castellas, no terrawoods, severs, chrysens and fallowoods. Nor were there Allogrenia's steep stony places, its streams and springs, its places alive with birds and brightwings, and its quiet places of emerald light. There was no Shelter here, just an empty sky and an empty plain and a man who denied her people.

She walked away, barely aware of where she went, her gaze on her shadow as it spidered over the ground before her. The hope that help lay in the north had driven her for so long that now that hope had gone, she felt directionless.

A horse appeared in her line of vision and she stopped. She knew it was the Northern leader but she kept her gaze on the horse's muzzle. It was the color of storm-clouds and she stroked it, surprised by its softness. The horse's eyes were long-lashed and luminous, and she wondered how Kasheron had turned his back on these glorious creatures, walked deep into the trees, and never returned.

'Kira, come,' said Tierken softly. 'There's something I want to show you.' She did not move. 'Come.'

She took his hand reluctantly and he pulled her up behind him and urged Kalos to a canter. He kept the pace gentle and after a while the land dipped away to reveal a steep-sided hill with a massive tor atop it. Kalos snorted as his powerful haunches propelled him up the near vertical slope to the small summit, and he stopped there, his flanks heaving as Tierken set her down, then thumped down beside her.

'The Terak call this *Terak's Tor* but the Kessomis call it *Helin's Twin*,' he said. 'It's due south of Helin Peak, the highest point in the Silvercades and made of the same stone. To the Kirs it's *Mindolin,* the spear, and to the Illians, *Fleam*, the sword.'

The tor had chips of crystal and Kira was reminded of waking in the Warens after the first Shargh attack and knowing everything had gone. 'What think you?' he asked gently.

'That it's unusual,' said Kira in Onespeak.

'I didn't bring you here to show you Terak's Tor no matter how *unusual* it is. Come, or you'll miss it. He turned her so her back rested against him, and folded his arms around her shoulders. 'Watch,' he said, his gaze on the mountains.

Kira stifled the urge to shrug him off and dutifully watched the sun slip to the horizon. The Silvercades' snow burned with a golden fire, then with an intense pink, and then with a gentler rose. Its beauty undid her and Tierken's proximity woke an intense need for Shelter. She turned in the circle of his arms and drew his mouth to hers. His surprise was momentary and then his kisses intense but all too soon he drew back. 'You're under my protection,' he said, his eyes as bright as the sunset.

'There's only *now*,' she said in Tremen, craving the Shelter of his arms, but he held her by the shoulders so she could not return to them.

'I will make it well for you in Sarnia,' he said. 'You'll be happy there.'

Kira said nothing, even as they rode back to camp. She was angry she had given into her need for Shelter and angry with Tierken for believing she would desert the Tremen. The men had gathered around a single fire and they watched Tierken lift her down. 'Stay with Marin,' he said, and rode off.

Kira had intended to sit behind the Commander, but Marin shifted sideways so she must sit beside him, in full view of the men. 'And how did you like Terak's Tor?' he asked loudly.

Kira sensed he protected her and Tierken from gossip and forced a smile. 'It's big,' she said.

Marin laughed. 'The Kirs, Illians and Teraks might agree with you, but not the Kessomis. They've been known to call Terak's Tor a pebble. Eat up,' he added, as he passed her a bowl of roasted nuts. A mug of cotzee followed. 'It's your last meal on the Sarsalin. Tomorrow night you'll sample Sarnia's finer offerings. The Rehan and Lehan valleys are rich and traders bring more fare from the northern ports.'

'I will look forward to it,' she managed to say.

Marin settled back with his cup of cotzee. 'Niria will have a rare feast waiting to welcome me home,' he said, with a sigh.

'Doesn't she miss you when you're on patrol?'

'We've been a long time together. Niria knew I was a patrolman when we married.'

'How often do the patrols go out?'

'The Feailner's been in Sarnia three seasons and in that time he's been out about once a moon. This patrol's been short. Some last more than a moon half.'

'That must be hard for your wife.'

'I'm not the only Commander,' said Marin. 'I don't always go.'

'Why does the Feailner patrol so often?'

'The Northern people were herders, so we've always journeyed,' said Marin then lowered his voice. 'It's a good way to show the younger men *all* their lands too and train them in horsemanship and battle skills. If fighting comes, they'll need to know what they're fighting for.' Marin took a swig of his cotzee and grinned. 'And young men with time on their hands are likely to turn it to ill use. The patrols put their energies to *good* use.'

The talk around the fire ebbed and then Slivkash began to sing, his pure voice soon joined by the other Kirs. 'Are there herders nearby?' whispered Kira.

'Not according to the scouts,' said Marin softly. 'We always sing on the patrol's last night. We sing of our time together under the stars and thank Meros *and* Irid, *if* you're a Kessomi, for our safety *and* the true hearts of our comrades. Kirs sing with Kirs, and they usually start, for they have fine singing voices. It's where the Feailner got his. The Teraks go next, then the Illians, then the Kessomis and back to the Kirs. We make our *own* lay-link.'

The Kirs' voices drew out in a final single note, Tierken singing with them, but before it ended, Jonred, Shird, Vardrin and other Teraks she did not know took up the song and Tierken sang again. He would sing with them all, realized Kira, for they were *his* people, but *his* people did not include the Tremen or *her*.

The lay-link was another forcible reminder of being exeal but the singing also reminded her of Allogrenia's celebrations of Turning and Thanking. Her eyes burned and she stumbled from the fire. 'Do you wish time alone?' asked Marin, suddenly at her shoulder.

'I am alone whether I wish it or not!' She wearily pushed the hair from her face. 'I'm tired, Marin. If you show me my gifan, I'll go to my rest.' Marin pointed to a gifan and she crawled into it but the singing was clear through the walls and Kira clamped her arms around her ears and wept.

9

Kira rode behind Marin the next day because he told her Jonred was on scout with Slivkash. The Commander turned out to be a lot more talkative than Jonred and kept up a commentary on everything they passed. She learned the steep juts of land to the east and west were the Lehan and Rehan Spurs and that the broad grassy swathe the patrol galloped over was the Rehan Valley. It was home to two rivers, said Marin, fed from the Silvercades' snow-melt: the Rehan River to the west, and the Steelwater to the east. There were many small settlements in the Rehan Valley for the soil was rich and much of Sarnia's food was grown there.

Kira took the opportunity to ask Marin about those who helped the Feailner rule and learned of men called the *Marken,* and of a man called the *Keeper of the Domain*. The Marken had advised the previous Feailner, *Darid,* said Marin, but there was something about the way Marin suddenly chose his words, that suggested the Marken were not well disposed towards the current Feailner, or him to them. She was reminded of Adris chafing under King Beris's rule and wondered whether, even if she managed to convince the Marken of the kin-link, the Feailner would heed their advice.

The *Keeper of the Domain* seemed a more promising possibility. Marin's words held warmth when he spoke of him and Kira gathered there was friendship between the Keeper and the Feailner. Apparently the Keeper of the Domain's father was one of the Marken and, while Kira briefly considered how to make use of the link, she had a nagging feeling that *nothing* was going help her quest for aid.

She knew she should turn for the south now but also knew the Feailner was unlikely to allow it. Every stride of Marin's horse took her further from Maraschin where Caledon might already wait with the Tremen volunteers, where she *knew* there was aid and, as the day drew on, dread grew that she was abandoning the Tremen.

The lands' strangeness added to her churn. There were trees laden with strange fruit, rows of lush plants, goats confined by fences rather than free to roam, animals with massive shoulders that bellowed, and fat birds that pecked the earth and did not fly away, even when the patrol galloped past. There were also oddly truncated longhouses. The people who worked nearby bowed low but Kira turned her face away, painfully aware of how unkempt she was.

Marin's sudden enthusiasm for describing Sarnia did not help the knots in her belly either. The city had stone paving and cleverly constructed domed roofs of stone, he said, for Terak had brought stonewrights from afar who had built in the manner of their own country.

She could see snatches of Sarnia between the trees: the buildings as pale as bone, the domed-roofs like the halves of shattered eggs. The stone buildings marched up into the Silvercades' foothills and the whole sprawl was encircled by a massive wall that, like Maraschin's wall, kept people in as well as out.

Tales of the Terak Kutan that Tremen children told each other on moonless nights to elicit squeals of fright swirled about in her head. This was the place Kasheron had fled and the home of its present ruler who called Kasheron a *traitor* and a *coward*; who denied Kasheron's

73

people aid; who accused *her* of being a *liar* and a *spy*. And what did they do to *liars* and *spies* in the stone city? Certainly nothing good.

Her breathing quickened and she started to sweat. She reminded herself the Terak had rescued her from the Shargh and treated her with courtesy, but the northern leader had threatened her more than once and she was now essentially his prisoner. Nausea surged and she frantically tapped Marin on the back. 'I need time alone,' she choked.

Marin shouted an order to slow but Kira threw her leg over the horse's rump and half slid, half fell to the ground as they galloped. There were shouts as the following patrolmen swerved to avoid trampling her and she managed to right herself, and ran back the way they had come.

Orders were barked behind her and, as a horse pounded at her shoulder, the horror of how the Shargh had snatched her, added to her panic. 'Kira!' It was the Feailner's voice but she sped on, and then the Feailner's big grey suddenly blocked the way ahead. She darted left, but the Feailner thumped to the ground, and caught her in his arms.

She tried to wrench herself free but it was hard to even get air into her lungs. Blackness intruded and then she became aware of the tussocky grass under her backside and a hand on the back of her neck that pushed her head between her knees. She sucked in air, the sweat cold on brow.

The Feailner crouched beside her but she kept her eyes on the grass as she concentrated on breathing. Another pair of boots appeared in her line of vision and Marin's voice sounded. 'I can mix her a stimulant, if you wish, Feailner.'

'No need,' said Tierken tersely. 'Pull the men back to Suran Spring. We'll join you there.' Marin's footsteps

74

receded and Kira was able to raise her head enough to watch Kalos graze. His dark grey muzzle wrinkled as his teeth gripped the grass, then he jerked his head sideways and tore it from the ground.

Tierken put his hand under her elbow and lifted her. 'Come,' he said. 'There's a better place to sit under the trees.' He took Kalos's reins and glanced sideways at Kira as they walked. She was still unsteady but he did not think she had been afflicted by a sudden illness; the ill did not leap from horses and run. There was an allogrenia in the grove he headed for, thank Irid, and even a convenient log beneath it. He lowered her onto it and passed her his waterskin. 'Drink,' he said, and was relieved when she did. She handed it back and he settled beside her. 'Tell me what you fear.'

She had looked at him rarely since his rejection of her ridiculous claim of kinship and she did not look at him now, but as she pushed the hair from her eyes, the rope burns on her wrists reminded him of just how little he really knew about her.

His intention to question her more fully had ended with her spurious kinship claim and it had been a mistake not to have persevered and found out more. He needed reasons to convince her to enter Sarnia and everything suggested Sarnia was the last place she intended to go.

'Tell me what you fear,' he repeated.

'Is the Rehan Valley safe?' she asked in Onespeak, her gaze on Kalos.

'Of course. Why do you ask?'

'Then you have fulfilled your obligation to deliver me to a place of safety.' She rose and bowed, her gaze on a point over his shoulder. 'I thank the Terak Feailner and his men for their rescue of me from the Shargh, and for safe passage across the Sarsalin, and for their care of me since. And I wish the Terak Kirillian Feailner and *his* people well.'

He stood too in case she intended to bolt. She still used Onespeak with him, which was not an encouraging sign, but her little farewell speech had given him the chance to see her eyes. They were as dark as the allogrenia's leaves which confirmed her fear. 'We need to speak,' he said, careful to keep his voice soft.

'With respect, Feailner, there's nothing left to say. According to you, my forebear Kasheron was a *treacherous coward*, I am a *liar* and a *spy*, and my people's histories are *false*. I am also *exeal*, as are my people. The only reason I came north was to seek aid for them, and as you've now refused it, there's no need for me to enter your stone city.'

She had used the phrase *my peop*le more than once but it was the Protector Commander's task to make the dangerous trek north to negotiate aid, not that of a seventeen-year-old girl. 'Seeking aid for the Tremen is their leader's responsibility, not yours,' he said tersely.

She bowed again, this time ironically. 'Tremen Leader Feailner Kiraon of Kashclan, that is *Kasheron's* clan, greets the *Terak* Feailner.' She paused. 'In Allogrenia, a *feailner* is a taker of pain, not a custodian of fire.'

Tierken stared at her incredulously. 'Are you telling me the Tremen are led by a seventeen-year old girl?'

The green in her eyes was abruptly replaced by gold. 'The Tremen are led by their best Healer, whoever that happens to be! Kasheron didn't believe that leadership should result from a simple accident of birth.'

Tierken stifled a retort at the insult. Her gold eyes told him anger had replaced fear, and that was very useful indeed, because he knew exactly where her anger came

76

from. 'All patrols must travel fast,' he said carefully, 'which gives very little time for *thorough* conversations about *anything*. On my return to Sarnia, I must spend time with the Marken, but after that, I would like to meet with you to discuss the Tremen histories *in far greater detail.*'

She hesitated and he knew he had her, but the softening of her eyes was more important. He had first seen them turn to liquid honey when they had kissed at the spring near Cover-cape Crest, and again at Terak's Tor, and the change told him her attraction to him was as strong as his to her. It might not be powerful enough to overcome her anger at his rejection of her preposterous claim *yet*, but he was determined it would be.

'Are you feeling well enough to go on?' he asked. She nodded, and he mounted Kalos and offered his hand, but she made no move to take it and he wondered if he had congratulated himself too soon. Then noticed her eyes had darkened again.

'Here,' he said and shifted behind the saddle. 'Sit in front.' He settled her so she was enclosed by his arms and felt her tension ease as he kept Kalos to a gentle gallop. He was gratified his proximity reassured her but the wash of chimes from Sarnia told him watchers had seen their approach.

Marin met them a little way from the spring. 'I can take her again, Feailner,' he said.

'I'll keep her with me, Commander,' said Tierken. 'She's fearful of Sarnia.'

'At least put her behind, Feailner. We both know the gossip that's run before us and how those of Sarnia will see it.'

'And how will those of Sarnia see it, Commander?' he asked dryly.

'That you bring back a bride.'

Kira stiffened but for once Tierken was in no mood to accommodate Sarnia's gossips *or* the Marken. He spent his days being polite to the Marken's daughters, unexpectedly thrust into his path, and to the daughters of other highly placed Sarnians intent on enhancing their personal power by joining the *Feailner's* family. It might be good to disrupt a few machinations with a new, and unexpected, competitor.

'Let the city think that I *do* return with a bride, if it gives them pleasure,' he said. Marin nodded, but his disapproval was clear as he ordered the patrol into formation and they set off again. The sound of bells increased as they neared the wall and Tierken smiled sourly as he noticed the wall's walkway was crowded with watchers. Perhaps he should have heeded Marin's advice *not* to excite Sarnia's gossips. Patrols often returned at night and the fine day meant large number of Sarnians had gathered to watch the Feailner's return.

'Why is there music?' asked Kira.

'It's a Sarnian tradition to ring bells to welcome a Feailner home. They are rung at a Feailner's birth too, at his marriage, and at his death.' He felt her tension grow as they neared the wall. 'How is a Tremen leader welcomed home?' he asked to distract her.

'I don't know. No leader has left Allogrenia before.'

They were almost to the gate and Marin bawled to the patrol to bring them into entry formation. The spectators were focused on Tierken, as they always were, but also on Kira, and he heard the hum of their exchanges above the bells. Kira obviously did too and shrank against him.

'You are safe,' he murmured in her ear. 'Trust me.'

10

Kira's heart thudded as they passed under the wall and only Tierken's Shelter stopped her fleeing again. She stared straight ahead as Marin led most of the men off to stables set against the wall but Tierken remained at the gate. The bells fell silent and although she now had her back to the watchers on the wall, a crowd of on-lookers were gathered on the paving too.

They kept a respectful distance but their attention was fixed on her and Kira stared up at the broad paved path that ran up to gates in a second wall. From what Marin said, she presumed the wall enclosed the *Domain*, where the *Keeper* dwelt. Sarnia's layout reminded her of King's Way but there was no Queen Alitha's grove here to soften the stone.

The paving was smooth but the path had been roughened and, as the gates opened and two silver horses galloped down, she saw why. The crowd whispered excitedly but Kira's heart raced. Their pace seemed too fast for the slope but neither horse slipped and the black and silver-clad riders were soon beside them.

Kira decided they must be Terak, being too tall and too muscular for Kirs or Illians. They reminded her of King's Guard and, like them, they wore a lot of metal in their uniforms. The flash of silver against the black was striking but Kira recoiled.

'The Domain Guard is sworn to protect the Feailner and his family,' said Tierken loudly. 'Guard Leader Tharin and Guard Second Daril will accompany you wherever you go. This is my guest, the Lady Kira of the Tremen,' he said to the Guard.

The Guard bowed and Kira nodded awkwardly, nonplussed by Tierken having suggested to the crowd she was part of his family. He had also given her a title he had never used before, but she did not want to be a *Lady* in Sarnia, any more than she had in Maraschin. The Guard brought their horses behind them and Tierken turned Kalos up the path. He kept the big grey to a walk but Kira would have been happy with a flat gallop to escape the crowd.

The Domain walls were high and the gates manned by more black- and silver-clad Guard.

They passed through into an enormous square and Kira's nerves jangled as a storm of whinnying broke out from another set of stables. Kalos whinnied too and Tierken laughed. His mood had changed, she noticed. He was happy and relaxed because he was *home*.

He set Kira down, then nimbly leapt off. 'Wait here,' he said, as a grey-haired man appeared. Tierken went forward to meet him, taking Kalos with him, and the older man looked towards her and nodded at regular intervals while Tierken spoke. Then Tierken handed over Kalos's reins, and with final clap on his horse's neck, came back.

'That was Horse Master Ryn who's in charge of the Domain Stables. He will continue your riding lessons once you've settled in and things are more familiar.'

Kira's stomach resumed its churn. Tierken spoke as if he expected her to be there for many moons. He took her hand and squeezed it as he led the way across the square towards the immense domed building in front. It was abutted by two other buildings that ran down either side of the square. Both were double storeyed with balconies supported by colonnades.

'The Meeting Hall,' said Tierken, nodding to the domed building, 'from which Sarnia and the Terak lands are administered. The building to our left is the Rehan wing, where the Marken stay during the Feailmark, and the one to our right is the Lehan wing, where the Feailner and his family live. I've had a room prepared for you there.'

It was the second time Tierken had alluded to her being part of his family but Kira's attention was taken by the immense, shining window set high in the building's dome. 'It's colored glass,' said Tierken, as he followed her gaze. 'By all accounts, it took nearly two seasons to finish and a bag of gold traders. It looks well enough when the sun shines on it.'

'It's got the *alwaysgreen* on it,' gasped Kira.

'And the running horse. Both are the mark of my people.'

'They're on the ring too,' she said in wonder.

'What ring?'

'The one Kash—'

'Tierken!' It was a cry of pure delight, and a young woman clad in a gown of brilliant red, dashed from behind the colonnades, across the open paving, and threw herself into Tierken's arms.

Kira could not see the woman's face because it was buried in Tierken's shoulder but the man who hurried after her seemed equally happy. Tierken released the woman and the two men embraced. The man looked like a younger version of Marin, but was darker, with wider set eyes. The woman laughed, dark-eyed and dark-haired like the man, but with flawless creamy skin.

Kira waited uneasily until Tierken turned back to her. 'Kira, this is my sister Laryia, and my friend Farid, the Keeper of the Domain. He administers Sarnia in my absence *and* when I'm here,' he added with a smile.

Farid bowed but Kira lost sight of him as she was enfolded in Laryia's arms, her sweet scent and glossy braids reminding Kira uncomfortably of her own unwashed state. 'You are *most* welcome, Kira,' said Laryia warmly, 'and you are *so* like Tierken!' She laughed as she held her lightly by the shoulders. 'When the scouts reported they were bringing a gold-eyed woman back whose face was a looking-glass of the Feailner's, I didn't believe them! But they were right!' Laryia laughed again as her eyes darted between Kira and Tierken.

'As I explained in the Rehan, Kira, I'll be taken up with the Feailmark for the next few days,' said Tierken. 'Laryia will look after your needs and show you Sarnia's sights. Mid-market's soon, which I know you will enjoy, and I'll be free after that for us to speak again.'

He smiled but Kira abruptly wondered whether he had used the *hope* he would change his mind about the Tremen to trick her into entering the city. Out on the plain, he had been absolutely certain of the falseness of *her* histories and she had a feeling he would not be changing his mind.

The silence stretched and Tierken nodded to her and moved off with Farid, his arm draped over Farid's shoulders. His whole demeanor told her he was well content with how he had arranged things and as she glared after him, Laryia's smile became less certain.

'Come,' she said finally, and linked her arm through Kira's. 'You've had a long ride and men are not the most thoughtful when it comes to washing and clean clothes. I'll show you to your rooms and you can bathe and then we can eat.'

Laryia led her under the colonnades to a stone staircase with carved balustrades. 'The Domain is massive and both wings are full of rooms that are rarely used,' said Laryia, as they exited the stairs onto the balcony. 'In Terak's day, it housed many more families.'

Kira wondered if she alluded to Kasheron and his followers but Laryia was intent on the sky. 'I hope it stays fine. There's so much I want to show you.' She smiled, and Kira glimpsed Kandor again, but Laryia shared little else with Tierken. She must resemble one parent and he the other.

'Come and see the Owl Fountain,' she said, tugging Kira along the balcony. 'I think Terak designed the pool but the fountain was added by his mother, Queen Kiraon.' *Kasheron's mother too*, added Kira rebelliously. They looked down on a circular pool rimmed with a low stone wall and set with a central fountain shaped like a tree. Water cascaded from the uppermost branch and dripped from the others back into the pool. 'The branches have little owls carved on them,' said Laryia, 'but you can't see them from here.'

'It's very pretty,' said Kira politely, and it was but she mainly liked the tinkling of the water. It was a relief after so much stone and she resolved to look at the fountain more closely later, especially the owls.

'The rooms directly below belong to the Domain servers,' said Laryia. 'They prepare the Domain meals, clean the rooms and the courtyards, and order the records. Mouras, the Room Master, will assign a server to look after your needs.'

Kira blinked. 'My needs?'

'Keep your clothes, clean your rooms, dress your hair,' said Laryia, avoiding looking at Kira's hair.

'I'm happy to do these things myself.'

'That's what I said when we first came from Kessom,' said Laryia dryly. 'In Kessom, you do *everything* for yourself but here servers are *part of the dignity and respect of the Domain*,' she mimicked.

'So, is Farid a server?'

'By Irid no! He's Keeper of the Domain, and Tierken's closest friend, *and* he's Rosham's son, of all people.'

The last part was delivered in a mutter which told Kira Laryia did not like Rosham, but Kira was so overwhelmed with the flow of new information she did not ask why. The balcony gave a good view of the symmetrical pattern of the paving below, which she had not noticed before; of the pool and of the stables near the Domain gate.

Laryia turned to the rooms behind them. 'These are Tierken's rooms,' she said, gesturing to a heavily carved timber door, 'but he doesn't use them much. He usually sleeps and eats in the Meeting Hall *when* he's here. These are my rooms, and these are yours.'

The doors looked identical and Kira made a mental note that hers were the third from the end, mortified by the possibility of blundering into Tierken or Laryia's by mistake. Laryia turned the heavy metal key in the door and pushed it open to reveal a large room furnished with an ornate table, carved chairs, storage chests of pale wood, and shelves fixed to the walls. Lamps sat on the shelves as well as animals carved from wood and stone.

'Your rooms are a little plain, I'm afraid. The scout told me to remove everything of metal. I had to leave the lamps, of course, or you would be in the dark, and there are some metal fixtures in the bathing-room. If I've misunderstood Tierken's instructions, I can get the servers to bring the bowls and candle-holders back. They're Kir work and beautifully enameled.'

'No . . . I thank you,' said Kira, touched by Tierken's thoughtfulness.

'Your sleeping-room is through here,' said Laryia, leading the way through another door into a large airy room with three large windows. There was an enormous bed set under them, with a rich green covering embroidered with dark swirling leaves. The plush floor rug had leaves on it too.

'I've had the servers shift your bed under the window so you can see the Silvercades,' said Laryia, as she pushed the shutters wide. 'It's a lovely view when the sun sets.' She turned back. 'The scout said your home was in a forest so I tried to find things you might like.'

'They're very beautiful,' said Kira thickly.

'You can see Helin Peak,' said Laryia, peering out the window again. 'The smaller peak to the left is Kalin, and the one to the right, Mintlin. Kessom is south of Mintlin but you can't see it from here.'

'Tierken told me your grandmother lives there,' said Kira as she stared across at the mountains.

'We used to as well. Eris took us there after our mother Lyess died.'

'Didn't your father want you here?' asked Kira in puzzlement.

'Merench drowned a few moons later. I don't remember either of them but Tierken does. Perhaps that's why—' Laryia stopped. 'Anyway, after our father's death, the Feailner, *my uncle Darid*, was happy for Tierken to go to Kessom.' Her face hardened. 'He hoped for his own, *brown-eyed*, son.'

'But Terak had gold eyes.'

'Yes, I know. Terak built Sarnia and his mother, Queen Kiraon, who had gold eyes too, was greatly loved but after Kasheron deserted, gold eyes took on the stain of faithlessness.' She glanced at Kira and colored. 'Even after Darid's wife died he refused to send for Tierken,' she added, angry now. 'But Eris made sure Tierken was trained for the feailnership even more rigorously than if he'd been raised here.'

'Does Eris come to the Domain often?'

Laryia snorted. 'Sleep in the *city of stone*? Not Eris. She didn't even come to Tierken's Rites of Rulership, despite how much they meant to her.'

'That must have been hard for Tierken,' said Kira slowly.

'Not as hard as not seeing Eris for three seasons.' Kira stared at her in astonishment. 'We had to—*Tierken* had to break from Kessom.' She smiled bitterly. 'Kessom's the heart of healing in the north and Kasheron was a Healer. It doubles the *taint* Tierken carries. Eris understands.'

'But Tierken said he'd take me to Kessom,' said Kira, wondering if he had lied.

Laryia's eyes widened. 'To Kessom?'

'To meet your grandmother. I'm a Healer.'

'*You're* a Healer?' She stared at Kira for a long moment before she recollected herself. 'Forgive me. You've had a hard ride and have yet to bathe and eat. Come, I'll show you to the bathing-room.'

The bathing-room contained a deep bath crafted from smooth, pink stone; a large metal washing-bowl with fish engraved on it and, on the far side of the room, a low seat with a lid, which Laryia explained was a latrine, with pipes that ran away beyond the city's walls.

There were metal spouts above the bath that delivered hot and cold water via taps and a large looking glass that revealed Kira's tangled hair and her gold eyes, stark in her thin face. Gold-eyes *and* a Healer; a *double taint*, she thought grimly as she turned away.

'Tierken asked me to choose some gowns for you,' said Laryia, pointing to the neat pile on the chair, but I think they're all going to be too large.'

Kira thought of Adris and suppressed a sigh. 'I thank you but I don't wear gowns.'

'But . . . Tierken asked for them especially. It's the way Terak women dress in Sarnia.'

'I'm not a Terak woman.'

Unexpectedly, Laryia grinned. 'I haven't seen Tierken's eyes catch fire like that since we were children.' She sobered and frowned thoughtfully. 'I have clothes I brought with me from Kessom. I was younger then and smaller. Kessomi women wear hip-length tunics with trousers underneath. They're not new though and I don't think Tierken will be happy.'

Kira resisted the urge to tell Laryia making Tierken happy was not her priority. 'They would suit me very well. Thank you, Laryia. You've been very helpful and welcoming but there's no need to stay. I'm sure you miss Tierken when he's gone, as he misses you.'

Laryia's clear eyes regarded her worriedly. 'You're our guest. I can't just leave you. Besides, you haven't eaten.'

'If you could bring some food, I'll eat later. What I really need is some time alone to write, that is, if you have paper and ink.'

'Write? Yes, of course. I can get you some paper and ink, but—'

'Go to Tierken, Laryia. Then on the morrow, you can show me Sarnia. I might have a bath now,' said Kira, and slipped off her pack.

Laryia hovered. 'My rooms are the very next door remember. If you need anything, even in the middle of the night, you are to knock.'

11

Kira heaved a sigh of relief as the outer door shut and for a moment simply stood, eyes closed. Then she turned on the water taps, and shrugged out of her jacket and shirt. The looking-glass revealed the angry red scrapes from her slide into Ember Chasm; the rope burns on her neck and wrists; and the welt the Shargh had left on her back.

The injuries told the story of her journey north but her father's ring lying between her breasts, and the faint scar under her cheekbone it had inflicted while he'd worn it, told a story too. It would be comforting to believe the north was full of violence and the south free of it, but it would not be true.

She clambered into the bath and heaved another sigh as she stretched out. Laryia had been kind and helpful and, one way or another, had told Kira a lot of *private* information about Tierken. And yet, Laryia did not strike Kira as someone who chattered away thoughtlessly.

She sat up and searched the wooden pots nearby for a potion that smelled like Laryia's hair, found one, scrubbed the potion into her own hair, rinsed, and scrubbed again. Then she hauled her pack nearer next, fished out the comb, and worked at the tangles. When she had finished, she wrapped herself in one of the enormous drying cloths and tossed her dirty clothes into the water.

Laryia had left the new clothes on the bed for her, along with a comb, fashioned from pale wood and carved with owls in flight. Kira smiled wryly. It seemed Speri was not the only one who thought Kira should do *something* with her hair, and she *would*, when it was longer. The clothes *were* the same as the Tremen's and she smiled as she dressed.

There was a stack of paper squares on the table in the outer room, with ink and a pen, and a beautifully arranged platter of nuts, fruit, fine maizen bread, and small crusty balls of what smelt like sweetfish. A jug of water with rounds of orange and yellow fruit sat nearby with cups of fine clay.

Kira took a seat at the table, dipped her pen in the ink, and smiled sourly. She was tempted to write the *true* history of the Sundering, of Kasheron's epic journey south, of all that he had endured to carve out Allogrenia, but her duty as a Healer demanded she write of healing first.

She began with fireweed for she feared the Terak would soon have need of it, and worked steadily. It were as if Kasheron had sneaked back into the Terak's city and brought his despised Healer's kit with him, she thought, as she methodically filled each sheet. She ate as she wrote, oblivious to the sun blazing on the Silvercades, to the snow turning pink, and to the slow slide of stars into the night sky.

Tierken stretched his boots to the fire and yawned. Farid had drawn up a summation of Sarnia's affairs with his usual thoroughness and that meant there should be nothing to annoy or alarm the Marken, although Rosham would be sure to find *some* minute point of contention and convince Borsten and Gelf of its importance.

'So, tell me of our *Tremen* guest,' said Farid, as he collected the Writings into a neat pile and set them aside.

'I'm sure you know all there is to know already,' said

Tierken. 'We rescued the Lady Kira of the Tremen people from the Shargh, and I intend to make her my bride.'

'Her resemblance to you is remarkable,' said Farid, refusing to be drawn. 'But I've not heard of the Tremen. Where do they dwell?'

'In the Southern Forests beyond the Azurcades apparently. Her people shared Kessomi blood and entered the forests when all peoples were exeal.'

'But you came across her on the Sarsalin, I understand. How did she come to be so far from home?'

'She said she journeyed to Maraschin after the Shargh attacked the Tremen then left Maraschin to gather herbs and the Shargh took her.'

'Do you think they intended to use her against you?'

Tierken straightened. 'What mean you?'

'She looks every part your kin, Tierken. If the Shargh believed her so, she would be a rich prize indeed.' Tierken's blood ran cold. The possibility provided another reason she must remain safely Sarnia. 'So, the Tremen are in Maraschin,' said Farid, as he lounged back in his chair.

'Not that I'm aware of.'

'So, she travelled from the forests alone?' Tierken shrugged, annoyed he had not thought to ask. 'You don't seem to know much about your *bride*,' said Farid lightly.

There was a knock and Laryia appeared. Farid drained his cup and rose. 'The Meeting Hall's prepared and the Marken know of your return, Feailner,' he said formally. 'They will be in attendance at dawn.'

'I thank you, Keeper,' said Tierken ironically. Farid smiled at Laryia and pulled the door closed behind him. She settled at the table and selected a piece of redfruit. 'Kira's sleeping?' asked Tierken.

'Not that I'm aware of. She asked for paper and ink to write.'

'To write what?'

'She didn't say and she wouldn't wear the gowns you sent either. I'm guessing Tremen clothes are similar to Kessomi ones, so I gave her some of mine.'

'She's not in the forests now *or* in Kessom,' said Tierken tersely. 'She will dress as Terak women do.'

Laryia grinned. 'I'll watch when you tell her. I'd forgotten how interesting it is to see gold eyes change color.' Her smile faded and she leaned forward. 'Is it true the Shargh had her?'

'Yes.'

Laryia shuddered. 'What of her family? They must be frantic.'

'They were murdered by the Shargh. After that, Kira went to Maraschin where she worked in their Haelen before the Shargh captured her.'

Laryia stared at him in horror. 'But this is terrible. Why didn't you take her back to Maraschin? There must be Tain there who care about her and who *she* cares about. The scouts said you found her on the edge of The Westlans.'

'That's correct.'

'Then you should have taken her back to Maraschin.'

'You're telling the *Terak Kirillian Feailner* what he should do, *Lady Laryia*?'

'I'm wondering whether, for once, the gossips speak the truth, *my Lord*.'

'The gossips have had you married to Farid a dozen times and me to every husbandless woman in Sarnia. I brought Kira north because she was under my protection and I was coming north.'

Laryia eyed him speculatively. 'Is that the only reason?'

Tierken wandered to the window and stared out. The Domain was in darkness except for a dim sheen of lamplight from a window in the Lehan Wing. He turned back. 'Kira's safest here. The Shargh hunt her and the Tain have shown they can't protect her. She's only seventeen seasons, Laryia, and she's seen a lot of death. I want her happy and safe, and this is the best place for both things.'

Laryia's shrewd gaze was unwavering. 'But is that what Kira wants?'

Tierken threw himself back into the chair. 'Kira needs time to settle, that's all, and I want you to help her do that. Show her the city and take her around at Mid-market. Once her riding skills are better, you can take her on your favorite rides too. I hope you'll be friends.'

'I hope so too,' said Laryia. She rose and kissed Tierken on the cheek. 'I'm glad you're back, Tierken.'

He smiled. 'So am I.'

Tierken remained in the Meeting Hall long after Laryia had gone to her rooms. He knew he should be sleeping but the back of his neck crawled as it always did before a Feailmark. The records of the dues each dwelling paid were in order, the receipts from the traders that paid the Domain Guard complete, the tributes the stall-holders at Mid-market gave fully recorded, and the lists and tabs were as they should be. All thanks to Farid.

When Rosham had suggested his son as Keeper of the Domain, Tierken's first instinct had been to refuse. The last thing he wanted was a spy to report his every movement, but Farid had made it plain from the start that his loyalty was to the Feailner, and Tierken was confident

Farid never spoke of him outside the Domain except in the most general of terms.

The Marken were only advisors, but their power had grown over the long seasons of Darid's failing rule. Now that Tierken had the patrolmen's loyalty, he could dispense with their *advice* altogether, but he was loath to cause *unnecessary* discord. The Marken were kin-linked to Sarnia's most powerful trading families and his rule would be smoother with their approval than without it.

Poerin extolled the value of patience *and* of small victories, and while Tierken sat courteously through the Marken's interminable discussions, *and* their thinly veiled complaints, there were fewer and fewer things he actually changed.

He sighed as he wandered about the room again and rubbed his stiff neck as he glanced out the window. The lamplight he had noticed earlier was still there and he realized it came from Kira's rooms. By Irid! She should be sleeping. He strode from the Meeting Hall, down the steps and along the balcony, knocking but barely pausing before he entered her rooms. She *was* sleeping, *at the table*, head resting on her arms, ink-stained fingers still clutching her pen.

He gazed at her face, bathed in the gentle glow of lamplight. The shadows made her fairness less obvious and it was like looking at his younger self. Queen Kiraon and her sons had had gold eyes, but there had been no others in the north until him. And yet in the south, growing to womanhood in the forests, there had been another, who bore Queen Kiraon's name and claimed to be the seed of her other son. It was not possible, and over the coming weeks, he would convince her of the fact.

He reached over and carefully extricated the pen from her grasp but she jerked awake and the chair crashed to the floor as she sprang backwards in fright. It was one thing to tell Laryia Kira's family had been murdered but another to see the terror of it written all over her face.

'I'm sorry I startled you,' he said, feeling jarred himself. He watched the calm façade reassert itself and his guts tightened as he was again reminded how little he really knew of her. He righted the chair and glanced down at her Writings. Not only did Kira wear Kessomi garb, but she recorded her knowing in both Terak and Onespeak like a good Kessomi Healer.

'Why are you recording healing when you should be sleeping?' he demanded irritably.

'My healing comes from those who went before me and so I must leave it for those who follow.'

'There are no Healers in Sarnia,' he said. 'You're wasting your time.'

'I'm only wasting my time if you destroy my work.'

He looked at her surprise. Her opinion of him must be lower than he thought. 'Of course, I won't destroy your work,' he said. Kira made no reply, simply stared down at her Writings. 'Do you like your rooms?' he asked with forced lightness.

'They are very nice. I thank you.'

'But rather empty. There are many beautiful things at Mid-market. You can choose some to make your rooms more homely.'

'They are never going to be *homely*.'

'Not like the forest,' he conceded.

She moved restlessly, again reminding of his younger self and her gold eyes flashed to his. 'Why didn't Terak plant shrubs or trees in Sarnia?'

Tierken shrugged. 'I don't know. It was before my time.'

'It's *your* time now. Why don't *you* plant them?'

'There are far more urgent things in Sarnia than planting trees. The Marken wouldn't be happy to have the city's dues traded for greenery and, for once, I would agree with them. Sarnia is beautiful as it is.' He almost said she was beautiful too but recalled her reaction to the compliment on the Sarsalin.

She had washed her hair and it floated about her face like a golden cloud. He smoothed it back, gratified when she did not step away. 'Do all Tremen women wear their hair short?' he asked softly.

'They wear it like Laryia.'

He wondered briefly why she had cut it but her proximity roused every nerve in his body. He brought his mouth to hers, intending the kiss to be fleeting, but her hunger was as great as his and it took every part of his strength to pull back. Her trust was still tenuous and he was determined their time together would be far more than stolen kisses. 'It's late,' he said, with a small bow. 'I need to sleep and so do you. I wish you fair dreams for your first night in Sarnia, Kira.'

12

Caledon moved swiftly into the trees of the Azurcade's southern foothills, palmed and silently thanked the stars, all without breaking stride. Their light was hidden by clouds and the darkness thick, but their beneficence had gifted him a safe trip across the Dendora. He neared where Kira had come to his aid during the Shargh attack and, even as the thought crossed his mind, a figure stepped from the shadows.

Caledon drew his sword but as the figure advanced, two more emerged behind it. Caledon had faced similar odds before but not with a sword arm yet to regain its strength. A breeze woke and, as the cloud shredded, starlight spilled to the ground. 'Lord Caledon! Praise be to Meros!' the first figure exclaimed.

'Guard Archorn,' said Caledon, and silently thanked the stars again. More men emerged from the trees, their relief palpable as they formed a loose circle around him. They were King's Guard, despite their dark capes.

'We've waited ten days for you and our orders were to wait another two,' said Archorn.

'I've been much delayed,' said Caledon.

'With your leave, we will journey on to the Aurantia Cave this night,' said Archorn. 'We've seen no Shargh but it's best to be quit of their lands. Prince Adris awaits your return.'

'By all means. But tell me, is the Lady Kira still in Maraschin?'

'No, my Lord.'

Caledon hid his disappointment. 'Prince Adris provided her with an escort north?'

'It's best you speak with the prince, Lord Caledon.'

Caledon sensed the grimness of the waiting Guard and gripped Archorn's arm. 'Tell me what's happened.'

Archorn ordered the Guard to proceed to the Aurantia Cave and the trees were quiet before he turned back to Caledon. 'The Lady Kira was taken by the Shargh.'

Something inside Caledon drained away to leave him as empty as a husk. 'When?' he heard his voice ask.

'Close to a moon ago. She left Maraschin to gather and the party was attacked.' Archorn dropped his voice, despite them being alone. 'But there's still hope.' Caledon looked at him numbly. 'Dead horses were found near The Westlans.'

'Dead horses?'

'The Lady Kira was taken by Shargh on *Ashmiri* horses. Two dead Ashmiri horses were found near The Westlans.'

'How were they killed?'

'By the time Prince Adris returned and ordered a search, the wolves had been at them.' Archorn glanced uneasily at the trees. 'We need to start back, Lord Caledon. We are very late and Prince Adris awaits.'

Caledon remembered little of the journey back to Maraschin. He knew he must have traversed the path that had all but claimed his life, passed through the sida grove, and slept in the Aurantia Cave. It was likely they camped near where he had sheltered from the storm with Kira, and when the Guard reached the rosarin groves, he was aware he had played the thumbelin for her there. Even the thunderous ride across the Scharn Grasslands failed to rouse him from the darkness of despair and it was only as he stepped into the Crown Rooms and Adris's haggard face swam into view, that he roused.

Adris enclosed him in a crushing hug. 'I'd lost all hope of seeing you again, my friend. Come, sit and eat. The scouts tell me you're hurt.'

Caledon slumped into a chair. 'A fall from Shardos—old injuries now.' He smiled grimly. 'I was careless, Adris, as you were with Kira.'

Adris passed him a cup of metz and gulped his own. 'She wanted to find a herb she said would cure Shargh wounds. I sent Guard with her to the Pelaval but she found nothing. Mendor Spur was attacked so I took Guard there. She sought me twice in my absence and when the king authorized gathering, she followed the gatherers to the gates. Ather tried to stop her leaving, but the king had issued no prohibition and she knew it. It's likely the Shargh knew she was here and watched for her leaving.'

'Archorn said you found horses.'

'What was left of them, but there was something else there only Guard Leader Remas and I know about.' He set his cup down, retrieved something from one of the wall-chests, and lay it on the table. It was an arrow, the haft dark with blood.

'I don't see—' began Caledon.

'The wood's allogrenia.'

'A *Terak* arrow,' hissed Caledon, his mind suddenly clear. 'The Shargh were attacked by *Terak*!'

'The Shargh might have got Kira away,' cautioned Adris. 'If the Terak rescued her, they would have brought her here.'

'Not necessarily.'

99

'They were virtually within our bounds!'

Caledon relaxed back in his chair. 'What do you know of the new Terak Feailner, Adris?'

'He's the old Feailner's nephew and was raised in Kessom. Like most Kessomis, he's a good horseman. He spends more time out of the city than in it and wasn't favored by Darid as heir but there was no one else,' listed off Adris.

'Do you know why he wasn't favored?'

'Darid hoped for a son of his own,' said Adris.

'That might be so, but it wasn't the main reason. Darid's nephew carries the taint of something most Terak would prefer to forget. He has gold eyes.'

Adris stared at him in astonishment. 'You think the Terak took Kira north because she's got gold eyes?'

'If the Terak Feailner led the patrol, I'm certain of it.'

'He still should have returned her here,' growled Adris.

'Perhaps the stars decided otherwise,' murmured Caledon. 'Perhaps they intended the two of them to come together after all.'

'Or the Shargh to kill her.'

Caledon glanced at him sharply, noticing his weariness for the first time. 'How goes it with the king?'

'The king has sunk into a sleep from which there will be no awakening.'

Caledon rose and went to him. 'Forgive me, my friend. My thoughts were only for Kira.'

'There's nothing to forgive,' said Adris, and gripped Caledon's shoulder. 'I hardly know what to feel myself. Part of me grieves while another part feels only relief.'

There was a long silence. 'I need to go north,' said Caledon.

'Yes, it's time. The Tain can't send greetings from their king but they *can* send them from their prince. Give me a couple of days to prepare, Caledon, so that at least you can go in safety. I don't want to lose you as well.'

Kira stared out at the Silvercades, or at least, in their direction. They were hidden by a heavy fall of dark clouds and everything beyond the window smudged with rain. She wandered to the table and then back to the window. She had plenty of paper and ink and no excuse not to be working at her Writings but she felt too restless.

The rain had postponed the second day of her tour of Sarnia, which was a relief. Laryia had been good company but having Guard at their heels the entire time had made Kira reluctant to speak at all. The stares had been even worse and by day's end she had found it hard to raise her eyes from the paving.

She craved the forest's deep quiet but Sarnia held nothing that grew at all. At least Maraschin had Queen Alitha's grove. She sighed and took another turn around the room. The rain might have allowed her to escape Sarnia's stares but it gave her too much time to think.

If she were in Maraschin now *and* Caledon had returned, she would know whether Kest's patrol had survived the trek back to the Warens; whether *Tresen* had survived; and whether the Shargh attacks had ceased.

She also feared she delayed in Sarnia not because of some faint hope Tierken would accept the kin-link but because she was too cowardly to leave his Shelter. His arms had gifted her a reprieve from the nightmares of Kandor's death and she dreaded being alone again.

Not very leaderly behavior, Tremen Leader Feailner Kiraon of Kashclan. She could almost hear Kest's acerbic voice, in fact, she wished she *could* hear it, because it meant *he* was still alive. She stared at the neat stack of paper on the table sightlessly. Recording her healing was important but her only reason for being here was to prove the kin-link.

She needed to speak to Farid. As *Keeper* of the Domain, he would know where the Writings on Terak histories were stored. A good plan, *Tremen Leader Feailner Kiraon of Kashclan*, except Laryia had told her Farid was taken up with the Feailmark too.

Stinking heart-rot! Kira wrenched open the door and strode out onto the balcony. The air was chill and water-logged and she sucked in a deep breath. Rain plinked the stone, gurgled down the roof-pipes, and sluiced along the gutters below. They crisscrossed the square like miniature rivers, ashine as they carried the water away. Rain pocked the surface of the Owl Fountain too and made the stone tree gleam. A *stone* tree, she thought in disgust, and paced along the balcony.

Tierken watched her from the Meeting Hall as he sipped his cotzee. He was too far away to see her expression but her restlessness was clear. The Marken had paused in their discussions to eat and were gathered around the platters the servers had delivered. There was a rumble of informal conversation behind him and Tierken grimaced as Rosham's voice rose above the rest.

'Good weather for redfruit,' said Milsin at his shoulder.

'But not for herders,' said Tierken and moved away from the window.

'Good pasture growth and full springs,' said Milsin, his smile revealing gappy teeth. 'Not too much to complain about there.'

'Unlike here,' muttered Tierken, under his breath.

Milsin's good natured face became thoughtful. 'A bird is happiest when it is allowed to sing,' he said.

Tierken looked at him in surprise. 'Well, there are many happy birds in the Domain today,' he said, and Milsin nodded gently.

The weather got no better and, as dusk neared, Kira interrupted her writing to light a lamp. The lamp on the table was full of oil and she was considering where flints might be when there was a knock at the door.

The woman who stood there was a stranger. 'Good evening, Lady,' she said with a small bow. 'Mouras has sent me.' She used Onespeak and her broad face was unlined despite the grey in her hair.

'Mouras?'

'*Room Master Mouras.* He directs the servers. I am here to see to your needs, Lady.'

'I don't have any needs, I thank you . . .?'

'Niria.'

'*Niria*,' repeated Kira. She had heard the name before.

'You are acquainted with my husband, Lady.'

'Your husband?' repeated Kira, aware she sounded like a half-wit.

'Commander Marin. He rode with the Feailner in the last patrol and gave you escort to Sarnia.'

Kira smiled in delight. 'Ah, yes. Marin spoke of you and was most kind to me during the journey. I'm sorry I didn't have a chance to say goodbye to him.'

Niria smiled too. 'It would be my pleasure to be your server, Lady.'

'We don't have servers in my lands, Niria, so I'm well used to doing things for myself.'

'In the *Terak Kirillian* lands, servers are an important part of the Domain,' said Niria, with quiet dignity.

Kira's face warmed. 'I . . . please come in,' she said. 'I'm having trouble lighting the lamp. If you know where the flints are . . .'

'I will light the lamps, make up your bed and ensure the bathing-room is clean. I work quietly and won't disturb you,' she added, as she glanced at Kira's recordings.

'I thank you,' said Kira, despite disliking the intrusion. She settled at the table again and pushed the hair from her eyes.

'I can braid your hair for you too if you wish, Lady,' said Niria.

'It's too short.'

'When my daughter was just a wisp, she cut off her braid and we had tears worse than this rain. I know how to braid short hair.'

'Very well,' said Kira, heartily sick of it being in her eyes.

Niria fetched the comb and some ties from the bathing-room, settled on a chair in front of her, and set to work. The slight tug and pull reminded Kira of how Tena had dressed her hair at Turning.

'Marin tells me you are from Tremen lands,' said Niria, as she worked. 'Is it the custom there for women to wear their hair short?'

'No.'

'It's very fair, Lady,' said Niria, obviously too polite to probe further. 'Are the Tremen a fair people?'

'Generally, though some clans are fairer than others. Some in Morclan have hair as bright as snow and eyes as blue as the sky,' said Kira. Her throat tightened as she wondered again if Kest still lived.

Niria smoothed back the hair from Kira's forehead and wove it into a flat braid that circled Kira's head. 'It suits you, Lady,' she said, when she had finished. It was certainly a relief to have it out of her eyes, thought Kira. 'I'll braid it every day if you wish and for the banquet,' continued Niria. 'With hairlets, it will look very well.'

'Banquet?'

'When a Feailmark coincides with a Mid-market, the Domain holds a banquet to celebrate the Feailmark's ending. The trade leaders and their ladies attend and the Marken and *their* ladies, as well as those highly placed in the city. It's held in the Meeting Hall and is very grand indeed. I know the Lady Laryia intends to trade for a new gown at Mid-market.'

Being *exeal* might have advantages after all, concluded Kira dryly, glad she would not have to deal with the stares and whispers of such *illustrious* company. And once the Feailmark had finished, Farid would be free to discuss the Terak Writings or better still, show them to her. In fact, it would be good to examine them *before* her next conversation with Tierken.

Niria took her leave, taking Kira's soiled clothes with her, but Kira had only just settled to her work again when she reappeared. 'Horse Master Ryn sends message that you're to start your riding lessons on the morrow at dawn. Let's hope the weather is kinder,' she added.

Niria got her hope. The rain cleared during the night and the sky was empty of clouds as Kira made her way to the Domain stables. 'The Feailner tells me he's made a start,' said Ryn, by way of greeting, as he unlatched the stable door. He led out a horse, already saddled and bridled. 'He's had this mare brought from Kessom for you.'

The horse was beautiful in the same way Kalos was, her coat the darker grey of storm clouds and mottled more lightly on her shoulders and haunches. 'She's three seasons, and will silver in time, but won't be as light as her brother, the Feailner's mount,' said Ryn. 'The Lady Laryia's mount's a full sister too, though she's but a season younger than the Feailner's mount.'

Kira stroked the mare's silky neck. 'It's kind of the Feailner to let me ride her,' she said. 'What is she called?'

'That, you'll have to ask the Feailner. Now, show me how you mount.'

Ryn did not bawl instructions at her like Tierken had but his piercing gaze missed nothing and by the time the sun was well up and he called a halt, Kira felt even less competent than after her first lesson. 'I will see you at dawn on the morrow,' said Ryn, as he led the mare away.

Kira had bathed, changed and started on the platter of fruit that had appeared in her rooms, when Laryia arrived, dressed in a dark brown gown. She seemed to have countless gowns in countless colors, thought Kira, as she recalled the red one she had worn on Kira's arrival and the blue one she had worn on their sight-seeing tour. The brown picked up the color of her eyes and hair, and Kira was struck again by how unlike Tierken she was.

Laryia smiled cheerfully as she settled opposite and selected a piece of sweet yellow fruit. 'Your hair looks beautiful like that, Kira. Did Niria dress it?' Kira nodded.

106

'I like Niria. I'm glad Mouras appointed her.' She finished the fruit and licked the juice from her fingers. 'I thought we could go to the North Wall gate today. It gives a good view over Sarnia towards Kessom then we can come back through the Kir Quarter and trade for *shirin*. That's sugared fruit in the Kir tongue.'

13

Kira followed Laryia across the square to another paved area at the back of the Meeting Hall to the *North Domain Gate*, which was manned by two black and silver-clad Guard. Kira hoped they were forbidden from leaving their posts and they probably were because *another* two Guard appeared and fell into step behind them. She irritably wondered why, if Sarnia were as safe as Tierken claimed, they needed Guard at all. Laryia ignored them, as she had previously, and Kira tried to as well, by concentrating on Laryia's description of Sarnia's layout.

The city had originally been divided into quarters and, although the boundaries had blurred over time, the Kirs and Illians still tended to live side by side in the western quarters while a third quarter was allocated to Teraks and Kessomis, although in truth, few Kessomis chose to live in Sarnia.

'And the fourth quarter?' asked Kira, staring at the buildings they passed. Unlike parts of Maraschin, Sarnia seemed clean and in good repair.

'It's become known as the Caru Quarter,' said Laryia briefly. 'It has a lot of gambling and alehouses that keep the Sarnia Guard busy. Some of the younger patrolmen drink too much too quickly when they come in from patrol and get into fights.'

'And then what happens?' asked Kira, wondering if they were beaten.

'They can be fined or expelled from Sarnia for a time. If they're in the cells when their patrol's due to set out, they're handed over to the Patrol Commander for punishment.' She smiled and glanced at Kira. 'How do the Tremen punish their wrong-doers?'

Kira had not grown up in the longhouses but nor could she recall her father or Merek speaking of fighting or overindulging in withyweed ale. Kashclan elders sometimes commented on Morclan's wildness or on the occasional recklessness of their own young but the Tremen believed the young were like saplings that became more stable as they grew.

'The Tremen live in much smaller groups than here and there's much love and respect between them,' said Kira eventually.

'It sounds like Kessom. But I don't understand . . .'

'What don't you understand?'

'Anything! Everything!' said Laryia with a laugh. 'How is it you speak Terak?'

'I'm speaking Tremen.'

'But you speak it like someone who's grown up in Kessom.' She looked at Kira with an intensity that had been missing before. 'I *want* to understand you, Kira. I *want* us to be friends and to make your time in Sarnia happy.'

'Hasn't the Feailner spoken of me?' asked Kira, acutely aware of the Guard behind them.

'He told me your people are called the Tremen and live in the Southern Forests and that they went there before peoples such as the Kirs, and Illians, and Kessomis came into being. He said your people were attacked by the Shargh and . . . you left.' Laryia swallowed and hurried on. 'He said you went to Maraschin and worked as a Healer and that the Shargh took you when you left to gather.'

Tierken had managed to omit *everything* important, concluded Kira grimly. Laryia loved her brother and Kira did not want to cause upset but she refused to deny her people. 'My people *are* the Tremen and we do live in the Southern Forests,' she said carefully, 'but we came from the north, *after* the Kirs, Illians and Kessomis came into being. It's why I speak like a Kessomi.'

Laryia stared at her in confusion. 'But . . . but how is that possible? Who were your leaders?'

'Ask the Feailner.'

'You've told him?'

'Yes.'

Laryia's dark brown eyes searched Kira's face. 'You've argued over this?'

'Yes.'

Laryia looked so troubled that Kira regretted saying anything. 'The Feailner was kind to me on the journey here and continues to be kind, as you do,' she said. 'Come, I'm looking forward to the shirin,' she added.

Laryia talked more about the Marken as they went on and Kira listened closely. 'Do they have a knowing of the Terak histories and treaties?' she asked.

'Yes, but less so than Tierken. The Marken are more concerned with trade. Poerin instructed Tierken in our histories, alliances, and treaties, as did Eris, but Tierken probably knows less of the Writings than Farid. As Keeper, Farid oversees the Writings Store. Why do you ask?'

'I'd like to find out more about Sarnia. Where *is* the Writing Store?'

'At the end of the balcony where our rooms are.'

'Do you think I could see what's kept there?'

'I'm sure Farid would be happy to show you, once the Feailmark's over but I'm not sure you'll find what you're looking for.' She dropped her voice. 'Darid had little interest in record-keeping during the final seasons of his leadership and the store is *very* disordered.'

Laryia waited until the Marken had retired for the night before she sought out Tierken in the Meeting Hall. Kira's revelations troubled her and so did her brother's behavior. After three hard seasons of *not* antagonizing Sarnia's most powerful citizens, he now seemed intent on goading them. His return bearing a gold-eyed woman perched afront his saddle was the talk of Sarnia and she knew many in Sarnia looked forward to learning more of the Feailner's *bride* before the festivities of the Feailner's marriage.

She found Tierken lounging at the table, half-heartedly perusing a list of dues. 'I recognize that look in your eye, Laryia,' he said sardonically. 'How have I offended you?'

'You haven't offended me, Tierken, you've puzzled me.'

'How so?'

'I went to the stables this evening to see Chime and Rin tells me you've brought a full-blood sister to her and Kalos to Sarnia for Kira. Everyone in Sarnia knows that bloodline stays in our family. I thought you wanted to douse Sarnia's gossip-fires, not add fuel.'

'Is that your only concern?'

'No. I want to know why Kira speaks Terak like Eris but has never been to Kessom; why she looks more like you than I do; why you brought her here when you should have returned her to Maraschin; and exactly what you have argued with her about.'

'A lot of questions Laryia, and some more suited to the gossips you mentioned.'

'Who were her forebears, Tierken?'

'I've already told you.'

'Tell me who *she* said they were,' said Laryia in exasperation.

'Kasheron.'

Laryia's eyes widened. 'Oh.'

'Exactly,' said Tierken, rising and pacing about the room. 'Kasheron who fled the warring peoples of the north to establish the healing community of Allogrenia in the Southern Forests. Her words, more or less, not mine.'

'Her settlement is called *Allogrenia*?'

Tierken nodded and came back to his chair. 'If she tells the truth, we have as our guest, Tremen Leader Feailner Kiraon of Kashclan, Kasheron's clan that is, Healer of Allogrenia, seed of the great, golden-eyed Healer, Prince Kasheron himself. Hardly news to make the Marken roll in their seats in mirth.'

'*Kiraon*?' gasped Laryia. 'And she's the *Tremen leader*?'

'So she *claims*.'

Laryia's eyes narrowed. 'You think she's lying?'

'Not about her settlement or being Tremen leader, but about Kasheron?' He shrugged. 'I believe Kira is truthfully repeating Tremen histories but it's obvious those histories are lies. The Tremen wouldn't be the first to concoct tales of a glorious past.

'The Tremen clearly share blood with those who later became the Kessomis, and while the only gold eyes we know of in *that* line are Kiraon and *her* sons, there might have been other gold-eyed people in the past who never came north. In which case, Kira's similarity to me isn't that unusual, especially since the Tremen have never mixed their blood.'

There was a long pause. 'Is it possible Kira's histories are true and ours are false?' asked Laryia.

'Drunken men have seen horses fly, so I suppose it's possible.

'But what if they are, Tierken?'

'You mean, what if *every* tale told in the north and *every* history recorded in the Writing Store is wrong? You would think that in all the seasons since Kasheron's desertion, at least one of his kin would have sought us out. But there's been no one.'

'So, there are more gold-eyed people in the south?' asked Laryia.

'Not according to Kira.'

Laryia half shook her head. 'But you are *so* alike! I find it hard to believe it's pure chance.'

'It isn't *pure* chance, for the reasons I've outlined, although I'd agree the *manner* of our meeting proves Irid has a sense of humor.' Tierken just hoped it wasn't a *malign* sense of humor or his present difficulties with the Marken were going to seem as trifling as grit in his boot.

Laryia gazed down at the table, deep in thought. 'Kira's called on the kin-link to claim Terak aid for the Tremen, hasn't she?' she said suddenly.

'Yes.'

'And you've refused it.'

'You know Terak law as well as I do. The Tremen are exeal.'

'So, when are you providing her with an escort south?'

'Never.'

Laryia's startled eyes came to his. 'But—'

'The Shargh hunt her and the Tain have shown they can't protect her. She'll remain here.' Tierken rose and rolled his shoulders. 'It's late and I have another long day on the morrow in Rosham's *pleasant* company. Don't fret about Kira, Laryia. She needs time to settle, that's all.'

The rain returned the next day and despite wearing an oiled cape for her lesson, Kira was soaked to the skin by the time she quit the stables. She padded along the balcony leaving a trail of drips and was almost to her rooms when Laryia's door opened and Tierken came out. He was in conversation with Laryia and Kira caught something about *tables* and *seating* before they saw her. 'You're drenched, Kira,' said Laryia. 'Best get dry. This rain's not helping me organize the banquet either,' she said, and hurried away.

Kira dragged off the cape and shook it before she entered her rooms. 'Ryn tells me you have a good seat and a light touch,' said Tierken, as he followed her in.

'He hasn't told *me* that,' said Kira, grabbing a drying cloth. She wiped her face and started on her hair.

'Horse Master Ryn is a man of few words. How do you like the mare?'

Kira smiled. 'She is beautiful.'

'What have you named her?'

'Named her?'

'It's the prerogative of the owner to name their mount,' said Tierken.

Kira looked at him confusion. 'But I'm not staying.'

She expected an argument but Tierken's tender expression remained unchanged. 'She's my gift to you,' he said softly.

His response confirmed her belief he was content she remain in Sarnia and she took a steadying breath. 'You told me the design of the big glass window in the Meeting Hall is the mark of your people,' she said.

'Yes, the allogrenia and galloping horse.'

'It's the same design as the ring of rulership that Kasheron took south.' Tierken's face hardened but Kira slid the thong and ring over her head and handed it to him. 'This is the Terak ring of rulership that Kasheron, as the first-born twin wore.'

'It's a common enough design,' he said, barely glancing at it before handing it back. 'You see it on rings and bracelets at Mid-market and even on chimes.'

'It isn't a *common* design in the south and nor are rings common. There is only one ring, the ring of rulership, which was *Kasheron's* ring.' Tierken said nothing and she glanced at his hands. Unlike his men, he wore no rings at all. 'Didn't Terak have another ring forged?'

'Terak had no need of a ring to mark his leadership and neither do I,' he said, and gave a brief bow. 'I must rejoin the Marken.'

Tierken shut Kira from his mind as Rosham held forth on his favorite topic of opening up the Caru Quarter. The city was crowded, he pointed out, and it made sense to use *all* of its available land before going to the expense of extending the wall. There was also the issue of the *unregulated* occupation of the Caru Quarter by those who paid no dues, but who were over-represented in drunken brawls.

What Rosham said was true, conceded Tierken. The Caru Quarter had become a dumping ground for refuse and a haven for ale houses happy to serve drunks; gambling houses with little regard for fairness; and for women who traded themselves like trinkets at Mid-market, and he had come close to agreeing to open up the Caru Quarter last

Feailmark. In fact, if anyone but Rosham had badgered him, he might have.

But now as Rosham regurgitated his arguments for the umpteenth time, Tierken's thoughts swung to the great Healer Queen, Kiraon. Heartbroken by the loss of her son, she had begged Terak to reserve a quarter of Sarnia in case Kasheron and his followers returned and, out of love for his mother, Terak had agreed.

It seemed an odd chance to Tierken, that Kira had appeared when he was on the verge of accepting what the Healer Queen had never accepted: that Kasheron and his heirs were lost forever.

Rosham finally fell silent and eyed Tierken confidently, as well he might, but Tierken's thoughts had turned to the things that might make Kira's life in Sarnia happier. 'I thank you for your words, Marken Rosham. As usual, they were well-considered and forthright. I will think on them until the next Feailmark.'

Rosham's smile faltered. 'With respect Feailner, that's what you said last Feailmark.'

'And it may well be what I say *next* Feailmark,' said Tierken with a smile. 'Terak left a quarter of Sarnia unused for a reason.'

'Surely you don't expect Kasheron's line to return, Feailner?'

Tierken kept his easy smile in place. 'I was thinking of future treaties, Marken. There might come a time when others settle in Sarnia and it would be useful to have land available.'

'What *others* would they be? The people of your *guest* perhaps?' The room had stilled; the remainder of the Marken suddenly intent on their cotzee.

'My guest?'

'The *Lady* Kira. It's said her people share our tongue and might follow her north, but I would suggest to you, Feailner, that Sarnian land should go to Sarnians before strangers.'

'I'm surprised you heed the idle gossip of the streets, Marken Rosham.'

'With respect, Feailner, anything that affects the city is of interest to the Marken.'

'The Caru Quarter will remain as it is then. If Kasheron's descendants return *or* those of his followers, I will give them leave to build there, as the great Terak himself intended. *If* we treaty with others in the future, they will be accommodated by extending the wall. Does that please the Marken?'

'It's not the Marken who must be pleased, but the people of Sarnia,' said Rosham with an icy smile.

'Then I must leave it up to you to ascertain their feelings, as I have neither the time nor the inclination to listen to their gossip,' said Tierken, and rose. 'I thank you once more, Marken, for your diligence and advice this Feailmark,' he said crisply. 'I wish you a pleasant day at Mid-market on the morrow and look forward to welcoming you as my guests to the banquet on Mid-market night.' With a nod to the Marken, he strode from the room.

14

Kira discovered that Mid-market was held on the grassy slopes *outside* the city walls and she was glad of the green even if it were soon churned to mud. Round huts like the Ashmiri's were set in rows and people crowded the narrow walkways between. The huts were full of metal cooking pots, ladles, knives, enameled bowls and cups; beautifully work belts and bracelets; ornaments; bolts of cloth; sacks of nuts, grain and fruit.

The huts' fronts were strung with cord to display scarves as light as air, and chimes of glass and silver that tinkled in the breeze, and the air held perfumes sweeter than lissium; odors of roasting meat and the scent of spices, that reminded Kira of Allogrenia, Maraschin and Caledon in turn.

Laryia linked her arm through Kira's as they strolled and their Guard, clad in their black and silver, had doubled to four. Laryia pointed out the Bishali horse-traders, the Naswali puppeteers, the Tallien cloth-cutters and the Kir metalwrights, and there were so many strangely clad people, and so many strange tongues being spoken, that for once Kira did not feel out of place.

Laryia came to a stop at a hut laden with bolts of cloth. 'This way,' she said and slid through a side-flap. The Guard followed and Kira edged forward in the cramped space to give them room.

The interior was filled with even more bolts of cloth and racks of clothes, and manned by a cloth-cutter whose height and slenderness keenly reminded Kira of Caledon. He was fairer though, with sandy brows, now low over his eyes as he appraised her. He took several gowns off a rack and Laryia smiled delightedly. 'You have the loveliest gowns, Warilin, and the best eye for fit. Come Kira, which would you choose?'

Kira blinked. 'I . . . I have no need of a gown, Laryia, but I thank you.'

'You do for the banquet,' said Laryia cheerfully.

Kira's heart sank but, conscious of the Guard, she resisted the urge to argue. The gowns were scoop-necked, long-sleeved, and encrusted with sparkling metal beads. 'I can't wear a dress with metal on it,' she said awkwardly. Laryia's smile faltered but strengthened again as Warilin searched the rack. 'I don't want to trouble you,' said Kira uncomfortably. 'I don't need to attend the banquet.'

'It's no trouble,' said Laryia firmly, 'and if Warilin hasn't a suitable gown, there are three more cloth-cutters we can visit.'

One of the Guard suppressed a sigh as Warilin all but disappeared into the rack, but he emerged with a dark green gown with gold metal buttons down the front. 'The buttons are easily removed,' he said.

'But it would be very plain,' said Laryia doubtfully. 'Do you like it, Kira?'

'It's pretty,' said Kira, with forced enthusiasm.

Laryia nodded and Warilin beamed, then Laryia selected a blue dress for herself and, as traders were exchanged, Kira edged towards the door-flap. 'Warilin will have the gowns brought to the Domain before the banquet,' said Laryia, as they strolled on. The way was crowded but the Guard in front meant people were quick to make way.

'The banquet's important for Tierken,' said Laryia softly. 'The Marken attend and Sarnia's most influential

119

traders. Tierken and I host it together to ensure it runs smoothly and our guests are treated with honor, so I've asked Farid to partner you.' She smiled. 'There will be dancing afterwards. Do you like to dance, Kira?'

Kira nodded, feeling more cheerful. She had enjoyed dancing from a young age and sitting next to Farid would give her the chance to quiz him about Terak histories. 'The Naswari puppet-masters,' exclaimed Laryia suddenly and seized Kira's hand. 'Quick, they're about to begin.'

Tierken strolled amongst the Mid-market crowds, enjoying the fine day and his relative anonymity. Most of the crowd were intent on the traders' wares or on navigating the mud, and his lack of Guard and the dark cape he had tossed over his black and silver garb meant he largely went unnoticed. His usual sense of relief at the Feailmark's conclusion added to his enjoyment, as did the prospect of spending time with Kira and learning more of Maraschin and the Tain prince.

By the time he returned from the next patrol, Kira should be settled in Sarnia and her riding skills strong enough to take her to some of his favorite haunts. *A natural, like all Kessomis*, Ryn had said, his slip understandable given Kira's slight build and insistence on Kessomi clothing.

She would need to adopt Terak customs but Tierken was willing to put the issue of clothing aside for the time being. Going from a small, isolated community to a large city like Sarnia was not easy, as he and Laryia had discovered, but Sarnia was home to him now, and would be to Kira.

The laughter ahead suggested a Naswali puppet show and Laryia's love of puppets made it likely she and Kira

120

were there. Laryia had pined for puppet shows when Eris had taken them to Kessom for the puppet-masters earned enough trade in Sarnia not to make the hazardous journey to Kessom.

He paused in the lee of a leather-worker's stall to survey the puppeteer's audience and sure enough, Laryia was near the front with Kira. He edged around the crowd's periphery until he had good view of them. Kira laughed as much as those about her and her happiness confirmed he had been right to bring her north.

The show ended and the crowd cheered and tossed traders into the proffered bowls before they wandered away. Tierken followed, staying near the back of the throng. He guessed Laryia would go to the Kir metalwrights next for she loved their chimes, and she had not gone far before she stopped at a chime-trader.

Kira waited at her side, but after a while, moved to a neighboring stall. It was another Kir metalwright, which surprised Tierken, given Kira's abhorrence of metal, and he was even more surprised when the trader handed her something and she took it. Intrigued, he made his way over.

The metalwright bowed low to Tierken and Kira glanced up, her eyes flashing gold in surprise and then suffusing to honey. He took the silver bracelet from her and turned it over. It was highly polished, the front beautifully engraved with the allogrenia and galloping horse, a design particularly popular with Kessomis. The bracelet was small too, obviously crafted with the finer-boned Kessomis in mind.

The metalwright started to extoll the bracelet's virtues in Kir and, as Tierken bargained, Laryia came to his side and a crowd formed as they noticed the Feailner, the

121

Feailner's sister, and the Feailner's *bride-to-be*. Tierken reached agreement with the metalwright, slapped hands, and handed over the traders. The bracelet was expensive, but it was the best workmanship he had seen in many seasons.

Kira's color was high, clearly uncomfortable with the attention they drew, but Tierken felt curiously carefree. He raised Kira's left hand and, with a small bow, slipped the bracelet onto her wrist. A gasp erupted from the gathering, not least from Laryia but Tierken ignored it. If he were Kessomi, he would have just pledged, and they would soon be married. But the Terak used the *right* wrist to pledge. He gave another small bow and moved away. Let the gossips chew on that for a while!

Kira was loath to offend Tierken *or* Laryia by taking the bracelet off, despite its cold slipperiness, but it was the first thing she did when she reached her rooms. She set it on the table and stared down at it. She had an uneasy feeling Tierken had used her in some sort of a game he played with the crowd and she wondered whether he scored points against the Marken as her father had scored points against the Clancouncil.

The gown had been delivered and she bathed and changed into it, surprised at how well it fitted, then Niria arrived to dress her hair. She twice asked Kira what necklets she was to wear and seemed taken aback when Kira answered none and refused the gold metal hairlets Niria had brought with her. Niria disappeared into the bathing-room and returned with shining green and gold ribbons and her mood seemed to improve as she wove them into Kira's braid.

'You look like Queen Kiraon come to life again,' she said, and had just finished when Laryia appeared carrying a carved wooden box. 'Ah,' said Niria, with a knowing smile. 'Is there ought else you need me to do, Lady?'

'No, I thank you,' said Kira, and Niria went out, closing the door softly behind her.

Laryia wore the sparkling blue gown she had traded, now ornamented with silver necklets and rings, and blue stones glittered in her dark hair. 'You look lovely,' said Kira, and she did.

'Tierken sends these for you,' said Laryia, clearly discomfited as she opened the box.

It was full of gold necklets, bracelets and rings, and Kira stared at Laryia is horror. 'Tierken *knows* metal is prasach!'

'Can't you wear metal just this once?'

'No!'

Laryia put the box on the table and took Kira's hands. Her color was high and Kira's tension increased. 'If you attend the banquet without the accoutrements of a *lady*, the guests will think you're Tierken's *woman*.'

'His *woman*?'

Laryia swallowed several times. 'Like the women in the Caru Quarter,' she muttered, unable to meet Kira's eyes.

Laryia was distressed but Kira still had no idea why. Attending the banquet *without* being decked out in metal seemed to dishonor Tierken in some way, which would hardly make him more amenable to the kinship claim but *wearing* metal dishonored Kasheron.

Laryia was on the verge of tears and Kira took a deep breath. 'I'll wear metal to please you, Laryia, because you love your brother, and if he's upset, you're upset, but *never* ask me to wear it again.'

Laryia enclosed her in a hug. 'I thank you,' she said. 'Do you want me to help you?'

'No, I can manage.' At least that way she could limit how much of the loathsome stuff touched her skin.

'Farid will be here soon to escort you to the Meeting Hall. You will have an enjoyable time, Kira.'

Farid turned out to be a surprisingly pleasant companion. He told Kira amusing stories about his early days in the Domain, described the peculiarities of particular guests, and made her completely forget the curious stares of those around her. He wore the Domain black with silver trim, as Tierken did, and when he smiled or laughed, which he did often, his whole face lit up.

The Meeting Hall had been set with a table running along a raised platform at its head, and tables running down each side of the hall. Tierken and Laryia sat at the centre of the top table with the Marken and their wives, and the wealthy trader leaders and *their* wives to either side. Kira and Farid sat at one of the side tables, but closest to the top table. The lesser traders, and the influential members of the city and their wives, took up the rest of the places.

A bevy of servers passed platters of food along the tables and the Hall hummed with voices, the chink of cups, and the scrape of metal against fine clay platters. Kira tried to ignore the sound of metal and, as the food dishes were finally cleared and the players took up their positions, she readied herself to turn the conversation to the Writings Store. But before she could, Domain Guard made their way over and Farid excused himself.

He spoke with them briefly then turned back to her. 'A dispute over dues I must attend to,' he said. 'Please accept my apologies. I will be back shortly. Why is it *always* the Bishali horse-traders?' he muttered, as he hurried away.

The Hall quieted as Tierken rose and delivered a speech of welcome and then the players began and Tierken led Laryia onto the floor to dance. They were soon joined by others from the top table and the players finished to polite applause before they started thread-the-leaves. Guests swarmed onto the floor until only Kira and an elderly woman with a stick remained at the tables.

The next dance was strange, but it did not matter because no one asked Kira to dance. A weave dance followed, and then thread-the-leaves again. Tierken remained at the top table, conversing with his guests, but Laryia was partnered by one of the Marken and Kira aware of her concerned glances as she whirled past.

Thread-the-leaves ended and Laryia said something to Tierken, but he barely interrupted his conversation with a finely dressed, silver-haired man and Laryia still stared at Kira worriedly as she was led back onto the floor by a trader leader.

Kira kept her face expressionless but her throat was almost too tight to breathe. Why in the 'green did she loiter in this loathsome *stone* city, *bedecked in metal*, betraying *everything* Kasheron fought for? And why had Tierken insisted she come to the banquet if he were to shun her? Was it his way of driving home that she was *exeal*? Not part of *his* celebrations? Not part of *his* people?

Well, she had better ways to spend her time! The music started again and she rose, intending to use the crowded floor to mask her escape, then froze. Those on the dance floor listened too, rather than danced, but Kira barely noticed. *The Parting*, the tune Kandor played for her at Turning, before the Shargh attack, before . . .

The Hall was gone, consumed by flames and the screams of the dying, and she was running back for Kandor, as she ran in nightmare, over and over again, but never fast enough, never *ever* fast enough ...

Figures stepped from the darkness and Kira cannoned into them. 'You cannot pass, Lady.'

Arms constrained her and she became aware of the night air, cool on her skin, and of the stone, gritty under her boots.

Her head swam and she gasped for breath. 'You have no right! You have no right . . .'

'Kira! What's got into you?'

It was Tierken and she turned on him savagely. 'I'm leaving your stinking city,' she shrieked. 'I'm—'

Tierken's grip replaced the Guard's and his gouging fingers stifled further speech. 'The Lady is unwell,' he clipped out. 'I thank you for your assistance, Guard.' He hauled her back across the square, up the steps, and along the balcony to her rooms.

'I'm not staying in your stinking city,' she panted, anger at his bullying replacing her terror.

'You've caused enough disruption for one evening,' he gritted. 'You will explain yourself to me later.' He thrust her into her rooms, slammed the door shut, and turned the key in the lock.

15

Kira beat on the door with her fists, then tore off the necklets and bracelets and hurled them across the room. They pinged and clanged on the floor and, shaking with rage, she dragged the dress over her head, pulled on her clothes and the ring of rulership, and yanked on her pack.

She must have been *mind-sick* to believe that this *Terak Kutan* would *ever* have the wit *or* intelligence to accept her claim. And if he thought he could *confine* her, he could add *delusion* to his list of flaws! She wrenched open the shutters, dropped her pack out, and clambered onto the sill.

A voice in her head said *don't* but it was no higher than she had jumped before and she pushed off. But the landing was not leaf litter, and the jarring shock left her curled on the ground. It was a long time before she could sit up and longer still before she could stand. Pain throbbed through her back and she knew she had been fortunate not to have broken anything. It was freezing too and shuddering with cold, she limped across the yard.

There was a disused stable against the Domain Wall and a stack of timber next to it that provided a rudimentary ladder and, weeping with pain, she clawed her way onto the stable roof, straddled the wall awkwardly and lowered herself down until she hung from her numb hands. It was an even bigger drop on the other side and she clenched her teeth and let go.

The pain was awful, but anger drove her on, and she limped north to avoid the Guard at the Domain gate. Laryia had not taken her to this part of the city and it was poorer, with mud rather than paving underfoot. Kira slowed as lamps heralded buildings ahead and cautiously peered out into the street. Music and voices flowed from the building opposite and then a door opened, slashing the ground with colored light.

A man staggered out, cursed as he collided with a low fence, and wove his way up the street. There was a woman there, Kira noticed in surprise, and despite the freezing air, she wore a gown that left her shoulders exposed. The man came to an uneven stop in front of her and Kira's heart thudded but the woman seemed unconcerned. She held out her hand and there was the chink of traders, and then she heaved the man's arm over her shoulders and they disappeared into a second building.

Kira slumped against the building as the patrolmen's bragging suddenly made sense. She thought of the wealth and poorness of Maraschin, the Domain's paving and the mud here, and of the forests. Allogrenia had none of the beautiful things she had seen at Mid-market, but it had none of the north's ugliness either.

She leaned her head back against the stone and closed her eyes. Her anger was spent and her back wracked with pain, and she was freezing. The sensible thing would be to return to the Domain Gate and beg admittance. *Please Domain Guard, let me go back to my nice warm bed and forget every principle I've ever had.*

Her father had used fear to confine her and Tierken had used a lock and key. She was not going back.

She scanned the street and then, teeth gritted in pain, hastened into the shadows of the buildings opposite and stopped. Beyond their ramshackle shells were not more buildings as she had supposed, but bushes, straggly vines, and clumps of grass. There was a strong smell of rot where rinds and fruit waste had been dumped but there was also the scent of silvermint.

Kira strained into the darkness. A great bowl of land had been gouged out, which explained why she had seen nothing from her rooms, and its sides cut into a series of terraces that disappeared into the gloom at the bottom. She had no idea *what* it was or *how* it came to be there, but it Sheltered the green and growing and she picked her way down.

Her jarred back made the going hard but there was a broken stone seat at the bottom and, as she drew near, she saw it encircled a tree. The tree had been cut down and she ran her fingers over the savage chop marks. The stump was too old to retain its spicy scent, but she knew what it was and she collapsed onto the seat, cradled her face in her hands, and cried.

It was late before Tierken farewelled the last of his guests and accompanied Laryia along the balcony to their rooms. He had managed to salvage the banquet's success by telling those who enquired that Kira had been taken ill, and by flattering and charming those who *had not* enquired but whose faces had showed their disdain. He had managed to hide his anger too, but he had no need to now and mentally rehearsed the stinging rebuke he was about to deliver.

Laryia eyed him anxiously as they reached their rooms. 'Tierken—'

'It's late, Laryia. Go to bed.'

'Kira was upset. You're not going to make things worse, are you?'

Tierken kissed heron the cheek. 'Fair dreams, Laryia.' Laryia still hesitated, her hand on the door to her room. 'Fair dreams, Laryia,' he repeated.

'And to you, Tierken,' she said, and disappeared inside.

Tierken unlocked the door to Kira's rooms and thrust it open. 'Kira?' It was dim inside, with only a single lamp on the table. Something crunched under foot and he cursed and held the lamp aloft. Jewelry flashed and glimmered all over the floor and he scowled as he picked his way through it to the sleeping-room. It was cold and he saw why.

The shutters were wide and he scanned swiftly The bed was untouched but clothes spilled from the chest and her pack was gone. He checked the bathing-room, braced himself, and peered out the window. She was not lying broken on the stones below, thank Irid, and he stared across the yard to the disused stables. The wall was only a little higher than their roof and his gaze took in the timber stack. It made for an easy climb out *straight into the muddy wastes of the Caru Quarter*.

It was the only way Kira could have gone without being returned by the Domain Guard and it was the worst place for a lone woman to be at night. He collected his sword and knives from his rooms, tossed a cape over his black and silvers, and set off at a run not pausing until he reached the ale- and wager-houses. They were quiet which was unsurprising given how late it was and he eyed where the Caru women lived.

Drunken men were poor judges of a woman's willingness to take them and his sword arm tensed as he wondered whether Kira had been accosted. The only way to find out was to have the Guard mount a search, but he was loath to involve them. Kira disliked crowds in any case and *if* she had come this way, would have avoided other people.

He strode across the street and on between the buildings where the weeds were waist-high and cursed as he stepped in a foul-smelling slop. Rosham was right. It *was* time the Caru Quarter was cleaned up! He used his sword to hack a passage and the stench gave way to the scent of herbs. It gave him hope she *had* come this way and he called softly. 'Kira?'

Nothing. He clambered down into the quarry, taking care on the ledges hidden beneath the tangle. Terak had taken stone from here for Sarnia's building but Tierken had not been here for several seasons and it was more overgrown than he remembered. There was someone there at the bottom, no, it was just the tree stump. Praise Irid! Kira was there too!

She was motionless, her head resting back against the stump, her eyes silvered by the stars. 'This is not a good place to be,' he said tersely as he scanned. 'Come. You need to be back in your rooms.'

'You cut down the alwaysgreen,' she said, her voice as empty as her face.

'It was an allogrenia,' he said automatically. 'It was before my time.'

'The Terak cut healing from their hearts.'

He took a steadying breath. 'Come back to the Domain, Kira. We need to talk.'

'You deny me. There's no point in talk.'

'I've never denied *you*!'

'You deny *me*! You deny *healing*! You deny the *Tremen*! I'm not going *anywhere* with you!'

'You can't stay here,' he said tersely.

'Why not? It's where you dump the things you don't want, isn't it?'

The words cut him to the quick and he sat down beside her. 'I want you, Kira. From that moment on the plain, when you raised your face and looked at me with eyes as gold as my own, I've wanted you.'

She half shook her head. 'You don't want what I am.'

Tierken took a deep breath. '*All* our tales and *all* our histories tell of Kasheron taking his followers north over the seas and there's no evidence to suggest any of them are false. But I've never had the Writing Store ordered, and in truth, I don't know exactly what may lay hidden inside. Tomorrow I will ask Farid to order it and to put aside for me *anything* that speaks of Kasheron. Would that please you?'

She nodded once.

'Come then,' he said in relief, but she could barely stand. 'You've hurt yourself!'

'I've jarred my back.'

'I'll carry you.'

'It will be better if I walk.'

Tierken brought his arm around her and they made their way up the slope. It was slow going, her every step agony and when they finally reached the steps to the balcony, he picked her up and she did not protest. His arms gave her the Shelter she craved and he pushed open the door to her rooms and lowered her onto her bed. She watched his face, its beauty illuminated by the lamp's dim glow, as he pulled the shutters closed. 'I'll set the fire,' he said.

'Stay, Tierken.'

He perched on the bed and brought the back of his hand gently down her cheek. 'This is not a good time, Kira. You're—'

She placed her fingers on his lips to still his words. The Shargh had taught her that the future could be obliterated in an instant. 'There's only now.'

'You're safe in Sarnia. There will be plenty of—'

She slid her hand under the silk of his hair and pulled him close. 'There's only now,' she repeated and brought her mouth to his.

Tierken prowled around the Meeting Hall. Farid waited at the table with Mid-market's records stacked neatly in front of him but all Tierken could think of was Poerin's advice to deal with *uncomfortable facts* sooner rather than later.

Last night had confirmed Kira's place was with him but she was no ordinary woman and the complications of the kinship claim made him feel as if he stood on Kristlin ice, and that it had started to crack.

As the Tremen leader, she demanded more *evidence* the Tremen histories were false than another leader's claim and he considered the ring she wore at her neck. The design *was* common in the north, as he had told her when she had first challenged him, but it had only come into existence when King Elrin had wed Kiraon, the gold-eyed Kessomi Healer. Such had been Elrin's passion for his new queen he had added the Kessomis' beloved allogrenia to his mark of the galloping horse.

It was around the same time silverwrights had perfected their art so that the bowls and candle-holders in his rooms, which dated from *Terak's* time, were not the dull silver of Kira's ring. It meant the ring had been forged *after* Elrin had married Kiraon but *before* silver had been properly purified, namely the time of Terak and Kasheron's princedoms. But the timing proved nothing.

133

Countless such rings had been forged then and traded far and wide since.

He stopped at the window and grimaced as he realized he was to repeat his forebear's actions but under far less auspicious circumstances. There had been no antagonism to Kessom when Elrin had married Kiraon, that had come later when Kessom had refused to support the fight against the Shargh and then the Healer Kasheron had dealt Terak's forces a near fatal blow by deserting with his followers.

It had seeded a bitterness that endured to this day and yet, oddly, many of the conversations he had shared at the banquet last night had been conciliatory. Thanks to the gossips, it was well-known Kira was a Healer and her gold eyes were obvious to everyone and yet, more than one of the powerful trader leaders, whose views the Marken subtly or not so subtly expressed each Feailmark, contained oblique gestures of support.

It had been Mirina, wife of the wealthy glass-trader Jarklin, who had been most plain in her speech. After congratulating Tierken on his three seasons on rulership, she had commented on the happiness Sarnia felt in Tierken having added to Laryia's gentle presence. *The Domain is a better place when it contains the women folk of the Feailners and their children*, Mirina had said.

His breath sifted between his teeth. Perhaps after the long uncertainty of Darid's childless rule, Sarnia was more concerned with procuring an heir than his bride's Healer tendencies!

'You're distracted this day, Feailner,' said Farid eventually.

'Forgive me,' said Tierken, and wandered back to the table.

134

'As I said last night, the Bishali horse-traders continue to believe their treatment is more ill than every other trader's,' said Farid.

'Did you offer them the usual choice?'

'Trade leader Udrun chose as he usually does, to be levied on the number of horses traded, rather than their value. I also offered him a flat rate on the land his traders occupied, as you suggested. He declined.' Farid selected a brecon nut and peeled off the shell. 'He's not going to be happy whatever he chooses.'

'No,' said Tierken.

There was a long pause. 'My father tells me Kira was distressed at the banquet. I beg your pardon, Feailner, that I absented myself for so long.'

'Kira wasn't distressed by your absence. She comes from a small community and finds crowds oppressive. And you had little choice. Udrun's never been quick to pacify and the fact you soothed his imagined injuries at all is testament to your skills.'

There was another long pause and Tierken wandered back to the window. He gazed towards Kira's rooms and his jaw clenched as he considered her leap from the window. 'The Writings Store in the Lehan Wing, Farid. Have you ever sorted through it?'

'When I first became Keeper, I examined the Writings of Darid's time, but I didn't go back any further. It appears the records have *ever* been ordered.'

Tierken turned back, hands on hips. 'Now the Feailmark is finished and you have more time, I'd like you to do so. Mouras can assign you servers to help. I want you to put aside *anything* that refers to the Sundering, Kasheron, the families he took with him, the ring of rulership he wore, and the Caru Quarter.'

'May I ask why? You're not thinking of releasing the land set aside for Kasheron, are you?'

'Your father would certainly like me to,' muttered Tierken, 'but it's not the reason I want the Writing Store ordered.' He threw himself into a chair. 'Kira's histories claim the Tremen are of Kasheron's line, which is obviously preposterous. But as she happens to be the Tremen leader, I need *evidence* to *prove* the fact.'

Farid stared at him in astonishment. 'The Tremen leader?' He took a steadying breath. 'Well, at least being Kasheron's line would explain her striking similarity to you.'

'Kira's exeal, like her people. The break between her forebears and mine happened long before the Kessomis were even a people. But she *will* be making her home here and I want that home to be happy.'

Farid's astonishment deepened. 'Are congratulations in order?' he asked uncertainly.

Tierken smiled briefly. 'Not yet, but soon.'

16

Kira had spent most of the morning in a hot bath, trying to ease her back when Niria informed her the Feailner expected her for mid-meal in the Meeting Room. She climbed out gingerly and dressed slowly, her thoughts on the previous night.

Tierken's love-making had been infinitely gentle, his warmth and scent and tenderness a balm that had soothed away her anger, and fear, and hurt, and afterwards, she had slept curled about him, drawing her breath with his, snug beneath the cover.

She had never known such peace but as the dawn's silvery light found the window, he eased away from her and dressed. She watched him, delighting in the line of his shoulder and flank, and then he had kissed her and gone.

She touched her fingers to her lips and the sweetness of his Shelter washed over her again. They were unbonded and her time in the north short, but she could not regret what she had done. It had taken the Shargh to teach her that yesterday was lost and tomorrow might never come.

Kira lowered herself into a chair as servers bustled about the Meeting Hall with platters of food and jugs of fruited-water. Her back throbbed, despite her morning in the bath, and she considered the salves she carried in her pack. They were not much use though given there were no Healers in Sarnia to administer them.

Tierken's face held none of tenderness of last night as he poured her a cup of water and she wondered if he needed to be *the Feailner* in front of the servers but his manner remained business-like even after the last of the servers had left. 'I've come to the Meeting Hall at midday as requested, Feailner,' she said formally, taking his lead. 'What would you have me do?'

'Tell me about the Tain,' he said. 'And eat.'

'Your people have a treaty with the Tain. Don't you know about them already?'

'My knowing isn't recent,' said Tierken as he sipped his water. 'There's been no contact since early in my uncle's rulership.'

It was what Caledon had told her and the reason he believed the Terak would not come south. Tierken wanted to know about King Beris and Prince Adris, the King's Guard, Maraschin's administration, the watch-walks, the Shargh attacks and the doings of the woodcutters, herders, gatherers and physics.

He probed and questioned, his brows drawn in concentration as he demanded more and more detail and challenged any apparent contradiction. His questioning took her back to her time in the Sanctum, to the garden where she sat after Jesin's death, and to Caledon. She was weary and her back spasming but he paused only to let the servers light the fire and the lamps and deliver cotzee.

'Did you like Maraschin?' he asked once they had gone. He filled her cup with cotzee and relaxed back with his own.

'There's a lot of stone in the city, and noise, and the smell of cooked flesh.'

'What of the Tallien ,Caledon, Prince Adris's friend?'

Kira contemplated the fire flames as she thought of how he had played the thumbelin and held her close as the storm had howled about them, and she thought of his sweet spice smell and Shelter. 'Is he your lover?' demanded

138

Tierken, no longer lounging in his chair.

'Caledon loves the stars,' said Kira, still intent on the fire, and for the first time, had a sense of what that might mean.

'That's not what I asked.'

Irritation at his badgering stirred and she glanced at him briefly. 'Caledon is a Placidien. He journeys to put things right in the world.' Tierken's expression remained hard and she looked back to the fire. If only things *could* be put right, the Bough be *unburned* and Kandor ...

'I didn't get the chance to tell you how beautiful you looked at the banquet,' said Tierken abruptly.

'That probably explains why no one asked me to dance,' retorted Kira, still smarting from the humiliation.

'That wasn't the reason. It was to avoid offending me.'

Kira looked at him in surprise. 'How could dancing with me possibly offend you?'

'It's widely believed I've brought you to Sarnia to marry.' Kira burst out laughing but choked to a stop when she noticed his gravity. 'Is the idea so ridiculous?' he said tightly.

Kira shrugged. ' Do Terak Feailners usually marry their *exeal* prisoners?'

'I've explained to you *more than once* why you need to remain in Sarnia's safety. You're no use to the Tremen dead.'

'And I'm no use to them alive either while I delay here,' she retorted in frustration.

His face hardened 'Is that how you see our time together? As a *delay*?'

Kira looked away and heard his cup chink down and then her blood fired as he came to her side of the table. He pulled her gently into his arms, and she pressed closer,

139

greedy for his Shelter, and he scooped her up and set her down again on the soft rug before the fire.

He undressed her slowly, his touch as delicious as the fire warmth, his caresses as gentle as the last night's, but her hunger for him was greater and grew in urgency until it coalesced into a surge of potent sweetness.

Afterwards, as she lay safe in his arms, she stared at his face, wanting to imprint his beauty in her memory as he had imprinted her with the hot essence of himself. His eyes were shut as he stroked her breast and then his fingers touched the ring and stopped.

He gathered his clothes and dressed, and Kira dressed too, but more slowly, made clumsy by her painful back.

'You can tell me about the Tremen on the morrow,' he said, as he sifted through the Writings on the table. 'Then I'll be taken up preparations for the next patrol. When I return, we will visit Kessom.'

Another patrol! Kira stared at him in dismay. 'But—'

'I've instructed Farid to order the Writing Store, as I pledged, but it will take time. We can discuss anything of relevance he might find on my return too.'

Kira winced as her back spasmed. 'If he finds Writings that say Kasheron went south, will you accept the kin-link and grant the Tremen aid?'

'Such a find would be highly unlikely,' said Tierken, frowning as he perused a Writing.

He continued to read and the understanding that Tierken would not aid the Tremen, regardless of what the Writing Store held, settled over her like a comfortless cloak. He replaced the Writing on the pile and glanced up. 'It's time you went to your bed, Kira. Your back needs rest to mend.'

Kira went to the stables early the next morning. Her back was still painful but she was keen to improve her riding skills and scour away her frustration. Tierken acted as if he had all the time in the world to decide the Tremen's fate but as the Tremen leader, she could delay no longer. The fastest way south was by horse and she needed to be a far better rider to survive the Sarsalin.

Ryn appeared towards the end of her practice and was surprised to see her. 'The Feailner said you'd injured your back and wouldn't ride for a time,' he said.

'I missed her,' said Kira as she patted the mare's shoulder.

'No name yet?'

Kira shook her head. There was no point naming a horse she must leave behind in the north. Ryn listed off the names of horses he had known or owned, and common Kir and Illian horse names and their meanings and Kira nodded politely, but her thoughts were elsewhere. 'I'd like to ride outside the city,' she said as she rubbed the mare's nose. 'Laryia says there are good rides to the north. Do you think I'm skilled enough?'

'You are skilled enough.'

'Laryia says that this mare, her mare Chime, and the Feailner's mount Kalos, are stronger and faster than the horses of the Domain Guard. I know little of horses, Horse Master Ryn. Is that true?'

'It is,' said Ryn. 'That line is like no other.' He glanced up at the sky. 'It will rain before the sun clears the Sarsalin. You know how to rub the mare down when you've finished,' he said, and with a nod, moved off.

Ryn's prediction proved accurate and Kira was soaked before she trudged back up the steps to the balcony. Farid came out of a room at the far end, his arms loaded with sheafs, and Kira hastened to the open door as fast as her back allowed. She wanted to ask him about the Writings, but he had disappeared by the time she got there and she peered into the small room.

It reminded her of the Waren's Sarnia Room and she scanned the shelves excitedly. Two servers sat at a table, sorting through Writings and placing them into piles, but the shelves were so jumbled it looked like someone had upended them.

'Is there anything we can help you with, Lady?' The questioner was so bald he looked like a Drinkwater pebble.

She wanted to read *all* the Writings but she needed a map and was suddenly glad that Farid *had* disappeared. 'I'm a stranger to Sarnia,' she said hurriedly, hoping he did not suddenly reappear. 'Do you have any maps of the lands all about? Of the Sarsalin?'

The server slowly shuffled through some sheafs and Kira glanced at the door nervously. The man finally extracted five or six squares of paper and handed them to her with a formal bow. 'May I take them to my rooms?' she asked. 'I'll bring them back by nightfall.'

'Of course, Lady,' he said.

Kira tucked them under her jacket, hastened to her rooms, and locked the door behind her. The first few maps were of the lands north of the Silvercades with Talliel prominently marked, but they showed smaller settlements too. Other maps showed the forested tracts of the Silvercade's foothills and then she found one that showed the lands between the southern Silvercades and the northern Azurcades.

She crouched over it, so absorbed, she barely heard Laryia's voice at the door, and then the door handle rattled. 'Kira?' She thrust the maps under her clothes in the clothing chest and hastily opened the door. 'You're soaked,' said Laryia as she came into the room. 'Surely you haven't ridden in this?'

'It was fine when I started.'

'And there's no need to lock your door,' she said, glancing at Kira's uneaten breakfast. 'The Domain is quite safe, with plenty of Guard and servers about.' Kira nodded and pulled off her wet jacket, shivering as drips ran down her neck.

'I'll run a hot bath for you,' said Laryia. 'We don't want you ill.'

Kira followed her into the bathing-room and steam billowed as water gushed from the taps, then perfume filled the air as Laryia tossed in a handful of pink soap-flakes. She swirled her hand through the water and glanced up. 'Tierken is waiting for you in the Meeting Hall,' she said. 'He's told me who you claim to be.'

'He doesn't believe me.'

'He doesn't believe your *histories*. There is a difference.' Laryia paused. 'Tierken's happiness is the most important thing in the world to me, Kira. I think he could be happy with you.'

'I have to go south again.'

'Tierken believes he's very different to his uncle, Darid, the previous Feailner,' continued Laryia, as if Kira had not spoken. 'And in many ways he is, but Darid only loved once, and even after Seren died, he didn't take another wife. Darid could have fathered an heir to supplant Tierken but Seren was too precious to him. I think Tierken will only love once too.'

'I have to go south again, Laryia, to be with my people,' said Kira desperately. 'I don't have any choice.'

'There are always choices, Kira,' said Laryia, and enclosed Kira in a hug. 'I think Tierken has chosen well.'

Tierken's questions about the Tremen was as methodical and unrelenting as his questions about the Tain. The relative authority of the Tremen leader, the Protector Commander, the Clancouncil and the clanleaders; the nature and frequency of patrols; the training and discipline of the Protectors; the relationship of each clan to the others; gathering and trading rights; the seasonal variation in food and forage.

He was particularly interested in the lack of metal. 'So only swords and herbing sickles. Does that mean Tremen men are bearded?'

'No, they use clear-root, a plant that takes off hair.'

'No jewelry either. Laryia would be most displeased,' he added lightly.

'There's wooden jewelry and beautiful beads made from tree sap,' said Kira defensively.

'Tell me of your growing.'

'I lived in the Bough, as I've said. My mother died after Kandor, my younger brother, was born. Helpers stayed with us to clean, cook and sew.' Kira shrugged. 'That's all.'

'How did you occupy your days?'

'I gathered, foraged with Tresen and Kandor, and played at the Kashclan longhouse.'

'Tresen?'

'My clanmate.' She did not even know if Tresen were still alive.

'Did the Shargh kill him too?' asked Tierken more gently.

144

'Nearly, and it was my fault.'

'How so?'

Kira smiled grimly. 'It took me a long time to realize the Shargh hunted *me* and that to stop the bloodshed, I had to leave. I knew Kest wouldn't agree so I went secretly but Tresen knew me too well. He caught up with me just as I had stumbled upon Shargh and led them away. They caught him before Kest's patrol arrived and he was terribly wounded.'

'Why *do* the Shargh hunt you?' asked Tierken.

'They hate my eyes. When they had me—' Her throat tightened making it hard to even breathe and Tierken was suddenly on her side of the table. 'They're never going to have you again,' he said, taking her in his arms. 'You're safe here.'

Kira stepped back, fighting the urge to believe she *could* hide away in the north. 'I'm the Tremen leader, Tierken. Before the Shargh took me, Caledon went south to Allogrenia to seek volunteers to fight with the Tain. They might be in Maraschin *now*. I *must* be there with them.'

Tierken's eyes narrowed. 'You trusted this *Tallien* to seek Protectors from Allogrenia?'

'He said you wouldn't aid us and that you might not even aid the Tain. He said the silence between your people and the Tain had been too long.' She paused, but Tierken was angry and she pressed on.

'He said the Tain wouldn't aid my people unless we aided the Tain.' She took several steps away and hugged herself. 'To *order* Protectors to fight and die on the plains would be to betray *everything* Kasheron fought for.' She smiled bitterly. 'So I asked for volunteers.'

Tierken paced to the window and then swung back to

her. '*If* this Tallien, *Caledon*, brings Tremen fighters from the forests, they will be led by Kest, not by you, and *if* the Shargh capture you again, they will fight *and* die in vain. The Shargh will trade your life for their compliance and once your people are dead, they will kill you too. You will remain here.'

'You have no right to keep me here!' cried Kira in frustration. 'According to you, *I'm* exeal *and* my *people* are exeal, and that means whatever happens to them *and* to me, is nothing to do with you!'

Tierken was to her in a stride. 'Yesterday you called our time together a *delay* and today it's something to be dispensed with like this!' he said, and snapped his fingers. 'I'm beginning to think that Tremen women are as faithless as Caru women!' Kira's fists clenched and she stepped back. 'I didn't mean—'began Tierken.

'In Allogrenia, love is a *gift* given without thought of reward,' she gritted. 'I realize things are different in the north, that here, *everything* is traded. You've given me Shelter, Feailner, and a sleep without dreams. If you also found pleasure in the moment, I consider the trade fair!'

'Kira!'

She was already at the door and wrenched it open. 'I don't have anything to trade for your rescue of me *or* for my food and clothes since. I can only give you thanks for them. I hope you find the trade sufficient!'

She slammed the door and Tierken was still ruing the exchange when there was a tentative knock. 'Enter!' he bawled.

It was Farid, carrying a Writing. 'I've been ordering the Writing Store as requested and I've found something of interest.'

'What?' demanded Tierken. 'That Kasheron had a daughter, who had a daughter, who had a daughter, who had a daughter, who had a daughter called Kira?'

'No, something else,' said Farid, eyeing him. 'When Kasheron and his followers left, they took Kessomi horses.'

'A sore point,' snapped Tierken, prowling around the room. 'Kasheron abandoned the horses when he sailed away and Terak had to trade every one of them back. It cost him dearly.'

'Terak traded them back from the Ashmiri, I believe.'

'Yes,' said Tierken. 'Ashmiri mounts are poor and Terak knew the Ashmiri would be a lot more dangerous on Kessomi horses.'

'When did Kasheron and his followers leave?'

Tierken threw himself into a chair. 'At the beginning of summer. Kasheron and his ilk's desertion weakened Terak's defences and the dry earth advantaged the Shargh who fought on foot. Yet despite everything, Terak had all his horses back by summer's end.'

'That's my understanding too,' said Farid, and laid the Writing on the table. 'But it's not what this says.'

Tierken scowled. 'What does it say?'

'More or less the same thing, except that Kasheron left at the start of *winter* and that Terak had all his horses back by *winter's* end.'

Tierken shrugged. 'It's a small difference.'

'Where do the Ashmiri graze in winter?'

Tierken stared at him and then swore. 'It contradicts *everything* we know but it's not *impossible*. Our histories could be *completely* wrong and Kira's completely right.' He laughed hollowly. 'Your father could even think me the best Feailner since Terak himself.'

'Terak was a meticulous record keeper,' said Farid evenly. '*If* this Writing is true, Terak had all his horses back, *traded from the Ashmiri*, by winter's end and, as the Ashmiri graze their animals *east* of the Azurcades in winter, the horses must have been traded from the *south*, not the north.'

'One Writing that contradicts *everything*,' muttered Tierken. 'It could be wrong or our histories could be wrong.'

'It's hard to judge without going through *everything* in the Writing Store,' said Farid.

'Do that, Farid, and get more servers to help you.'

17

Caledon stared up at the sky but the dawn light had eaten the last of the stars. Horses stamped and snorted behind him, ten in all, their riders the most experienced of the King's Guard. They had discarded their blues in favor of garb better suited to the Sarsalin and talked amongst themselves until there was the sound of a horse on King's Way.

The recklessness of its descent meant it could only be Adris and he appeared at full gallop, not wrenching his horse to a stop until it was almost on them. He thumped to the paving and strode forward with a leather message cylinder.

Caledon accepted it with a bow. 'I will deliver greetings from the Tain Prince to the Terak Feailner,' he said.

'You may deliver greetings from the Tain *King* to the Terak Feailner. My father died this night.'

Caledon dropped to his knee. 'Then I honor the Tain King. May his reign be long and wise.'

'There is no bending of knees between friends,' said Adris, raising him. 'I will send Guard over the Azurcades to await the Tremen fighters, even as the Guard awaited you. Billets have been prepared.'

'I thank you,' said Caledon.

Adris embraced him long and hard. 'May Meros guide your way, my friend.'

Caledon smiled. 'With all due respect to Meros, I prefer the stars.'

In the Cashgars' shadow, the rising sun lit a scene so extraordinary that Tarkenda had to remind herself it was not a vision. The spur's entire lower slope was crowded with sorchas. The Weshargh and Soushargh warriors had arrived in the night and their singing and shouting had kept her and Palansa wakeful.

The warriors were quiet now, the bravery the sherat had gifted them having been replaced with snores. Tarkenda wondered how much food they carried. No Shargh in the Grounds went hungry, even those on the lower slope, but there was little left for storage.

Tarkenda grimaced. There was so much hot blood and wild talk of what was to come, the stench of it still hung in the air like a summer storm. The only small comfort was that soon the hatred of Arkendrin and his followers would be directed north, and the struggle to protect Ersalan be a little less.

Kira started upright in her chair as the door to her rooms was flung open and the silhouette in the doorway resolved itself into Laryia. She wore trousers and a jacket, rather than her usual gown, and Kira blinked. 'You haven't slept,' said Laryia in dismay, 'and we have a long day ahead.'

'What?' said Kira, wondering if she dreamed. Her pen was still in her hand and she set it down and rubbed her stiff neck.

'We're going to Kessom; we're going to see Eris,' sang Laryia, as she danced across the room. 'Tierken's postponed the patrol, and he's at the stables, readying the horses. I've packed fur jackets and fleece shirts for us. It's freezing in Kessom this time of season but *so* lovely! The snow glitters and the Kristlin glows like a blue gem. Oh, how I long to see Eris and Thalli and Jafiel . . .'

Kira stared at her in bewilderment and Laryia laughed and took her hands. 'I'm probably not making much sense but Tierken said to let you sleep as long as possible. He came to my rooms a while ago and told me we were going.'

'But why?'

'He says he needs to speak with Poerin but I know he wants to see Eris as much as I do. Oh, I can't wait! Come Kira and dress. I know Niria put some warmer things in one of these chests,' said Laryia and darted towards one.

'I'll get them,' said Kira sharply.

Laryia stopped and Kira softened her voice. 'I'm sorry, I'm still half asleep. I'll change into warmer clothes and meet you at the stables.'

'I've got hats and gloves but we won't need them until after the Tiar Forests. We'll breakfast there too. Don't be long. It's going to be *so* wonderful.' Laryia laughed again. 'You're going to love Kessom *and* Eris, and Eris is going to love you.'

Kira changed and made her way down to the stables not knowing whether to feel angry at the delay to her journey south or excited at visiting Tierken and Laryia's *Healer* grandmother. Kessom was older than Sarnia, and she comforted herself with the possibility it might hold records that proved her claims of kinship were true.

Tierken led the way into the foothills, with Laryia and Kira next, and two Domain Guard bringing up the rear. Laryia kept up a constant chatter about everything from the Silver Falls, which were the most striking in the Terak lands, to the dwinhir hatchlings in the Torlands behind Kessom, to the wonders of the Kristlin.

Tierken spoke briefly to the Guard and occasionally responded to Laryia but said nothing to Kira. His greeting at the stables had been no more than a nod and she knew he was still angry with her for insisting on going south.

The climb into the Silvercades' foothills was steep but the path zig-zagged across the slope and rather than going straight up and, unlike the Azurcades, the Silvercades' stone seemed stable. The crisp morning air carried the tang of many plants and Kira's spirits rose. It was good to be away from Sarnia's stone confines, to breathe air filled with the green and growing and she enjoyed the mare's warm, horsey smell too.

After a time, the scattered trees came together in a dense grove and Laryia fell silent. The leaf litter filled the air with resinous scents and reduced the horses' hoofbeats to soft thuds. There was no undergrowth, just trunk upon trunk, that stretched away unbroken in the muted light.

'The Tiar Forests,' said Laryia. 'They are always dim but we'll be through them soon enough.'

'They're beautiful,' said Kira thickly.

Laryia grinned. 'I had forgotten your lands are forested. You're going to like the Frost Groves and the allogrenia stands in Kessom.'

They emerged back into the crisp morning air and the path steepened and narrowed, forcing them into single file until the slope levelled off again into a broad jut of flat land. 'This is the Tiar Lookround,' said Laryia. 'It's where we will breakfast.'

They dismounted and the horses were tethered. It was easy to see why it was called a *lookround*. Beyond the dark crowns of the Tiar Forest, a wintry sunshine lit

Sarnia's stone and the perfect circle of its wall. Kira stared beyond it, to where the Sarsalin glimmered in a golden mist, and birds appeared and disappeared as they dived and swooped.

'Courting dwinhir,' said Tierken, coming to her side. 'In winter, when the cock-bird seeks a mate, the hen-bird tests his strength and resolve to see whether he's in accord with her.'

'It doesn't seem very fair to him,' said Kira as she watched the birds.

'Oh, he gets his reward. If she chooses him, he'll have a mate for life. In Kessom, it's called the dance of the dwinhir, but some Terak call it the disappointment of the dwinhir, because the hen-bird sometimes shuns the male.' He glanced to where the Guard built a fire and Laryia was busy with the food. 'I need to beg your pardon for my words last night. They were ill-considered and untrue.'

'I wasn't much better,' muttered Kira.

Tierken's fingers gently turned her face to his. 'Are we in accord?' he asked softly.

'I don't think the Terak and Tremen will ever be in accord,' she said honestly.

'The dance isn't over yet,' he said, and kissed her.

'The cotzee's brewed and the nuts will soon be roasted,' called Laryia cheerfully. 'Time to eat!'

The meal was brief and they were soon on their way. The path continued to climb until it reached a narrow ridge and, as they turned along it, the ground fell away steeply on either side. The day was fine and the breeze gentle but Kira guessed the ridge would be very different in a high wind, especially as there were no bushes or sheltering trees and a river rushed along below them. They rode in pairs now, the two Guard positioned beside Laryia and

153

Kira. 'Glass Gorge,' called Laryia over her shoulder and Kira nodded.

It was close to midday before the ridge broadened and they crossed a shallow, fast-flowing river. There was a roar too and Kira stared around in mystification. 'The Silver River,' said Tierken, slowing Kalos so that Kira came alongside. 'You can hear the Silver Falls too. There's a good view of the Falls ahead where we will eat.'

The track forked and they continued north-east, the trees crowding close, and had not gone far before Tierken led them off along an overgrown path. Silvery foliage brushed against Kira's legs and she ducked under branches until they exited into a small clearing. They tethered the horses and the Guard set a fire-circle and collected wood.

'I'll show you the Falls,' said Tierken taking Kira's hand and leading her off through the bushes. His gaze flicked between the way ahead and the way they had come as he took his bearings, but Kira was content just to be with him, her hand warm in his. 'We need take care,' he said. 'The land drops away.'

The words had scarcely left his mouth when he brought her to a stop. A short way ahead, a mighty surge of water plunged down a yawning gulf and rainbows flickered, flung into space by the water's fume.

'Irid's sign,' said Tierken softly, but his gaze was on her, not on the rainbows. There was no slow arousal this time, just a fierce want of him. Kira forgot the Falls, the silvery plants, the crisp air sharp against her skin. She was so consumed by her need of his Shelter that she clung to him in the grass long after the storm of desire had passed.

'Laryia will come looking for us in a moment,' murmured Tierken, as he pulled his clothes back into place and helped Kira with hers. He took her hand to help her up but kept hold of it, his face curiously intent. 'Marry me, Kira.'

Kira blinked as the words penetrated the warm miasma of their love-making, and then twigs snapped as Laryia appeared, her gaze darting between them. 'I waited for you to come back and eat, and the food's cold now. At this rate it will be dark before we clear the Gorge.'

'You're right, Laryia,' said Tierken. 'It's getting late. We must go on.'

Kira replayed Tierken's words in her head as they rode on but they made no more sense than when he had uttered them. She knew from the patrol's gossip and the Marken's powerful webs of connection that kin-links, treaties and alliances were crucial in the north and that no Feailner would tie himself to an *exeal* woman, especially one who led an exeal people and she concluded she must have somehow mistaken his meaning.

The mountains soared around them and, as the sun dipped below their peaks, it took the warmth with it. Laryia donned a fleece hat and gloves and handed Kira a set. Kira took them gratefully and pulled the hat low over her frozen ears.

'The last part of a night journey to Kessom is cool in summer and icy in winter,' said Laryia and smiled. 'But Kessom's winter skies more than make up for the frigid air,' she added as she gazed upwards. 'It's not far now and soon we'll be warming ourselves with Eris.'

Kira stared up at the night sky too. The stars' brilliance reminded her of Caledon's faith in their prescience. 'The Kessomis call them star-storms,' said Tierken, waiting for her to come level. 'They are said to be the reason why so few Kessomis leave Kessom. Kessomis are star-bound to the Silvercades,' he added with a smile.

'You left,' said Kira, unable to imagine turning her back on Allogrenia.

'I went home. Laryia and I were born in Sarnia.'

'But raised in Kessom,' persisted Kira, much preferring her surroundings to the stone city. 'Where does your heart lie now?'

'You of all people should know that,' he said quietly.

'It lies in Kessom of course!' interjected Laryia, as globes of light emerged from the darkness.

A low building appeared first, then the pale wood of yards, and when a horse neighed, Kalos, Chime and Kira's mare gave answer. 'Kessomi horses know their own,' said Tierken. A door slammed and a lamp bobbed towards them. 'A good evening to you, Robrin,' said Tierken.

The man, *Robrin*, swung the lamp high. 'By the mists of Mintlin! It's you, Tierken, *and* Laryia. Ah, this is a happy night for Kessom.'

Tierken and Laryia dismounted and were enveloped in hugs. 'This is our guest, Kira,' said Tierken, catching Kira's hand and lifting her down before she had a chance to dismount.

Kira went to bow but found herself hugged as well. 'We've heard tell of your *twin*, Tierken,' said Robrin, raising the lamp and making Kira squint. 'For once Sarnia's tattle-tongues are right,' he said cheerfully. 'You are most welcome.'

'You've room in the stables?' asked Tierken.

'By all means, by all means,' said Robrin, busy taking their reins.

'And someone to help?' asked Laryia.

'Plenty of that too, Laryia. Go on off to Eris. We'll be seeing you in a few days, no doubt, for a proper welcome,' he said and headed off towards the stables, their mounts in tow.

Tierken spoke to the Guard, who followed Robrin, and then took Kira's hand again, as Laryia danced on ahead. They followed a path that wound steadily upward into the deeper darkness of trees. Their spicy scent was unmistakable and Kira slowed. 'Alwaysgreens,' she breathed, but Tierken tugged her on.

'Tomorrow,' he said, quickening his steps.

More lamps glimmered in the darkness, seeming to hang in the air, but lighting houses higher on the slopes. She heard the rush of water too and they crossed a small wooden bridge their steps echoing like a drum. 'The Zinaidi,' said Tierken, without pausing.

More alwaysgreens crowded forward, their glorious scent washing over Kira, and a house appeared, set close to the path. Laryia waited at its door. 'Everything looks the same,' she murmured, as she caressed a gnarled, leafless bush that over-hung the doorway. 'Even the freylin still grows.'

Tierken knocked and after a while, the door opened and a wedge of yellow light spilled out, illuminating a small, hunched figure. *Eris*, Kira presumed. Tierken bent low and Eris kissed him on each cheek, then did the same with Laryia. The welcome seemed very formal given Eris had not seen her grandchildren for three seasons and, after the stableman's hug, oddly restrained.

Kira stepped forward reluctantly, not wanting to intrude on their special reunion, but Eris kissed her on each cheek too, then cradled Kira's face between her papery hands and stared at her intently. 'It's good that you've come to Kessom, Kira,' she said. 'It was time.'

157

18

They shared a small meal and then Laryia bade her grandmother good night and took Kira to her childhood sleeping-room, leaving Eris and Tierken alone. For a while they sat in silence, Eris's keen gaze moving between her herb grinding and the grandson she had raised. It had been three seasons since the summons had come from Sarnia, and his face was harder now and his golden eyes warier. He looked more like Merench despite Lyess's coloring.

Tierken hefted another piece of wood onto the fire and sighed. 'It's good to be here,' he said.

Eris put her grinding bowl aside and rested her hands on her knees. They looked very old, even to her. 'You don't like being a Feailner?' she asked with a smile.

'What man would not like being a Feailner?' said Tierken. 'Life on the Sarsalin is good but in Sarnia? Nothing's simple there.'

'You knew the Marken wouldn't welcome you. What of the traders?'

'The traders are happy if the city is administered well, which it is, thanks to Farid.'

'Your patrols ensure all is secure so he *can* administer well,' said Eris, 'but you didn't come to Kessom to discuss Farid. Tell me of Kira.'

'I assumed you would know about her already.'

'The Kessomi patrolmen speak of what happens on patrol *and* of what's gossiped of in Sarnia, but I'm presuming you've come to Kessom to tell me the truth.'

'Well, I didn't come to please Rosham,' said Tierken dryly. 'You knew Kira was in Shargh hands when we came

158

across her?' Eris nodded. 'And now you've seen her, you know why she generates so much gossip. But there are things known only to me, Laryia and Farid. Kira claims to be Kasheron's seed and that Kasheron didn't go north, but to the Southern Forests, where he established a healing community called Allogrenia. He named his people the Tremen, and they are now under Shargh attack.'

Eris stared at the fire. 'A difficult claim for Sarnia to swallow,' she said eventually.

'And one completely at odds with Terak history. According to Kira, Kasheron set up a system of leadership where the best Healer becomes leader and that means Kira is the Tremen leader.'

'So,' said Eris slowly. 'She's called on the kin-link for you to aid her people.'

'Yes, which I've refused.'

'Why?'

Tierken glanced at her in surprise. 'You know Terak histories as well as I do.'

'I also know Terak prejudices. So, you deny Kira's people your aid and still she looks upon you with love.'

Tierken's eyes fluoresced in the firelight, a change she had not seen since childhood. 'It's a strange thing to find the other half of yourself,' he muttered.

'But not comfortable, for either of you. What do you intend to do, Tierken?'

'Marry her.'

Eris was not surprised. Darid had once sat in this very room and told her he was to marry Seren with exactly the same certainty. 'Kira's the leader of a people you've denied aid to, a people under attack. If you were her, would you stay or go back to them?'

'The Shargh have taken her once and still hunt her. Kira will stay in the north where she's safe.'

'Whether she wants to or not?' He made no reply and Eris considered him. 'Is it a wife you desire, Tierken, or a prisoner?'

'That's not how it is. Kira just needs time to grow used to Sarnia. It was the same with Laryia and me when we first went back there, but we're happy now and she will be too.' He yawned. 'I've an early start to Poerin on the morrow so I'll wish you a good night.'

'Will you ask Poerin's advice about Kira?' Tierken nodded. 'And will you take it?'

'I will listen to Poerin as I've listened to you,' said Tierken, and kissed her on the cheek. 'Fair dreams, Eris.'

Eris remained by the fire deep in thought. Tierken had spent his boyhood in fear the feailnership would be snatched from his grasp, a hard growing that had bequeathed him a dislike of uncertainty. She suspected it drove his unwillingness to accept Kira's claim as much as his reluctance to upset the Sarnians. The next few days would reveal what drove Kira.

Laryia and Kira joined Eris for breakfast the next morning and Eris watched Laryia's growing puzzlement when Tierken failed to appear. 'Does Tierken still sleep?' she asked finally.

'He's gone to Poerin.'

'I thought he'd at least stay here a day,' said Laryia indignantly. 'It's been three whole seasons since he saw you.'

Eris smiled. 'He saw me last night. That's enough for a young man.'

'Poerin trained Tierken in fighting and horsemanship,' Laryia explained to Kira, 'but he chooses to live where only dwinhirs frequent. It's a hard trip and too rough for horses. Tierken will be gone two or three days.'

Last night, Eris had seen how Sarnia had changed Tierken but it had changed her grand daughter too. Laryia had grown into a beautiful young woman but she was far more than that and, being female, the Marken had yet to suspect her strength. Her affection for Kira was clear too but Kira's gaze was mostly on the table. The daylight confirmed Kira's resemblance to Tierken but Kira had not learned to control her eye-color and Eris found its candor reassuring.

They had almost finished eating when there was a knock and Laryia set down her herbed bread and disappeared down the passageway. A squeal of delight floated back. 'It will be Thalli,' said Eris. 'It doesn't take long for news to spread in Kessom. Laryia and Thalli were close as children.'

Laryia re-appeared with her arm around a sandy-haired woman so heavy with child Kira thought she might birth on the spot. 'Kira, this is Thalli,' said Laryia. Thalli kissed Kira on the cheek but her attention was all for Laryia. 'Take breakfast with us,' said Laryia.

'I thank you, but Leos and Jafiel will soon be back from the Torlands. They're collecting tanich for dye. Why don't you come—' she stopped.

'Go along, Laryia,' said Eris. 'Kira and I have healing to discuss.'

'I'll be back early, Kira, and we can visit some of my favorite places,' said Laryia, by way of farewell.

161

The outer door thudded shut and Eris poured Kira another herbal tea. 'Tierken told me you're a Healer,' she said.

Kira's chin came up. 'When Kasheron founded the Tremen, he instilled in us a love of healing.'

'Kasheron's healing skills came from Kessom,' said Eris mildly. 'It's long been the heart of healing.'

'In the *north*.'

'In the north,' acknowledged Eris. 'Tierken also told me your kinship claims are false. Like those in the north, he believes Kasheron and his people went over the Oskinas seas.'

Kira said nothing but her anger reminded Eris of Tierken, when first Lyess, and then Merench had died. 'I came to Sarnia in the hope he would change his mind,' said Kira tightly, 'but . . .' She half shrugged but her eyes had darkened. 'As Tremen leader, it's my duty to go south again and treaty with the Tain. Caledon says that if the Shargh are victorious, they'll leave no one in peace.'

'Caledon e Saridon e Talliel?' asked Eris in surprise.

Kira's eyes fixed on hers, gold again. 'You know of him?'

'He's been here several times over the seasons.'

'But . . . then Tierken must know him,' said Kira in confusion.

'No. Caledon is known as *Saridon* in the north and Tierken was away with Poerin when he visited. How is it you know Saridon?' she asked curiously.

'I met him on the southern slopes of the Azurcades. He was the first stranger I had ever seen, apart from the Shargh.' She smiled dryly. '*I* was half-starved and *he* was under Shargh attack. He helped me cross the mountains and we ended up in Maraschin together.

'He told me the Terak wouldn't aid the Tremen, which is true, but that the Tain might, *if* we fought together. He took a message from me to my people to ask for volunteers.' Her eyes dimmed to green. 'I won't *order* Tremen to fight and die beyond the forest.'

She pushed her chair from the table and took several paces up and down. 'While he was gone, I was caught by the Shargh and then Tierken's patrol found me and brought me to Sarnia. I don't know if Caledon has returned to Maraschin or even if . . . he still lives.' She took a shaky breath. 'If he *is* back in Maraschin, he'll think *I'm* dead, and if he has brought Tremen to fight, I *must* be there!'

Kira was so distressed Eris thought she might turn and flee. 'I need to gather this day,' she said quickly. 'Will you aid me?'

Kira's eyes came back to hers, dark and unseeing. 'Yes . . . of course,' she said. 'I'll get my sling and sickle.'

Eris's thoughts were on Kira as she tidied away the platters. There was love there for Caledon e Saridon e Talliel, and she wondered if Tierken had realized it yet. She collected her sling, sickle and steady-stick and made her way slowly down the passageway. The day was cool and fine and she waited for Kira under the freylin. 'Your last season,' she murmured as she glanced up at it. 'And mine too.'

Eris could barely walk, which made the gathering slow, but Kira did not mind. The air was crisp, and the Silvercades snowy peaks brilliant against the blue sky. But best of all, there were stands of alwaysgreens. Kira sucked in their spicy scent as they passed them and when she scrambled down stony banks at Eris's behest, paused in their Shelter.

163

Eris described the herbs and distillations, brews, and pastes the Kessomis made, and many were the same as those of Allogrenia, which was to be expected given Kasheron's heritage. Eris spoke of the Kessomi Healers too, who were skilled in childbirth, bone-setting, soothing coughs, stitching, and salving wounds.

'The strongest Healers are still of Queen Kiraon's line,' she said. 'Both my sons Darid and Merench were inclined to healing, but Darid stifled it, for Sarnia wants no healing. Merench was skilled but drowned in a storm-flood while gathering. Healing is in Tierken and Laryia too, but strongest in Laryia.'

'Why *is* there no healing in Sarnia?' asked Kira, voicing the question that had long troubled her.

'It's a rejection rooted in the Sundering,' said Eris, panting as she harvested silversalve and straightened. 'But no place is totally without healing and Sarnia is no exception, despite the Markens' contempt. There are birthing-women there and makers of syrups for coughs and oils for aches, but skills kept behind closed doors grow poorer with the passing of time. Here there is a sharing and celebration of what gives life and healing stays strong. Is it not the same in the forests?' she asked with a smile.

'Yes. We thank the green and growing and honor its gifts.'

There was a shout and they turned. Laryia was on the path below and she hurried up. 'There's been an accident,' she panted. 'I've been to half the houses in Kessom looking for you. Jafiel's fallen in the Torlands and broken his ankle. The bone's through the skin. Leos had to carry him back and Thalli's distraught. I think she's started to birth.'

'You go,' said Eris to Kira. 'Laryia, run back and get sickleseed, sorren, bandages and splints.'

'Which house?' asked Kira quickly.

'The second one on the next path left,' said Laryia, pointing.

Kira sprinted away and was soon beating on a door. The haggard man who opened it seemed to know who she was and ushered her in. Her ears were met by the sound of groans and she hastened after him to where Jafiel lay, the bone of his shattered ankle stark against his bloodied flesh. 'You've got sickleseed?' the man asked anxiously, but Kira was too busy unbuttoning Jafiel's shirt to answer. The fire-filled tunnel was ferocious, as it always was, but when awareness returned, she still heard groaning.

'Who?' she asked, in bewilderment.

'My wife . . . our first child . . .' the man said, and pointed towards a second door.

'I need to wash my hands and then I'll set the ankle,' said Kira, struggling to still her nausea. 'When Laryia comes, we'll bind Jafiel up and give him something to make him sleep.'

A woman took Kira to a bathing-room to wash, and then she came back and eased the bone back into place. The break was ragged, but not the worst she had dealt with. Eris appeared, followed by Laryia, but neither spoke till Kira had finished. 'You had sickleseed with you?' asked Laryia in surprise, as she deposited sorren, splints and bandages on the bed.

'No,' said Kira, busy unplugging the sorren pot.

'But how—'

'I'll splint the ankle,' interrupted Eris. 'Kira, it would be better if you reassured Thalli her brother is on the mend and get Leos to rest too or we'll have a third patient to look after. You go as well, Laryia. Thalli needs you.'

Laryia held Thalli's hand while Kira checked all was well with the babe and, a short time later, Eris took Kira's position next to the bed. Kira curled up in a nearby chair and watched, weary as she always was after taking pain. There was really no need for her to be there. Eris was skilled and the birth progressed well.

Unless something went amiss, Kira predicted the babe would be born before nightfall, which would be quick for a first child, not that Thalli appreciated the fact. She was in pain, as birthing women always were.

Samari, Leos and Jafiel's mother, came and went with honey cakes, cotzee and biscuit bursting with fruit. Eris and Laryia ate but Kira was too queasy. She dozed and the sky was full of star-fire before Thalli's daughter slithered out onto the bed, sandy-haired like Thalli, with a perfect, serene little face.

'A good birth,' said Eris, as she placed the babe in Thalli's arms, 'and a beautiful girl like her mother.' She smoothed Thalli's hair back and kissed her forehead.

'Shall I wake Leos?' asked Laryia.

'Let him sleep,' murmured Thalli, her gaze on her daughter. 'He's had a terrible few days.'

Laryia hugged her. 'You sleep too,' she said. 'I'll see you both again on the morrow.'

Kira also slept, a solid dreamless sleep, not waking till late, and to an empty house. She set off up the path, passing others who nodded to her pleasantly, but was too restless to do other than nod back. The sight of Thalli holding her new-born daughter, surrounded by those who loved her, had reminded Kira how far she was from those who loved *her*.

She turned off the path into a grove of alwaysgreens and climbed, but for once the trees' spicy scent failed to comfort her. Eris's blunt words had confirmed what she had been reluctant to admit, that her quest to gain aid from her northern kin had failed.

But with Caledon's help, she could still gain aid from the Tain. Kasheron's legacy *must* survive and it was her duty as leader to ensure it did. Nothing else mattered, least of all her personal wishes.

19

Kira watched from her perch as the Silvercades burned with the brilliant pinks and golds she had first seen at Terak's Tor and when a chill blue reclaimed their peaks, she climbed down and made her way back to Eris's house. Laryia jumped up as soon as she appeared but Eris simply nodded in greeting and continued her grinding.

'It's fully dark outside,' said Laryia. 'Where have you been?'

'There's no reason to be concerned. I journeyed many days alone in the forests of home,' said Kira, as she held her chill hands to the fire.

'Have you eaten? Tierken says you need to eat more.'

'Tierken's not here,' snapped Kira and forced a smile. 'Don't fret about me, Laryia. I am well.'

'Well at least have some herb tea,' said Laryia mollified.

Laryia went to their sleeping-room soon after, but Kira remained by the fire, watching Eris at her grinding. The bright scent of the silvermint reminded Kira of healing in the Warens and the desperate search for fireweed. 'Do you have a herb in Kessom called fireweed?' she asked.

'Not by that name.'

Kira described it but Eris shook her head and Kira wondered whether the Silvercades had valleys like the Thanaval. If she started early on the morrow, before Eris or Laryia had risen—

'Leos told me what you did,' said Eris, 'though he didn't understand it. Are you the only Healer in the Southern Forests who can take pain?'

'There were two others that we know of,' said Kira uncomfortably. 'Tremen Leader Feailner Sinarki and her daughter, Tremen Leader Feailner Tesrina. It's rumored the first Kiraon could too.'

'The *first* Kiraon?'

'Kasheron and Terak's mother,' said Kira, puzzled by Eris's ignorance.

'Who's the *second* Kiraon?'

Kira flushed as she realized her mistake but was reluctant to lie. 'I'm the second. Kira's short for Kiraon. Tierken said not to use Kiraon in the north.'

'He had no right to do that,' said Eris, with surprising vehemence. 'It's your name.'

'It doesn't matter,' said Kira, keen not to cause upset. 'I was only called Kiraon by the Clancouncil on formal occasions, and by my father, when I was in trouble.'

'And were you in trouble often?' asked Eris.

'Yes.'

'You weren't in accord with your father?'

'No.'

'What of your mother?'

'She died after my brother was born.'

'So your clan-kin raised you?'

'My father was the Tremen leader, so we lived apart in a building called the Bough. I was four seasons when my mother died, so I didn't need anyone to raise me.'

'Then who looked after your younger brother?'

'I did.'

'That's a big task for a child of four seasons,' said Eris.

'It was no hardship. Kandor was beautiful. He—' Her head filled with flames and choking smoke and when the room finally reassembled itself, Eris's papery hands gripped hers. 'I'm sorry,' said Kira shakily.

'There's no shame in grief.'

'I don't have time for grief,' muttered Kira, self-consciously withdrawing her hands.

'What of Tierken?'

She forced a smile. 'I don't have time for him either now he's denied my people.'

'And yet you love him.'

There was a long silence and Kira pushed the hair from her eyes. 'I've allowed myself this little time of happiness, Eris, something the Shargh can't steal from me, but it's only a little time.'

'That's not what Tierken believes.'

'I've told Tierken *who* I am and *what* I am. I've told him my histories and I've shown him Kasheron's ring. I can do no more. I am the Tremen leader and the Terak's refusal of aid means I must go south again.' She forced another smile and rose. 'Kessom is beautiful, Eris. You're fortunate it's a long way from the Shargh.'

It was still dark when she set out the next morning her pockets full of nuts. She wore a cape over her jacket and the hat and gloves Laryia had given her for the trip north. She had no map but the path she had followed with Eris seemed to be the main route through the settlement, and the winding trails that led off to either side, the paths to houses.

The Kessomis lived closer than the Tremen, but nowhere near as closely as those in Maraschin and Sarnia. Lamps still burned amongst the trees but became fewer the further Kira went and she had cleared the last of them before the eastern sky blushed pink. The path steepened and grew rockier and she crossed a small wooden bridge over the rush of a gleaming stream. Probably the Zinaidi again, she guessed, which flowed between Robrin's stables and Eris's house.

She clambered down to its rocky bank and scooped the icy water to her mouth. The taste reminded her of the Breshlin and she realized the Zinaidi probably fed it. She climbed back up the bank and settled on a stone to breakfast on some nuts. It was at the Breshlin ford she had discovered Tierken was the Terak leader and where he had discovered she spoke Tremen, or Terak, as he had insisted on calling it.

A lot had changed since then and nothing at all. Those first kisses had turned into something far more but he had not accepted her people then, and he did not now. She got to her feet and went on.

Tierken paused to watch the star-storms then continued down the slope, choosing the best route through habit, while he mulled over Poerin's words. The old warrior was as irascible as ever and just as blunt. *Rosham and his ilk are an enemy just as dangerous as the Shargh, their tongues as likely to injure you as swords. Either force the Marken to bow before you, Tierken, or one day, be prepared to bow before them.*

Then there was Kira's kinship claim.

A woman with your face and your tongue, claiming to be Kasheron's seed, is surer to be who she says she is, than a joke by Irid. When you've a choice between the works of gods, and the works of men, the latter's more likely.

And on marriage.

If you want to satisfy your lusts, go to the Caru Quarter. If you want to build alliances, ask Rosham to choose your

171

bride. If you want to follow your heart, be prepared for it to take you where your head would never choose to go.

So much for that! Still, Tierken had enjoyed his time with Poerin, even though he had chopped an entire winter's supply of burning wood and carted enough water to last the old man a full season. He had drank with Poerin in front of a crackling fire, listened to his tales as he had as a boy, and felt Poerin's love surround him as thick as the Silvercades' snow. Poerin's farewell had been gruff, but his embrace had been that of an old man who knows it might be his last.

Tierken came to the slopes above Kessom and gazed down. Lamps glimmered in the trees and bira bats whipped overhead. The night was freezing, as winter nights in Kessom always were. He wore his fleece cape but left his ears unprotected so as not to dull his hearing. But it was movement not sound that made him draw his sword. He made no effort to mask his steps and the figure whirled. By Irid, it was Kira!

'What are you doing out here *alone*?' he demanded.

'I'm gathering.'

'Where are the Guard?'

'I don't need a guard.'

'You do if you're wandering about at night!'

Her chin came up. 'I'm not *wandering about*, I'm gathering. Sorren is best harvested in darkness, as is morning-bright.'

The star-sheen illuminated Tierken's likeness to Kandor but also his own beauty and then she was in his arms, his kisses as sweet as she remembered, his hunger as great as hers. He led her into the trees, spread his cape on the ground, and his jacket over them both. He undressed her under its warmth, as she undressed him and, as she

172

lay atop him, he cupped her breasts to his mouth, then caressed and parted her so that she took him in.

His body was in perfect harmony with hers and even after the crest of her longing and desire had ebbed, her lips moved over his face and her fingers explored the ridged muscles of his stomach and groin.

She slid off him and lay snug in the crook of his shoulder. 'I missed you,' she said softly, as she twined the hair of his chest. 'You didn't say goodbye.'

'I wanted to let you sleep. What have you been doing?'

'Gathering, working with Eris, preparing herbs, exploring Kessom.'

'Do you like Kessom?'

'Kessom is beautiful.'

'Is it like Allogrenia?'

'It *feels* like Allogrenia,' she said, 'but Allogrenia has no mountains and no breaks in the trees apart from the Arborean.' She thought of how she had last seen it; the grass charred, the trees brown-leaved and empty of brightwings and birds, and then an owl called. 'The mira kiraon,' she whispered, and sat up.

'It's a grenia owl,' corrected Tierken. 'They favor the allogrenia, hence the name.' Kira said nothing and he ran his hand down her back. 'Lie down, you'll get cold.' Kira still did not speak and he sat up too, the air like ice on his skin. 'What is it?'

'I've been gone from Allogrenia almost four moons.'

'I missed Kessom too when I first went to Sarnia. It takes time to settle.'

Kira dressed and Tierken followed suit, flicked the leaves from his cape and led Kira back onto the path, his warm hand enclosing hers. 'On the morrow's night, all of Kessom will gather in the Keshall to welcome us,' said

173

Tierken. 'There will be music and dancing. You'll enjoy it.'

'I didn't last time.'

'You will this time,' said Tierken, bringing his arm around her. 'And so will I.'

The gathering in the Keshall was nothing like Sarnia's banquet. There were only a few chairs set around the sides of the hall for older Kessomis to rest their bones, while everyone else formed a noisy, constantly moving throng. The Kessomis called Tierken by his name, not his title of *Feailner*, except for the younger men who were obviously patrolmen.

Tierken and Laryia were greeted with hugs and kisses, as was Kira, who was regaled with stories of Tierken's youthful misdemeanors. She had only been in the hall a short time before she knew Tierken had been knocked unconscious when thrown from a stallion Robrin had forbidden him to ride and had received a thrashing for his trouble once he had recovered.

Then there was the time he had been lost for three days beyond the Kristlin after going off in search of dwinhir nests. And he had once eaten so many roscakes at a Keshall welcome, he had been ill for a week.

'I've never eaten roscakes again,' he admitted ruefully. Kira laughed, enjoying Tierken's discomfort. 'I'll wager you have an equally long list of indiscretions,' he murmured, as another group of Kessomis approached.

'You'll have to come to Allogrenia to find out,' she said lightly.

'That's *very* unlikely,' said Tierken, as he was embraced by a woman with a long grey braid.

Kira smiled as the woman kissed her formally on each cheek, but Tierken's words stung, and then Laryia appeared from the throng with Thalli and Leos, Thalli's babe snug in her sling.

'She's beautiful,' said Kira as Thalli lifted the babe out, and handed her over.

'Two Kira's together,' said Thalli, and Kira looked at her in surprise. 'We've named her for you, for what you did for Jafiel.'

'There was no need—' began Kira, taken aback.

'There is,' said Thalli firmly as she settled the babe back into the sling. 'It's fitting *our* Kira knows how you aided her uncle on the day she was born.'

'What *did* you do?' asked Tierken curiously, after Thalli, Leos and Laryia had moved away.

'I helped Jafiel with the pain of his broken ankle.'

'With sickleseed?'

'No.' She glanced across at the players. 'I think the music's about to begin,' she said brightly.

'Then how?'

'I'm a Feailner and, as I told you on the Sarsalin, in Allogrenia that means a taker of pain.'

His eyes narrowed. 'But surely that must injure you. You're not to do it.'

'I'm a *Healer*, Tierken.'

He brought his face close to hers and she glanced around uncomfortably. 'You're *not* to—'

The music started and Laryia twirled to their side and grabbed Tierken's arm. 'I claim the first dance with my brother but you can have all the rest,' she added with a smile, and hauled him away.

Kira danced many dances before Tierken returned. Thread-the-leaves, the weave dance, then something like a wreath dance, with four steps back and to the side where Kira least expected them. She flushed in mortification as she upset the pattern of an entire row but those around her laughed good-naturedly.

'I'll get Laryia to teach you the wreath dance,' said Tierken afterwards, as they sipped fruited-water.

'I *know* the wreath dance,' said Kira, still smarting. 'The Kessomi version must have changed after Kasheron took the original version south,' she added. Tierken grunted but then the first notes of a pipe rang out and Kira's heart faltered.

Tierken said something but his voice was already lost beyond the roar of flames and the desperate need to run and she had no memory of leaving the Keshall, or of how long she stayed under the alwaysgreens before she came to her senses, but she was shivering violently before she stumbled back to Eris's house.

Eris was at her herbal work in the cooking place as usual and eyed her shrewdly. 'Have you argued with Tierken?' she asked, as Kira warmed herself in front of the fire.

'Yes, no—it was something else,' she said and took a shaky breath. She had never confided in anyone about the *waking* nightmares that had plagued her of Kandor's death but Eris was a Healer.

'Tell me,' said Eris quietly.

'The night the Shargh . . . killed my family, my younger brother . . . played a song for me on his pipe. It was a song I really liked and he had practised it . . . in secret for many days . . . to surprise me. Now *if* . . . *when* I hear that song, it's as if I'm there again . . . in the attack. There's smoke and I can't breathe and I'm always too late to save him, as I was then. But I *must* run; I *must* run . . .' Even speaking

176

of it risked the nightmare's return and she fought to steady.

Eris contemplated her thoughtfully. 'Do you dream of it too?' Kira nodded. 'When I was a young Healer, there was fighting between the Terak and Bishali. It didn't last long, but some of the wounded Terak were brought here. The Bishali would beat metal as they went into battle, and even the clash of a cooking pot lid was enough to make the injured shake.'

Her bony hand closed over Kira's. 'People are wounded by many things, Kira, and in many different ways. As a child, Laryia fell into the Kristlin and her fear of water remains. Give yourself time to heal.'

'Time is the one thing I don't have.' The outside door sounded and Tierken came in, nodded to them briefly, and went to his rooms. 'I might go to my bed too,' said Kira uncomfortably. 'I thank you for your words.'

20

'Tierken says we're to return to Sarnia tomorrow,' said Laryia at breakfast. 'And we've only been here a few days!'

Laryia was upset but Kira was relieved. She needed to start her journey to Maraschin. The silence stretched and Kira glanced around the empty table. 'Does Eris still sleep?' she asked, keen to change the subject.

'She was called out to a woman birthing during the night.'

'I could have gone,' said Kira, thinking of how frail Eris was.

'She wanted to let you sleep. Besides, it's what Eris does. She's a Healer and will heal until her last day.' Laryia smiled. '*Her* words, last night, when I suggested that she send you instead.' Laryia broke the small maizen loaf and handed half to Kira. 'And, in case you are wondering where Tierken is, he's with Kessom's council.'

Laryia eyed her but Kira knew she was too polite to ask about Kira's abrupt exit from the Keshall. Tierken's absence suited Kira too. She wanted to search for fireweed and she was sure he would have reasons why she couldn't. Laryia would want to spend her last day with Thalli and that meant Kira had the whole day to herself.

Her reconnoitre *north* of Kessom had revealed small valleys but, unlike the Thanaval, they were dry and rocky, with little leaf-fall and she needed to look south. 'I might go for a walk,' she said, rising and slipping the bread into her pocket.

'I'll come with you,' said Laryia hurriedly, rising too.

'Visit Thalli instead. It's so long since you've seen each other, it must be hard for you.' Laryia looked uncertain and Kira headed to the door. 'Say hello to little Kira for me.'

She hastened down the passageway but it was chill outside with a gusting wind that hinted at rain. Guard fell into step behind her and Kira ground her teeth. Why must *she* be guarded when Laryia and Eris roamed wherever they wanted? She ignored them and strode on and as the wind strengthened, regretted not bringing her cape.

The Guard were obviously concerned about the weather too. 'How far do you go, Lady?' one asked, his gaze on the sky. They Guard had no capes either but Kira shrugged, her irritation with Tierken robbing her of her usual courtesy. 'It will rain soon,' he said.

'I've been wet before,' said Kira shortly.

It was not long before ragged veils of rain misted through the trees but Kira trudged on and then, as the land grew rougher, set off down a side-track. The chill dampness penetrated her shirt, but her attention was on the southward-facing slopes. The leaf litter had thickened, raising her hopes, and she set off through the trees where the land fell away into a gully.

'Lady, it's too steep!' exclaimed one of the Guard.

'It's not,' retorted Kira. 'As long as—'

Her feet went from under her and slid several lengths on her backside before a rotted trunk brought her to a stop. The Guard scrambled down after her, their horrified gaze on her leg. A branch had snagged her trousers and left a scratch from ankle to knee. It was shallow but bled copiously and Kira grimaced as she hauled herself upright and continued down the gully. The Guard followed in silence, their disapproval palpable.

179

As soon as the slope gentled, she fell to her knees and trawled through the litter and, finding nothing, went on, scrambling up and down other small gullies. The rain grew heavier but she knew it would be her last chance to search Kessom for fireweed.

The miserable weather brought an early dusk and she finally climbed back up to the track. The rain and chill wind made for a bleak journey back and the Guard remained silent until they reached Eris's door. 'We leave you now, Lady,' one of them said, and they bowed.

Kira left her boots at the door and padded through to the cooking place. Eris was not there, but Tierken and Laryia were and Tierken stopped his prowl to take in her dirty, saturated clothing and bleeding leg. 'Where in Irid's name have you been?'

'Ask your Guard,' muttered Kira, going to pass him.

Tierken seized her arm. 'I'm asking you!'

'Tierken,' said Laryia rising. 'I think—'

'Keep out of it,' he snapped, his furious gaze on Kira. 'Answer me!'

'I won't!'

'You will!' he said, and gave her a shake.

'Tierken!' cried Laryia.

Tierken jerked Kira closer. 'Our *guest* needs to learn she can't just rush off from celebrations held in *her* honor *or* wander away whenever the whim takes her.'

Kira's anger flared, as hot as his. 'I'm *exeal*, remember! That gives you *no* rights over me *at all*!'

Tierken's voice dropped to a vitriolic hiss. 'We're talking about *manners* now, not false claims! I know you're only seventeen and that perhaps, in *your* lands, courtesy is unimportant, but you live with us now!'

A string of insults tumbled through Kira's head, but she resisted uttering them for Laryia's sake. She straightened instead and stared Tierken in the eye. 'Tremen Leader Feailner Kiraon of Kashclan requests the Terak Kirillian Feailner to *take his hands off her*.'

Tierken's eyes blazed but he stepped back and she pushed past him into the bathing-room and a few moments later, Laryia appeared with buckets of warm water. 'Kira . . .' she began tentatively.

'Leave it, Laryia,' said Kira, peeling off her soggy shirt.

'Kira, you need to understand something about Tierken.'

'I don't need to understand *anything* about him,' said Kira, as her blood-stained trousers followed her shirt to the floor. Her underclothes were drenched too.

'Tierken spent his growing not knowing if he would ever become Feailner. It's a hard way to live, but he's sure about that now. He needs to be sure about you too.'

Kira said nothing and Laryia emptied the buckets into the bath. 'I'll fetch some more,' she said.

The evening meal was taken in strained silence, as was breakfast, and their breath plumed in the icy air as stood outside Eris's house while she farewelled them. Kira gazed up at the Silvercades as Eris kissed Laryia and Tierken in turn.

Then she stepped forward, acutely aware of Tierken's proximity. 'I thank you for sharing your house and your healing,' she said formally. Let the Terak Feailner complain about her manners now! 'And for your care,' she added thickly as her throat tightened.

Eris held her face cradled as she had when Kira had arrived. 'Give yourself kindness, *Kiraon*, and time,' she said softly, and kissed her on each cheek. 'You know where I am if you need me.'

Kira nodded dumbly and followed Tierken and Laryia down the pathway. No one spoke. Tierken was still angry from their argument and she guessed Laryia was upset at leaving Eris and Thalli. They crossed the Zinaidi and Kira gazed up at its rushing flow, reminded of her trek into the Silvercades. The mountains were very different to Allogrenia but still beautiful.

The horses were ready and the Guard already mounted and Robrin waved them off. Tierken led while Laryia rode beside her, pointing out plants or interesting vistas they had missed in the darkness on the northward journey.

They cleared Glass Gorge and stopped at the Frost Glades to eat but did not delay long and rode on in silence, Laryia's attempts at conversation dwindling with the light. It was fully dark before they reached the Tiar Lookround and paused to gaze down on Sarnia's twinkling lamps.

'Sarnia is a beautiful sight,' said Tierken, bringing Kalos level with Kira's mare. It was the first time he had spoken to her all day.

'To a Sarnian,' she said, her gaze on the city.

'Is there nothing in the north you like?'

'Kessom's star-storms and alwaysgreens, the silence of the Silvercades, horses, the dwinhir, your grandmother and sister.'

'But not the Terak Feailner?'

Kira refused to answer despite feeling childish. Whatever Laryia said about choices, Tierken's denial of the kin-link left her with none, and the sooner she was gone from him the better.

She went straight to her rooms on their return, as did Laryia, but Tierken ate with Farid in the Meeting Hall. He was glad to be back and that most of all confirmed he no longer yearned for Kessom. As he sipped cotzee, his gaze settled on the rug where he had taken Kira in love. She was angry with him, but it would pass, along with her Tremen ways. Eris had admonished him to give her more time but Kira needed to learn Sarnian customs sooner rather than later, for her own sake, as well as his.

'I finished ordering the Writing Store in your absence,' said Farid, 'and retrieved the records on Kasheron and his followers, as you requested.'

'Anything more on the Sundering or the ring?'

'Nothing on the ring apart from what we already know. As for the Sundering, none of the Writings specifically mention the season Kasheron left, apart from the one we've discussed.' He frowned. 'It's odd that the *tales* speak of Kasheron going over the Oskinas but not the Writings. What does Eris say?'

'That Sarnia's prejudice against healing colors its view of Kasheron. In other words, Kira's histories might be true.'

'And Poerin?'

'Poerin has more belief in the machinations of men than gods. He thinks Kira's version of events is likely true as well.'

'And so?' asked Farid tentatively.

'The tales tell of Kasheron going over the Oskinas and I'll wager that you'll not find a single Terak, Illian, Kir or even Kessomi who disagrees. My uncle believed it and the Feailners before him. The Marken and the traders believe it. Only a single Writing disputes the season, and by implication, the direction of Kasheron's travel.'

183

'*And* Kira,' pointed out Farid.

Tierken drained his cup. 'I'm leaving things as they are for the time being. It's too dangerous for Kira to be anywhere else but here, but on my return from patrol, I'll discuss what you've found with her, and other matters that have since come to my attention. But for me to recognize the Tremen as kin *and* for Sarnia to accept them, *and* everything else recognition entails, such as opening the Caru Quarter to them, I'm going to need a lot more proof than a single Writing.'

'Are you saying you believe Kira's version of history?' asked Farid in astonishment.

'No.'

Farid looked at him in confusion and when Tierken said nothing, cleared his throat. 'How does Eris?'

'Frail, but still gathering in all weathers.'

'What did she think of Kira?'

'Healers tend to like each other and it was so this time.'

'Did Kira like Kessom?'

'Kira liked it better than Sarnia, but that's not saying a great deal,' said Tierken acidly. 'She's been used to going off where and when she pleases and, given the Shargh threat, that must cease. She'll become more settled here over time, as Laryia has. Now, we need to discuss the patrol's provisioning.'

Arkendrin marched at the front of his warriors, his spears over his shoulder, his flatswords and daggers at his side. In another day, they would clear the Braghans' western flank and turn east. The Sky Chiefs had at last granted him healing and though his leg still pained him, he had spurned the horses some of the Weshargh and Soushargh rode.

The Sky Chiefs had delivered the gold-eyed creature into his hands, then snatched it back, and Arkendrin would give them no cause to punish him a second time by again lifting his feet from the earth.

He pondered whether using the legs of beasts also risked the withdrawal of the Sky Chiefs' favor from their *greater* mission. Erboran's death meant the Sky Chiefs' intended *Arkendrin* to rid the Shargh of the creature of the Telling *and* reclaim their stolen lands, but did the Sky Chiefs smile on Orbdargan and Yrshin too?

Orbdargan's herds had grown too large for the Weshargh's pastures but Yrshin sought lands to silence those who wanted a chief who could still run and hunt. His quest was unlikely to have the Sky Chiefs' approval and, to add to the danger of rousing the Sky Chiefs' anger, Orbdargan and Yrshin continued to mock the Sky Chiefs by climbing into the mountains with their warriors. It was only because the Braghans were too steep for horses that the Soushargh and Weshargh who *had* chosen to ride, now trailed at the back of his men, rather than trod the mountains too.

Arkendrin spat as he considered the possibility of them tainting his fortunes. He had argued there would be plenty of the herders' and woodcutters' food in the Braghans' northern foothills, without burdening themselves with still more horses laden with provisions, but Yrshin had worried his fat belly would shrink, and Orbdargan had sided with the old Soushargh Chief *again*.

21

Kira wandered along the top of the wall, her gaze on the southward sweep of the Rehan Valley, gold in the westering sun. Tierken's patrol would leave in two days and she in three. Given she was exeal, she should have no difficulty quitting Sarnia, because Tierken's authority did not extend beyond *his* people, and if it did, she would simply take a pleasant ride into the Rehan Valley and outrun the Guards' horses over the plain.

She had managed to avoid Tierken by riding early and pretending to sleep whenever he knocked. Her locked door had prevented him entering *and* maintained his irritation with her. She no longer needed his Shelter but the nightmares had returned and she had woken more than once with the Guard in her rooms, drawn by her screams.

She came down from the wall, the Guard at her heels, and kept her eyes on the paving as she set off back up to the Domain. Whispers followed her as they always did and she unclenched her hands and smoothed down her shirt. She had lost weight again, having disguised her theft of food for the journey, by eating less at each meal. The map she had copied meant the Northern lands were more familiar to her, but the map did not show *everything* that might kill her.

The Domain Guard opened the gate for her and she glanced up at the glass window as she strode across the square. The running horse *and* the alwaysgreen; she supposed it proved it *was* possible for the two things to co-exist, just not in her time. The Owl Fountain tinkled and she detoured to perch on its edge. The carved owls were pretty in the sunshine and Kira wondered what the first Kiraon had been like, and Queen Alitha, who had planted the grove in Maraschin.

'A good evening to the *Lady* Kira,' said a male voice.

Kira looked up startled, then stood. 'Good evening . . .'

'Marken Rosham,' he said, stopping so close Kira had to resist the urge to step back. He was not much taller than her, but broad set, with hair as silver as swords. 'I wouldn't expect the *Lady* Kira to know me, given her lands are far away and somewhat *rustic*, I hear.'

Rosham's tone was contemptuous and Kira searched her memory for what she knew of him. Laryia had rolled her eyes but he was Farid's father, and Kira liked Farid.

'How does the *Lady* Kira occupy her time when she's not *keeping company* with the Feailner?'

'I ride and record my Healer knowing,' said Kira reluctantly.

'*Healer knowing*? Ah, of course. I had forgotten you dabble in the things that play to men's weaknesses. How did you enjoy your jaunt to Kessom?' he continued before she could respond.

'Kessom is beautiful,' said Kira defiantly.

Rosham's gaze moved over her slowly. 'Yes, I thought it might suit *you*. Things are laxer there perhaps like the lands you're from, a point the Feailner sometimes forgets.' His mouth bent in a smile. 'I wish you a good night, *Lady* Kira.'

Kira's stomach churned as she stared after his receding back. Was that how she was seen in Sarnia? Like a Caru woman? She pushed the hair from her eyes. Laryia had alluded to it when she had insisted Kira wear metal at the banquet, and Tierken had as well. He had apologized later but Kira suspected the words reflected how he saw her too.

She went slowly up the stairs to her room, shut the door, and closed her eyes as she rested her head back against it. She thought of Merek and Kesilini and wondered whether they had shared a bed before they had bonded. She had seen countless bonding ceremonies at Turning but had never thought of what came before or after. She had been too busy at her gathering, and drying, and making of pastes. She had noticed *nothing* until Caledon. She hoped Merek and Kesilini *had* known the sweetness she had shared with Tierken. Its briefness did not make it less worthy and nor did being unbonded, as Rosham implied.

'Are you tired, Kira?' Kira started violently. Tierken was seated at the table. 'I beg your pardon for invading your privacy, but I decided it might be the only way to see you.'

'You need to take care, Feailner, that you're not seen as being as *lax* as those in Kessom,' she said, heart rattling with fright.

His brows drew. 'Whose words are they?'

'Does it matter?'

'Yes.'

'Well, it doesn't to me. I don't mind being compared to a Caru woman, for at least they're honest. They take traders for their bodies and no one pretends anything else is being exchanged. I don't mind being called a *dabbler* in things that pander to men's *weaknesses* either, because I know how to set bones so that a man might walk without a limp, and how to bring babes into the world without them losing their mothers.'

Tierken sprang to his feet. 'Who said these things?' he demanded. He wore the black and silver she had last seen him wear at the banquet.

'It doesn't matter. It's how Sarnia thinks, isn't it?'

Tierken made no reply, which was answer enough, and Kira stepped around him and sat down at her recordings. The paper lay ready but she was in turmoil and could not remember what she had last written, let alone what she should write next. 'What did you want to see me about, Feailner?'

'Before I go on patrol, I'd like an answer to the question I asked you in the Frost Glades.' Kira looked at him with bewilderment. 'Did it mean so little to you that you can't recall it?'

Her heart started an uneven thump. 'I thought I had mistaken your words.'

'How can you mistake *marry me, Kira*?'

Kira stared down at the neat Writings in front of her. 'You mean marry like the Tain marry? Wear metal and stay together even if love fails?'

He took her hands and gently pulled her upright. 'Look at me Kira,' he said softly, and she reluctantly raised her eyes. 'I love you and want you with me until the end of my days. In Sarnia, the pledge of this is a bracelet, worn on the right wrist until the marriage takes place. Then, at the time of the couple's choosing, usually within three moons of pledging, they come before the Marken to make their pledge publicly. The pledge is binding. The woman continues to wear the bracelet, but you needn't as I know metal is unpleasant to you.'

He reached into his pocket and produced a beautifully scrolled silver bracelet. 'This is the bracelet my father Merench used to pledge to my mother Lyess. Retrieving it was one of the reasons I went to Kessom.' He gently raised her right wrist. 'Will you marry me, Kira?'

His eyes were so full of love she had to look away. 'I can't marry you,' she said miserably.

189

His grip on her wrist was still gentle but she sensed the tension sweep through his body. 'Because of Caledon?'

'Caledon?'

'I've asked you before whether you are lovers, a question you've never answered.'

'You *know* I'm the Tremen leader. You *know* I have to go south.' She took a shuddering breath. 'When . . . when I've seen the Tremen Protectors at Maraschin, and spoken with King Beris, I'll come back.' The thought of leaving Allogrenia forever was so terrible she could scarcely breathe but the look on Tierken's face was worse. 'I'll come back and bond with you, Tierken, if that's what you want.'

'But not marry me?'

'The Tremen way is to bond,' she said desperately. 'We pledge before those important to us, but there's no metal, and the bond can be broken if there's unhappiness.'

He dropped her wrist. '*If there's unhappiness*? So, you can just wander off with another lover as the whim takes you?'

'Bonding is rarely broken and never lightly!'

'But it can be broken?'

'Yes.'

He slipped the bracelet back into his pocket. 'And that's all you will offer me? An arrangement you can *break* when it suits you?'

'It's not like that!'

'It obviously is,' he said, and gave a curt bow. 'I'm sorry I mistook your feelings for my own, Tremen Leader Feailner Kiraon of Kashclan. I can assure you, it won't happen again.'

The door slammed and Kira collapsed onto her chair and cradled her face in her hands. Having Tierken had always meant *not* having Allogrenia; *not* having Miken, Tresen, Kest, Tenerini, Mikini and all the others she loved. A small part of her had *always* known it but she had been greedy for Shelter and pushed its consequences away.

She sleeved her eyes and fought to steady. The choice of staying with Tierken or going back to Allogrenia was not hers anyway. It depended on winning the battles to come and for that to happen, she *must* go to Maraschin. Tierken's refusal to bond actually removed a major complication so she should be grateful, so then why did she feel like her heart had been torn out.

There was a knock, but before she could rise, Laryia burst in, clearly upset, and Kira groaned inwardly. 'I *thought* I'd told you how things are with Tierken. I *thought* you understood what it was like for him to grow in Kessom knowing Sarnia didn't want him; that Darid might father an heir; of the harsh winters training with Poerin; of the Marken's snide animosity; of leading the patrols on the Sarsalin, fighting windstorms and snowstorms, wolf attack and fanchon strike, to earn the patrolmen's loyalty. I *thought* you understood and cared. I *thought* you loved him!' Kira said nothing. 'Well?' she demanded.

'You seem to know everything already,' said Kira grimly. 'Maybe you've talked to Rosham. He seems to know everything too.'

Laryia sat beside her and caught Kira's hands. 'What's Rosham said to you?' Kira shrugged. 'Take no notice of him, Kira, that man's poison. How he ever spawned a son like Farid is beyond me.' She paused. 'Tell me you don't love Tierken.' Kira half shook her head. 'Then why won't you marry him?'

'The Tremen don't marry. We bond. I explained it to Tierken and he refused it.'

191

'Perhaps he didn't understand. Tell me,' said Laryia.

Kira sighed, wondering how many more times she must explain it. 'We have a ceremony at Turning, which is once a season, where those wanting to bond pledge their love and loyalty before the Tremen leader. It's a very serious pledge and most Tremen remain with their bondmates for life. But the bond can be broken if things turn out ill.'

'Surely the difference between marriage and bonding isn't insurmountable? He loves you, Kira, and you love him. I can see it in your eyes.'

'I loved Kandor too, but it wasn't enough to save him,' said Kira bitterly. She pulled her hands from Laryia's and paced around the room. 'You haven't seen what I've seen, what the Shargh did to Allogrenia, what they might *still* be doing. I left to gain help from the Tremen's kin, from *you*, the Terak Kirillian. I've told Tierken the truth, and every question he's asked me about the Tremen I've answered honestly but *still* he refuses aid. There's going to be awful, bloody, fighting, Laryia, and my people won't escape it. I *must* be there with them.'

There was silence and then the sound of horses intruded from the square below. 'That's odd,' said Laryia. 'The Domain Guard never ride past the stables.'

22

C aledon stared up at the magnificent building ahead. A massive dome crowned its central part and set directly below it was the largest colored glass window he had ever seen. It blazed in the last rays of the sun and held both the mark of the Tremen and that of the Terak Kirillian. Two vast double-storey wings splayed out on either side of a paved courtyard, their balconies supported by rows of stone columns. He had heard tell of the Domain's wealth but it was the first time he had actually seen it.

Their escort of guard ordered them to a halt, and Caledon repeated it in Tain to the King's Guard behind him. It was crucial this first contact with the Terak went smoothly. One of the black and silver clad guard disappeared through large double doors directly ahead, but the others remained with their backs to the buildings, swords in hand, attention fixed on Caledon and his party.

Allowing them to remain armed and mounted was a good sign the long-neglected Alliance could be salvaged, but honor did not replace trust, and the black and silver clad guard outnumbered Caledon's party two to one.

The doors ahead opened and two men appeared, both dressed in black with silver trim. But there was no mistaking the Terak Feailner, his Kessomi blood giving him his lighter build and his Kir blood his darker skin.

Caledon turned to the King's Guard behind him. 'Dismount, kneel, and place your weapons on the ground in front of you,' he ordered in Tain. They complied, and Caledon dismounted, put his own sword and knives down, and went forward. He stopped two paces away, knelt, bowed his head, and offered the message cylinder with both hands. 'I ride for King Adris of the Tain city of Maraschin and northern lands of the Azurcades, The Westlans, the Spur and Torlands,' said Caledon in Terak. 'King Adris sends greetings to the Feailner of the Terak Kirillian, and to the Terak Kirillian people who have long been friends to the Tain.'

The Feailner took the cylinder and opened it and Caledon snatched a glance up. The Terak Feailner was a masculine, darker version of Kira! His thoughts whirred as he considered the stars intent and he became aware of watchers on the balcony. Two young women, one dressed in a gown of crimson, the other in Kessomi garb.

'By the grace of Aeris!' he exclaimed and then Kira raced along the balcony, disappeared, then emerged from behind the colonnades and sped towards him, and then she was in his arms. He had broken protocol by rising but all he could think of was the veracity of the stars. 'Beyond all hope,' he muttered, holding her close. 'Beyond all hope you are safe.'

Kira raised her head and Caledon wiped away her tears. 'You're hurt,' she said, touching the gash on his forehead.

'Almost mended, thanks to Tresen,' he said, and became aware of the shift in tension in the courtyard. The Terak guard were now focused entirely on him, and animosity radiated from the Terak Feailner like heat from a fire. Caledon swiftly released Kira and bowed low. 'Forgive my breach of manners, Feailner,' he said. 'The Tain believed Kira to be dead. There will be rejoicing in Maraschin to know the Terak Kirillian have secured her safety. King Adris is in your debt.'

'And you are?' demanded the Feailner.

'Caledon e Saridon e Talliel. I am honored to have been friend to the late King Beris, and to his son, Adris, the new King.'

'Beris is dead?' asked Kira in wonder. Caledon nodded but kept his eyes on the Feailner.

'I have heard of you, Saridon,' the Feailner clipped out, 'and I thank you for your journey. The Keeper of the Domain will arrange food and rooms for you and your escort. We will speak tomorrow.'

'Tell me of the Tremen, Caledon,' said Kira eagerly. 'Tell me—'

Caledon raised his hand. 'Later,' he said, without looking at her. He bowed low to the Feailner once more and Kira watched in frustration as he followed Farid away.

She wanted news of Allogrenia, of how he had been injured, of how Tresen had healed him. He had been with Tresen! So Kest had got the patrol back safely, or at least some of them. The square emptied swiftly, stablemen taking the horses, and the Domain Guard taking the King's Guard's weapons. Laryia was still on the balcony, and even from a distance, Kira saw her face was icy, but none of it mattered. Caledon brought news of Miken and Tresen and Kest, and now he was here, she could go south with him.

Tierken waited, his face no warmer than Laryia's. 'I would have speech with you, in the Meeting Hall, *now*!' he said, and strode off.

Kira stared after him, excitement at seeing Caledon again, doused by Tierken's bullying. She considered going back to her rooms and locking the door but, in his present mood, Tierken would probably break it down. And antagonizing him was not going to help anything either.

She followed him more slowly, overcome with relief Tresen still lived and Caledon was safe.

Tierken waited by the window, hands on hips, and swung round when she entered. 'I'll ask you this question a third time,' he said. 'Is this Tallien your lover?'

Despite her best intentions, Kira's anger roused. 'I've loved a lot of men, Tierken. Caledon's one of the few who's still alive.'

'That's not what I asked!'

'How many women have you shared your body with?'

His hand slammed down on the table. 'We're talking about you!'

'No, we're not! We're talking about your lack of trust! Do you think I would have offered to bond with you if I didn't intend to spend the rest of my life with you? But *you* think I've gone from Caledon's bed to yours, and that I'll go from yours to someone else's! I can see your point. After all, I've lied about *everything* else. My histories are false, I'm not Kasheron's seed, and my people are exeal!'

'I need to be sure of you,' he ground out.

'There *is* no surety, Tierken. Allogrenia was breached, the Bough burned, my family was murdered. Wounds that should have healed, didn't. Truth became lies and healing killing.' She choked to a stop and sleeved the wetness from her eyes. 'I'm going south with Caledon to meet with my people and then, if you wish, I'll return to Sarnia.'

'You will remain here!'

She straightened. 'I'm the Tremen leader and *will* be with *my* people, as you will be with *yours*.'

There was a brief knock and Farid appeared. 'I beg your pardon,' he said, and stopped in the doorway.

'There's no need,' said Kira, as she brushed past him. 'The Feailner and I have finished our conversation.'

The Domain Keeper escorted Caledon to the Meeting Hall the next morning, bowed courteously and left. Given the obvious friendship between the Keeper and the Feailner, Caledon found his absence interesting and that the Feailner had no advisers with him. He either wanted no witnesses to their exchange or was content to make his own decisions.

The Feailner acknowledged his bow with a nod, gestured him to a seat and poured him metz. Then he broke a fresh loaf of maizen bread and handed it to him on a platter. It was a ritual welcome practiced by the wandering Bishali and Ashkals but they passed the bread directly to the guest's hand, and Caledon wondered whether the custom had changed among the Terak Kirillian, or whether it signaled the limitations of the Feailner's goodwill.

Caledon sensed none of the anger Kira's welcome had generated but no warmth either and had spent a good part of the night considering the stars' intent. The symmetry of what unfolded was breath-taking in its beauty but not in its clarity. The Shargh's blood-thirst had brought together the long-sundered seed of Kasheron and Terak, leaders who shared the title of feailner, their faces and their remarkable eyes.

. The passion the Terak Feailner had for his southern kin was obvious and added to the stars' design but what of Kira's feelings? Caledon dare not meet with her to find out until he had gained some measure of the Feailner's trust and, even then, he must be *very* careful. The star pattern suggested her task was to make Terak and Kasheron's peoples whole again and, *if* that were so, he must put aside his own feelings but the stars might have other purposes yet to be revealed.

'Tell me what unfolds in the Tain lands,' the Feailner said.

197

Caledon began a methodical description of the Shargh attacks and what he thought they portended and the effects of Beris's long illness and recent death. He also spoke candidly of the difficulties the prince had faced prior to the king's death and *still* faced in repelling the Shargh.

'The Shargh seek the Tain's destruction for a number of reasons,' said Caledon. 'It will weaken you and, with the Tain eliminated, the Shargh can focus their attacks on the north, without fear for their backs. The Tain's demise will also serve as a potent warning to other small peoples whose support or acquiescence the Shargh need.'

'King Adris doesn't call on the Alliance.'

'There's been a long silence between your peoples,' acknowledged Caledon. 'No king wants to use a request for aid to break it.'

'*If* what you say is true, they *will* need our aid.'

'Certainly,' said Caledon, ignoring the Feailner's qualification, 'but the Tremen send nearly a hundred and fifty men to strengthen the Tain defences.'

'*Protectors*?'

The Feailner's contempt was plain. 'I am not aware of what Kira's told you of her people or of herself,' said Caledon carefully. 'When Kasheron established Allogrenia, he didn't abandon his brother's warrior ways entirely. The Protectors are skilled fighters but have never fought in the open. I spent time training them before I left.'

'Our histories record that Kasheron went north,' the Feailner said curtly.

'I'm familiar with the Terak Kirillian's histories,' said Caledon evenly. 'And I admit that when I first met Kira, she puzzled me greatly. A gold-eyed Healer who spoke Terak with a Kessomi lilt, whose face and form bore the Kessomi's fineness, and who shared the Kessomi passion for healing. And she wasn't quick to trust either. I was on my way to the Tremen lands before I realized *Kash*clan wasn't a Kir word as I had supposed, but came from *Kasheron*, and what I saw in Allogrenia confirmed it.'

The Feailner straightened in his seat. 'And that was?'

'The Tremen hate metal and smelt none and yet they have an abundance of northern swords and herbing sickles. They have a vast store of Writings too that stretch back to before they entered the trees.'

The Feailner shrugged. 'They could be false.'

Caledon inclined his head. 'I considered the possibility, of course. The Tremen's earliest records are written on paper made from scartch, which doesn't grow in the south, and the later ones on paper made from patchet, which does. I've been to Kessom a number of times, as you might know, and have seen the Writings there, some recorded by Kasheron himself. He had a distinctive hand. I've seen the same hand in the Tremen's Writing store.'

Caledon sipped his metz to allow the Feailner time to digest the news. 'Kira also carries the ring of rulership that Kasheron took with him.'

'I've seen it.'

'Then you will know it bears the same design as your magnificent glass window outside.' Caledon took another sip of metz. 'There are other reasons I believe Kira's people are of Kasheron and his followers' line. Their hatred of metal, yet acceptance of herbing sickles and swords, is nonsensical, and a sign of a peoples who have lived a long time alone, constructing their own beliefs and ways of doing. The perversion extends to their memory of their Northern kin.'

The Feailner's lip curled. 'The Terak *Kutan*?' Caledon nodded. The Feailner emptied his cup, refilled it, and topped up Caledon's. 'Do you know why the Shargh hunt Kira?' he asked abruptly.

'No, but the Shargh are superstitious. They are likely to believe gold eyes ill-omened, especially as the leader of the hated Northerners is gold-eyed too.'

'So, they kill because of gold eyes,' muttered the Feailner.

'Killing is rarely that simple,' said Caledon, starting on the maizen bread. 'It's been years since the loss of their northern grazing lands, long enough for hatred to fester and the new crop of warriors to forget the bloodiness of their defeat.'

The Feailner's eyes did not change like Kira's, which made him hard to read, and given his youth, his words and movements were surprisingly considered, in stark contrast to Adris's explosions of speech and energy.

'Kira wants to go south with you to Maraschin. I'm denying her permission.'

Caledon considered the Feailner calmly but his thoughts raced. *She wants to go with you but I'm keeping her with me*. Given Kira's greeting of him last night, the Feailner probably suspected they were lovers. He would not ask Caledon outright but it would affect all their dealings together. Allowing the Feailner's suspicion to remain might serve the stars' purposes or *destroy* them, depending on whether the stars intended Kira to be with him, or with the Northern leader.

Caledon smiled to ease his words. 'I spoke with many in the Southern Forests who love Kira and on one thing they were agreed: Kira will go her own way.'

'Not this time.'

'Protector Commander Kest attempted to keep her in Allogrenia for her own safety and failed. Had he succeeded, I would now be dead, for Kira killed to save me. Prince Adris and I attempted to keep her in Maraschin for her own safety and failed.'

The Feailner's eyes lightened betraying the strength of his emotions. 'Because of *your* failure, the Shargh took her! Because of *your* failure, she screams in her sleep!'

'The failure meant she came north, *to you*, perhaps as the stars intended,' said Caledon quietly.

'I am aware of the Placidien's belief in the benevolence of stars but I don't share it. Kira has paid a heavy price for their *benevolence*.'

'Kira's arrival in the north opens the possibility of your peoples being one again,' said Caledon.

'My people *are* one: the Terak, the Illians, the Kirs, and the Kessomis!'

Caledon inclined his head, acknowledging the Feailner's correction, and realized he had misjudged the Northern ruler's capacity *or* willingness to change. There was a brief silence, while he considered what the stars might intend, and then the Feailner rose.

'I thank you for your words. I will think on them and take advice. I would be pleased if you and the leader of the King's Guard would join me for this evening's meal.'

Caledon rose and bowed. 'Thank you. I look forward to it, Feailner,' he said.

23

Kira perched on the edge of the Owl Fountain, her chin resting on her knees. The water's splash seemed loud now Caledon had fallen silent and she blinked hard. His words had woken an unbearable longing to be with Miken and Tenerini and Tresen; to walk among the dance of dappled sunlight and shadows; to hear the whisper of leaves. 'So, there were no more attacks after I left,' she said thickly.

'No.'

'I delayed too long. Tremen died because of me.'

'The Shargh kill the Tain, Kira, and you're not there. As I've said before; this isn't just about you and the Tremen.'

Again only the fountain's ripple and splash filled the silence. 'How many of the Protectors who volunteered will survive to go home, Caledon?'

'That is unknown.'

'They could all be killed.'

'Yes.'

'That will be the ending of Allogrenia,' said Kira hoarsely.

'*Your* Allogrenia ended the day the Shargh found you,' said Caledon gently.

The shadow of the Lehan Wing crept inexorably towards them and Kira shivered. 'Come to my rooms, Caledon. It's warmer there.'

Caledon glanced towards the Meeting Hall. 'I don't think that would be wise.'

Kira followed his gaze. 'He doesn't believe Kasheron went south or that I carry his blood,' she said bitterly.

'According to him, the Tremen are exeal.'

'You ask the Terak Feailner to declare his peoples' histories false and to publicly acknowledge a blood link that's long been despised. Your people call his the Terak *Kutan*, and his have sent yours out of memory and time. Don't underestimate the gulf that lies between the Tremen and the Terak, Kira.'

Kira's heart gave a sickening thud. 'Are you saying Tierken will *never* accept who the Tremen are? Who *I* am?'

'I think it could take more time than has been given. The coming fighting will be long and bloody and leave no one untouched.' Kira stared at the fountain numbly. 'I could be wrong about the Feailner,' he said, lightening his tone. 'I've been wrong before.' He winced as he eased his position.

'Let me see your arm,' said Kira, suddenly business-like. She removed the bindings and probed gently along the bones. 'Nice and clean,' she said, and rebound it. 'Tresen's done well.'

'Did you doubt it?' asked Caledon with a smile.

'What other injuries did you suffer?'

'Just my leg, all healed, and I gashed my forehead.'

Kira smoothed back his hair and leaned in to examine the wound. His sweet spice smell roused memories of their time together and of his comfort. Caledon accepted who *and* what she was *unlike* Tierken.

'All healed too,' he said then hurriedly rose and bowed.

'Forgive my interruption,' said the Feailner. 'I require speech with Kira.' Caledon bowed again and moved off towards the stables. 'We'll speak in my rooms,' added the Feailner. She followed him up the steps and along the balcony, feeling suddenly weary. The last thing she wanted was yet another argument.

His rooms were the same as hers but decorated with pots and bowls of metal, and animals fashioned from colored glass that winked in the light. Chimes hung in the windows, metal and wrought in the form of horses in various stages of galloping. The room was warm, thanks to the fire and she was surprised to see the table set with a platter of maizen loaves and fruit, a jug of fruited-water, and two beautifully patterned cups.

He gestured her to a seat. 'It seems too long since we last ate together,' he said with a smile, breaking a loaf and handing her half.

Kira nodded her thanks. It *had* been too long and her gaze took in the soft curl of his hair where it touched his shoulder. She craved these moments of peace between them, and of love, when she could be in his arms, free from the fear that arguments would follow.

'You've grown thin again, Kira. Is Sarnia's food not to your liking?'

'No, the food in the Domain is very nice. I thank you.' His gaze was measuring and she suppressed a sigh. 'You don't look very happy,' he continued, as he filled her cup. 'I thought the arrival of your *friend*, Caledon e Saridon e Talliel, would alleviate the hardship of living in the *stone* city.' He filled his own cup and relaxed back in his seat. 'What did you and your *friend* discuss?'

'We discussed you, amongst other things.'

'May I ask exactly what you discussed about me?'

'That it's unlikely you will ever accept me for what I am.'

'That's *not* what I said to him!'

He was no longer relaxed and Kira placed the bread back on the platter. 'Not in those words perhaps, but it's true, isn't it?' she said, and forced a smile. 'To accept me, you have to accept that my histories are true and that yours are false.' She shrugged. 'Caledon helped me realize there's been too many seasons of separation and bitterness between Terak and Kasheron's seed for us to mend it. I think our peoples *will* come together again one day, but not in our time. In the meanwhile, I'm going south with him.'

'You will remain here.'

She took a deep breath. 'If you lock me in my room, Tierken, I won't eat. If you lock me in the city, I'll remain at the gate until hunger and cold claim me. If you let me *out* of the city, I'll ride south alone. But if you *allow* me to go south with Caledon and the King's Guard, I will speak with my people then return here. You will have no need of locks and keys, and no need to fear *your woman* will embarrass you by dying at the gate.'

He thrust back his chair and prowled around the room. 'I don't want you as *my woman*, I want you as *my wife*! But that's not part of the trade you're offering me, is it?'

'I told you *what* I was early in our time together. I'm willing to bond with you in the Tremen way. That's all I can offer you *as a Tremen*.'

He swung around to face her. 'And what does the *Tremen* offer the Tallien?' he asked sneeringly. 'The same trade or something else?'

Kira rose too, and pushed her chair back into the table. 'It's not what I offer him, but he what he offers me,' she said. 'He offers me trust, Tierken, something you refuse.'

Tresen was glad he marched beside Arlen. Being with his clanmate and knowing he would soon be with Kira again were the only things that kept him putting one foot in front of the other. The awful emptiness that confronted them as they left the trees behind, still sent a shiver down his back, and he had reminded himself more than once that Kira had made the same trek alone.

The Protectors had journeyed at night, with little speech and no fires despite the hard, frosty mornings. Even wearing all the clothes he carried, he had been cold in his sleeping-sheet and had endlessly rehearsed Pekrash's instructions on what to do if attacked. But he had done none of it when they had reached the Azurcades' foothills, and the Guard had stepped from the shadows.

Tresen was the only Protector who knew more than a few words of Onespeak and the lack of common tongue had caused confusion when they had finally cleared the pass over the Azurcades and the leader of the King's Guard had ordered them to *follow* each other, rather than walk spread out through the trees.

Tresen wondered how many other misunderstandings would arise. At least they were under trees again even though he did not recognize them or the bird calls. They were under different command too, that of tall, muscular men, who looked every bit Terak Kutan despite being Tain. None of it seemed real but in one more night he would be in the Tain city of Maraschin with Kira, and it all would have been worthwhile.

They were nearing the edge of the trees on the northern slopes when one of the scouts hastened back, grim-faced. There was an urgent exchange Tresen could not understand and it was only when they came out onto the grasslands that Tresen saw that a pall of black smoke rose to the west. 'The Westlans burn,' said one of the Guard. 'The battle has begun.'

Kira worked away at her Writings, the lamp oil low and the fire all but out. Her eyes were gritty but even if she took to her bed, she would not sleep. Caledon's departure must be near and she was determined to leave with him; she just had to work out how. In the meantime, she wanted as much of her Healing recorded as possible.

There was a brief knock but before she could struggle from her seat, Tierken was in the room. 'I've reconsidered your trade and decided to accept it. You will journey to Maraschin to see your people and then you will return to Sarnia, where you will remain. You will travel with Caledon e Saridon e Talliel, the Tain Guard *and* a Terak patrol led by Commander Marin. You will spend seventeen days beyond Sarnia's gates: seven in travel south, three in Maraschin to rest the horses and speak with the Tremen Commander, and seven to travel back. Are we agreed on the terms of trade?'

'Yes,' said Kira, grappling with what he had said.

'Smack hands then.'

Kira raised her hand and Tierken's slapped it briskly. 'You will need to prepare a pack. Take warm clothes and a cape. Then try to get some sleep. You are leaving at dawn.' He strode back to the door and paused with his hand on the handle. 'Oh, and I'm traveling with you.'

Kira got no sleep at all and not just because her head was full of all she must do when she reached Maraschin. A northerly wind whined over the Domain like the howl of wolves and by the time she reached the stables in the predawn murk, an icy rain had joined it. Most of the men were already mounted and being heavily caped, made it hard to recognize anyone. Kalos was easy to pick though, as was Tierken, as he barked orders.

The King's Guard formed up together and while she could see no sign of Caledon, she guessed he was with them. Rin held her mare steady while she mounted and then Marin came alongside. 'You're to ride directly behind me,' he said, 'and remain there unless ordered otherwise.'

Kira nodded. 'I'm glad you're with us.'

Marin gave a small bow. 'We have a foul start though, Lady. It's a bad time of season for traveling the Sarsalin.'

'I must meet with my people in Maraschin,' said Kira defensively. 'Perhaps the weather will improve as we go south.'

'Or worsen.'

They set off, Tierken leading, followed by Marin, then Kira with patrolmen to either side, the rest of the patrol, and the King's Guard. The wind strengthened, straight off the Silvercades, and drove the rain into their backs. Her backside was soon wet despite her cape and the reins grew slippery. Dawn gave way to a gloomy day that scarcely brightened as they rode south. She caught the words *Ges Grove* amongst the patrolmen's mutter and her heart lifted as she recalled their dense shelter. There might be fireweed hiding there too!

The wind and rain were unrelenting and they stopped only once to eat maizen biscuit, using their horses as shelter. It was dark before they reached the Grove and Kira unsaddled her mount and stowed the harness. Rin had never shown her how to attach a tether rope, and she copied Jonred as best she could, and was halfway to the fires when Tierken ordered her back. 'Tether her like that and she will tangle and burn her legs,' he said.

He stood over her while she forced her numb fingers to undo the rope and shorten it. 'I thank you for your help, Feailner,' she muttered. Tierken had not ordered she remain with the patrol, *while they camped*, and she went to fire where Caledon sat with the King's Guard. 'Always he wants his own way,' she muttered, smarting from his rebuke.

'A Terak Feailner must always be that in front of his men,' said Caledon mildly. 'I'm surprised he allowed you to come south,' he added. Kira said nothing as she grimly considered the trade she had made and Caledon handed her roasted nuts. 'Eat Kira, we've a long day ahead on the morrow.'

The wind dropped during the night and the rain dwindled to a fine mist, but it remained bitterly cold. They were on their way again before dawn, Kira's request to search for fireweed refused. She had noticed no soaks in the Grove anyway, she comforted herself, so it was unlikely fireweed grew there but it was frustrating not to check.

Their second camp was at the Breshlin Ford, and Kira unharnessed the mare and tethered her next to Jonred's mount. 'An improved effort,' said Tierken, and stalked off to the patrolmen's fire. He had barely spoken to her since they had set out and she was keen not to make the situation worse by being anything other than compliant.

As they traveled the next day, she considered what she must say to the Protectors in Maraschin *and* how to acquire fireweed supplies for the north.

'Ashmiri,' muttered Jonred beside her. Kira could see nothing, but her heart quickened as the patrolmen unclipped their bows. The day remained cold but it did not rain again and the sky was full of stars before they zig-zagged down the steep, grassy slope of Cover-cape Crest.

'I'll take the mare,' said Marin, as they came to a stop.

'There's no need. I'll—'

'Feailner's orders.'

She dismounted and he led her mount away, along with Jonred and Vardrin's horses, and then Jonred took her arm. 'This way, Lady,' he said. The patrolmen were tense and she knew there would be no search for fireweed here either. Several fires were set and Jonred pitched her gifan close to one, but most of the patrolmen remained on their feet, as did the King's Guard.

Kira sat on her sleeping-sheet next to the fire, an ache in her belly she had not felt for many moons. *Put some flesh on your bones or you'll never carry*, Sendra had once admonished, before her father had sent the helper back to her own longhouse. Of all the helpers who had come and gone from the Bough, Sendra had been the only one to comment on how rarely Kira bled. It had never worried Kira; mothering was the last thing on her mind.

She drew her knees up to ease the ache and thought of what she carried in her pack. 'I need some time alone,' she said to Jonred when he returned with windfall.

'The Feailner orders you're to remain here until he returns.'

The guards kept a constant patrol beyond the circle of light and Kira rested her head on her knees and must have drowsed, starting as grass crunched underfoot. 'Jonred says you request time alone,' said Tierken. 'Come.' She struggled to her feet and followed him into the trees. 'Here will do,' said Tierken. 'I'll turn my back.'

'I need to go to the spring to wash.'

He shook his head. 'You'll have to accept being grimy for a while.'

'It's not because I'm grimy . . .' Stinking heartrot! Must she beg his permission for *everything*?

'No further,' he said, hands coming to his hips. Kira sat down on the grass and pulled off her boots. 'What in Irid's name are you doing?'

'I need to change my underclothes. To do that, I have to take off my boots and trousers.'

'There's no reason—'

'I bleed, Tierken.'

Comprehension dawned and for the first time since they had set out, he looked other than angry. 'Kira, I—'

'Just turn your back.'

24

It was dark again before they reached the ridgelands of Shally Spring where Kira had gathered on the northward journey. Given the number of herbs that grew there, she was hopeful fireweed might too, although she could recall no drifts of leaf-fall. Tierken would refuse if she simply *asked* for time to search so she waited until he had eaten before she approached his fire. 'I request speech with you, Feailner,' she said formally.

The patrolmen's conversation faltered and he rose and came away from the fire. 'What is it?'

'I wish to search the ridges for fireweed.'

'Our trade was for a southward journey of seven days. I'm not extending it to eight.'

'I wish to trade with you for the time between dawn and midday.'

His eyes glittered in the drift of firelight. 'What do you offer?'

'The mare.'

'She was a gift!'

'And so mine to trade,' said Kira steadily.

'I thought you had affection for her but you don't seem to have affection for anything *or* anyone.'

The words hurt and she winced. 'I need time, Feailner, and if you won't gift it to me, I must trade for it.'

His gaze remained hard but when he finally spoke, the anger had gone from his voice. 'Have your time, Kira, but you'll have the patrol with you. And keep the mare, she's yours.'

'I thank you, Tierken.'

Despite the patrolmen's aid, Kira's search elicited nothing more than sorren, silvermint and frost-burned tagenwort. They went on and she scanned her surroundings with increasing urgency. If Caledon were right and the fighting was widespread, the wounded would end up in Sarnia and without fireweed, they would die.

That night they camped without shelter and water. It was another half day's ride to Barrow Soak, Jonred told her, and the horses would have to wait till then. No one said it, but Kira knew she had delayed the patrol for nothing.

Cloud rolled in overnight making for a grey morning and they reached Barrow Soak and watered the horses, then ate maizen biscuit as they rode. It was as dusk closed in again that a darker stripe appeared in the distance. 'The edge of the Tain lands,' said Vardrin, noticing her gaze.

'We'll reach Maraschin tonight?' asked Kira eagerly.

Vardrin shook his head. 'We're to make camp at Mendor Soak but that won't be until after the night's turned. Tomorrow we pass east of Mendor Spur and cross the Baia Plain. All going well, we should reach the Tain city by nightfall.'

Cloud drowned the moon and it had started to rain, a fine veil of chill droplets, when a scout galloped back. Kira's heart lurched. She had no idea what he yelled but Tierken shouted orders in Terak and Caledon bawled them in Tain, and then they spurred off into the gloom with King's Guard pounding after them.

Marin's commands were quieter but patrolmen formed up in front and behind her, Jonred and Vardrin drew so close their knees rubbed hers. She strained into the murk, heart pounding, unable to see anything, but she could hear some sort of commotion ahead and, as the patrolmen set arrows, Kira realized they had stumbled on an attack.

213

Tierken galloped beside Caledon and threw himself sideways as a spear whistled past his head. Caledon shouted orders in Tain and Onespeak for the King's Guard to split to encircle the attackers but Tierken kept Kalos at a gallop and braced as Kalos's mighty chest slammed into an Ashmiri horse. He slashed down with his sword as he hacked a passage through the Shargh, the Guard driving forward too, using swords rather than arrows, to reach the herders trapped in the melee.

As the battle raged, the Shargh grew desperate to break out of the Guard's encirclement. Spears were flung and a Guard's horse went down. They hacked at its rider and as Guard surged to their comrade's defence, the circle was breached and the Shargh stormed through and fled. A volley of Tain arrows followed them, felling two, and their riderless mounts disappeared into the night.

Tierken and Caledon set off in pursuit and the Shargh ponies strung out, no match for the speed of Kalos and Caledon's mount. Shargh favored spears and flatswords, not bows, and Tierken suspected they had spent their spear supply.

He galloped in parallel with the hindmost Shargh and Caledon galloped on the other side. The Shargh could neither diverge nor outpace them and Tierken dispatched him with a single arrow, then he and Caledon increased their pace to hem in and kill two more.

The night was suddenly quiet and Tierken wrenched Kalos to a halt. 'They've had the wits to separate,' panted Caledon.

'I counted seven, four remain,' said Tierken.

'They won't be far. They'll be watching.'

'You've fought the Shargh often?' Kalos snorted, keen to resume the chase, but Tierken held him steady.

'Too many times, of late. With your leave, Feailner, we should return to the herders. There might be some there who can still be saved.' Tierken nodded. Apart from anything else, he wanted the King's Guard back with Kira.

Marin had imposed order on the chaos by the time they returned. Fires had been set, the surviving herders corralled safely together, and the dead removed. The Shargh lay in a heap beyond the firelight and the herders had been laid out respectfully to one side. Tierken received Jonred's brief report then went to where Marin and Kira tended the wounded. Marin stitched the Guard called Remas, whose chest and arms were covered in stabs and slashes; a second Guard lay next to him unconscious; and a third, a patrolman, lay gasping on his side. His back was slashed and Tierken's jaw clenched as he recognized Kanil.

He watched Kira turn Kanil so he lay on the wound. It contradicted everything he knew of healing but he resisted the urge to intervene. Kira's face was almost as pale as Kanil's as she unbuttoned his jacket and shirt, shut her eyes and lay her hands on his chest. Even in the firelight, Tierken saw her blanch, then she turned her head and retched.

He caught her arm. 'Kira. Are you ill?'

'Fetch my pack, will you,' she said, her attention on Kanil. Tierken hurriedly retrieved it from beside Marin. 'Help me turn him,' she instructed. Kanil's eyes were open and he no longer panted.

'You took his pain,' said Tierken in wonder. Kira was busy cutting Kanil's jacket and shirt away from the wound and he watched her lathe on a paste. Tierken had seen Eris

215

heal all through his growing, and had gathered with her, but he had never seen or smelled this herb. 'What is it?'

'Fireweed.'

Kira recapped the pot, wiped her hands on her trousers and pulled out a length of stitchweed. The second wounded Guard groaned and she glanced at him anxiously. 'Fireweed? Isn't that what you searched for at Shally Spring?'

She looked at him for the first time, her eyes dull in the fire's flames. 'It burns away the filth the Shargh put on their swords. Without fireweed, men die. I searched in Kessom for it but found nothing. Laryia tells me there's no dense leaf-fall and soaks around Sarnia, so it's unlikely to be there. I fear it mightn't be *anywhere* in the north. I *must* have it, Tierken.'

'It's what you searched for near Maraschin, when the Shargh took you,' he said slowly, the risk she had taken suddenly making a terrible sense.

'Yes. I found a supply and managed to get some to one of the gatherers before—' she faltered then the second Guard groaned and her attention jerked to him. 'Can you stitch?' she asked.

Tierken nodded, Eris had insisted he and Laryia learn. 'You're not going to take pain again, are you?'

She ignored him and he gritted his teeth as she unbuttoned the Guard's shirt and jacket and lay her hands on his chest. Her face contorted and she swayed.

'I'll stitch him, Feailner,' said Marin, taking the stitchweed from him.

Tierken helped Kira away from the fire and held his waterskin while she drank. 'I told you in Kessom you're *not* to take pain.'

'Tremen Healing doesn't bow before Terak swords.'

216

She said it ironically but she was still unsteady and he tightened his grip on her arm. 'I've *never* asked you to bow before me!'

'Not in as many words.'

'Have you the fireweed, Lady?' asked Marin, appearing beside them.

Kira nodded and as he watched her go back to the fire, it struck him that she healed with the same desperation that he fought and that, for all Poerin's training, until this night, he had never actually *had* to fight. Caledon had, and for a Placidien who charted his life by the stars, he had done so with brutal efficiency. He was a man Tierken could learn from *if* he chose.

Arkendrin and his warriors sheltered in an abandoned wooden sorcha in the place the Tain called Westlans. They were well-protected from the foul weather, unlike the Weshargh and Soushargh further north. Messengers moved between them and Arkendrin knew the attack by Orbdargan and Yrshin's warriors on herders had been thwarted by the arrival of Northern fighters, an ill chance that demonstrated the Sky Chiefs' disfavor.

The Ashmiri missed nothing that moved on the plain and reported the Northern fighters included the Northern chief *and* the gold-eyed creature. Ashmiridin's seed had granted it protection but that was irrelevant to Arkendrin. Only the Sky Chiefs determined what lived or died! The Sky Chiefs had delivered the creature into his hands before and if he granted them the respect they demanded, would do so again. And this time, there would be no delay to its destruction.

Tierken grimly surveyed their party knowing their pace made them vulnerable and there was nothing he could do about it. The wounded must be carried and now they had herder children with them too. They rode atop the horses, the surviving adults having gone in search of their scattered animals, despite the new Guard Leader, Belzen, remonstrating with them to stay under the Guard's protection. Tierken glanced at the grubby, blood-stained children. Death by the Shargh's hand or death by starvation at the loss of their animals; it was a cruel choice.

The plain was open here, between the jut of Mendor Spur and Task Tor, which made a surprise attack impossible, but it would be a different tale when night fell. He slowed Kalos so that Caledon came level. 'Twenty-eight to protect eight,' said Caledon, echoing Tierken's thoughts.

'It should be enough.'

'*If* more warriors haven't joined the attackers and *if* they don't know Kira's with us. I learned in Allogrenia just how desperate they were to take her and of how she survived only because the honor of her death was reserved for the Shargh leader.'

'*If* they know she's with us, their attack will be very precise,' said Tierken grimly.

'Yes *and* ruthless. Protector Commander Kest told me they drove straight through his men, reckless of their own lives.'

'And we've got children and wounded.'

Caledon nodded. 'The Shargh know we won't sacrifice them. Their intention might be to take Kira rather than kill her, as they did last time. *If* they know she's with us, *with you*, they'll judge her more useful alive than dead.' Caledon paused. 'After all, what would the Terak Feailner not give to get her back?'

Tierken eyed him coldly. 'And what would the *Placidien* Caledon e Saridon e Talliel not give?'

Caledon held his gaze. 'Caledon e Saridon e Talliel would give everything, including the stars.'

They set camp soon after sunset, Tierken having decided it would be easier to defend a stationary group illuminated by well-placed fires than a group strung out in the darkness, especially one that included children and the wounded. He placed Kira, the wounded, and the children around the central fire, so that to reach her, the Shargh must fight through the mounted guard and the rest of the men, *unless* they used fire as weapon, as Caledon said they had in Allogrenia.

He'd had most of the day to consider other strategies to protect her and once camp was set, he took Jonred, Vardrin and Anvorn aside. They were his most trusted fighters and he kept his voice low as he gave them their orders.

If things turned ill, they were to abandon the patrol and take Kira straight to Maraschin. Terak horses had the speed and stamina to outrun anything the Shargh rode but his plans would go amiss if Kira delayed them by arguing.

Tierken waited until she had finished changing Remas's bandages and washed her hands, before he took her to where Kalos and her mare were tethered, and outlined his men's orders. 'Do you think they know I'm here?' she asked.

'If they attack they will and then we can expect attacks all the way to Maraschin.'

She looked back to the fire. 'I've often wondered why I, a Healer, cause so much death.'

She looked so desolate he fought the urge to take her in his arms. 'The Shargh are a brutal people,' he said brusquely. 'The fault's not yours.'

'So, I've been told and yet death follows me.'

'Not this time. I've described what will happen if we come under attack but unless you obey Jonred's orders *immediately*, you will risk *everyone's* lives. No argument and no delay, Kira. I need your pledge.'

The drift of firelight gilded the fine planes of her face and he cursed his men's proximity. He wanted her in his arms and he wanted her safe. '*My* pledge, Feailner? Something I can break if the *whim* takes me? I didn't think *my* pledge was good enough for you.'

'I need your pledge, Kira,' he repeated, ignoring her allusion to bonding.

'Tremen Leader Feailner Kiraon of Kashclan pledges the Feailner of the Terak Kirillian, that should we come under attack, she won't risk his men's lives by arguing with them.'

Sarcasm had replaced irony but he had what he wanted. 'The Terak Feailner thanks the Tremen Feailner,' he said with a bow.

The night passed uneventfully and by dawn, the men not guarding were breakfasting. Kira still slept and Tierken glanced at her as he drank cotzee with Caledon. One of her hands lay palm upward on the sleeping-sheet, beautiful but bare. No rings or bracelets; nothing to show she was his.

Caledon followed his gaze. 'There was much I didn't understand about Kira until I went to the Southern Forests,' he said keeping his voice low. 'I didn't understand why she had so little regard for her own safety.'

Tierken shrugged. 'The young don't look beyond the moment.'

'She grew without a mother.'

'That's not unusual,' said Tierken shortly. 'My own mother died when I was less than five seasons.'

'I understand you and your sister were raised by your grandmother,' acknowledged Caledon. 'Forgive me, Feailner, if I intrude, but I understand you were raised with love. From what the leader of Kira's clan told me, that wasn't so with her. She was left to her own devices until her healing rivaled her father's, and then he sought to suppress it. Kira poured all her affection into her younger brother Kandor. When he was killed, there was nothing to hold her in Allogrenia.'

'Why tell me this?'

'To help keep her safe.'

Tierken rose and tossed his cotzee dregs into the fire. 'I need *no* help to keep her safe,' he said and strode away.

The rain started again later that morning, making for a cold and miserable journey and Kira felt the men's tension increased as low cloud obscured the juts of land to either side. The bearers meant they could not quicken their pace either. Kira was wet despite her cape and her discomfort worsened by anxiety for the wounded, especially Remas. If the rain did not ease, there would be no fires tonight to warm him.

She wondered if she could— Kira's mare snorted and then scouts screamed warning and she looked around wildly and gasped. Horses pounded towards them with terrifying speed. She heard Tierken's voice ring out, and then Jonred's. 'We go!' he shouted. Kira nodded and threw herself forward as spears rained down and then she was at a hard gallop, Jonred racing beside her, Vardrin and Anvorn thundering behind.

The screams of battle faded and the night filled with the pound and snort of their horses. The rain was full in their faces and the night so thick she could scarcely see ahead. She shook her head savagely to clear her sight and then there was a sickening thwack and a thud, and Jonred was no longer there. Vardrin shouted but Kira wrenched her mount around, her speed throwing the mare off balance, and the mare floundered, slipped, and went down.

Kira was aware of being airborne, of a sharp crack and pain when she hit the ground, and of hoofs pounding all around her. She struggled to get breath, to scrabble clear, but terror froze her. Shargh screams filled the night and then she was seized by rough hands.

25

The Shargh screamed their battle chants and broke in waves upon the patrol's defences but as Tierken parried and thrust he felt curiously calm, as if Peorin stood at his shoulder instead of Caledon. He was aware of the solid circle of men to his left and right but not of how much time passed, that awareness came more slowly. The night gradually emptied of the clash of swords and filled with the harsh pants of his men and the sobs of the herder children instead.

His chest heaved as he leaned on his sword. Five Shargh lay unmoving while another two dragged themselves further into the darkness; one of his men was on his knees, Marin beside him, and the rest cleaned their swords on the grass.

'We need . . . to keep . . . moving,' panted Caledon, as he sleeved the rain from his eyes. 'There'll be no . . . safety in making . . . camp.'

'You're right,' said Tierken scanning the darkness. 'I thank you for your help.'

'There's no need of thanks, Feailner. We fight . . . for the same things.'

The rain eased as they continued their slow trek and dawn was close when they heard the unmistakable sound of hoofs. The men scrambled back into defensive positions and then Kalos raised his head and gave voice. There was an answering neigh and a silver horse cantered from the murk, reins trailing. It was Kira's mare and in the shocked silence that followed, the patrolmen's eyes slid to Tierken.

223

Marin strode forward and caught her. 'She's been down, Feailner.'

The mare's shoulder and knees were covered in mud and Tierken found his gaze drawn unwillingly to Caledon. The Tallien looked as grim as he felt. They went on and the growing light revealed the hoof prints of Jonred's party, deep cut and full of muddy water, a sign of swift travel.

The patrol stopped briefly to eat, but there was little conversation and Tierken could not choke down any food at all. 'What's done is done, Feailner,' said Marin, as he handed him cotzee. 'If she'd stayed with us, we'd have had a far bloodier battle, and they might have breached our defences.'

'They still might,' said Tierken.

Jonred scrambled up, seized Kira, and half threw her behind him, then slashed down at a dark shape and fended off another. Anvorn shouted as he drove his horse forward and metal squealed against metal. He wrenched her off the ground and she scarcely had time to clutch the saddle strap before Anvorn was at a flat gallop. The pain in her chest was agonizing and she screwed her eyes shut as she fought to hang on.

Another horse pounded behind them and she cringed as it drew inexorably closer. Then there was a shout in Terak and Kira was almost sick with relief to see Vardrin come alongside, Jonred behind. They were still galloping hard as dawn revealed the yellow stone of Maraschin's wall and a group of horsemen approaching at speed.

Anvorn cursed as he and Vardrin jagged their horses to a halt. The King's Guard stopped too and set arrows. There was an uneasy stand-off and Kira stuck her head out from behind Anvorn's back and winced as she sucked in air. 'I greet you . . . Guard Ather,' she called.

'My Lady, I didn't see you,' said Ather in astonishment.

'We've had a hard trip . . . and request your aid.' She struggled to get more air into her lungs. Speaking was harder than breathing and breathing was agony. 'May I present . . . Terak Kirillian patrolmen Anvorn, Vardrin and Jonred . . . without whom I would now . . . be dead. The Lord Caledon and your men . . . are behind us, escorting wounded. With them . . . are more Terak, and . . . the Terak Feailner.'

The King's Guard broke into excited speech and Ather ordered quiet, then conferred with the troop before he turned back. 'Guard Archorn will give you escort to Maraschin. The Guard and I will seek the rest of your troop, Lady,' said Ather. He shouted an order and the Guard galloped on past.

Archorn led Kira's party back to Maraschin and came alongside to speak to her as they passed through the gate. 'Your people are billeted in King's Hall, Lady,' he said. 'We go there now.'

Kira was desperate to see Tresen, but the pain in her ribs was making her light-headed. 'I need . . . to go to the Sanctum.'

Archorn peered at her. 'Are you injured, Lady?'

'Just cracked ribs,' she said, hoping they were not broken. 'Physick Aranz . . .will fix me.' They halted at the Sanctum and Anvorn carefully lowered her down. 'Go with Guard Archorn,' she told him. You all . . . need to rest. 'I'll join . . . you later.'

Jonred dismounted with a thump, his mud-covered boots stark against the paving. She was covered in mud

225

too, she realized dazedly. 'We stay with you, Lady,' he said.

Kira did not have the strength to argue and Jonred half carried her into the Receiving Room. Dumer stood in his usual spot and Kira had the wild idea that he had not moved since she had last seen him. He was in conversation with a troopsman dressed like a Protector, and Kira blinked. 'Tresen,' she mumbled, and fainted.

Tierken, Marin and Caledon contemplated Jonred's slain mount. The surrounding ground was so chopped up it was impossible to tell how many horses had been there, and Marin walked on, his gaze on the ground. 'Two riders went southward,' he said.

Tierken hoped they were his men, *with Kira*, but they could be Shargh, on Ashmiri horses, with Kira too. There was no sign of his men's bodies but there had obviously been a fight, and the whole party might have been terribly injured.

The scout yelled a warning and Tierken cursed and leapt back onto Kalos, and then bawled orders to his waiting men to take up defensive positions as a group of riders came into view. They went fast, but Caledon remained on the ground. 'King's Guard from Maraschin,' he said.

Tierken watched their approach. Twenty riders clad in the blue he had heard marked the King's House. They halted a little way off and Caledon went forward and spoke with their leader, then brought him back. 'I present Guard Leader Ather to the Feailner of the Terak Kirillian,' said Caledon formally. The Tain bowed low and Tierken nodded. 'Guard Leader Ather has word of those we seek.'

'Your men and the Lady Kira arrived in Maraschin a little after dawn, my Lord,' said Ather.

Tierken briefly shut his eyes. 'I thank you for your news, Guard Leader.

Tresen sat beside Kira's pallet, his fingers locked with hers as he watched her sleep. Her arrival, even with cracked ribs, was the only good thing that had happened since he had left Allogrenia. They had cleared the Azurcade forests in time to see the Tain Westlans burn and arrived in Maraschin to discover Kira had been captured by the Shargh over a moon earlier.

But he'd had little time to dwell on the appalling likelihood she was dead before the onslaught of carrier after carrier bearing wounded. Men, women, the old, children: the Shargh's slaughter had been indiscriminate.

If it had not been for the fireweed Kira had discovered on the day she was taken, the number of dead would have been horrendous. Even so, there were so many injured, that even with him and Arlen working with the physicks, he'd had little sleep in the half-moon he had been there.

Tresen sighed and smoothed the hair back from Kira's face. At least *she* lived and was here with him at last. One of the lesser physicks had washed the mud off and Tresen had dosed her with sickleseed, or *silverseed* as the Tain called it, and bound up her ribs. He had dressed the deep score on the arm of the man who had brought her in too. *Jonred*, he said his name was.

The men with Kira were Terak's seed but it seemed no more credible now, in the ripe light of midday, than it had at dawn. They were tall and muscular like the King's Guard and Archorn had invited them to bathe and eat,

227

but they remained in the Receiving Room, muddy and exhausted. Their orders were to guard Kira, one of them said.

Tresen knew from Jonred it had been their patrol that had rescued Kira from the Shargh and taken her north, and the fact Terak guards had brought her back suggested she had treatied with the Northern Leader, despite what Caledon had warned of.

More horses sounded outside and Tresen tensed as he listened for a summons, and when it did not come, relaxed again. Then he heard the march of feet, coming in his direction, and Dumer swept the curtain aside. He was accompanied by two men coated in dried mud and blood, and while Tresen recognized the Lord Caledon, he gasped as he noticed his companion. The man had golden skin and black hair, but Kandor's face and Kira's eyes.

Dumer nodded and withdrew, but the black-haired man was oblivious to all but Kira. He came to the pallet and lay the backs of his fingers on her cheek, the gesture so tender *and familiar*, that Tresen looked at Caledon in shock. His father said Kira was likely to bond with Caledon, but it did not look like it now.

'Healer Tresen,' said Caledon, 'I'm glad to see you made the journey to Maraschin safely.' Caledon was completely at ease and Tresen wondered if he had misunderstood Caledon's intentions towards Kira. 'I present Healer Tresen of Kashclan, Kira's clanmate, to the Feailner of the Terak *Kirillian*,' said Caledon, to the black-haired man.

Tresen used a deep bow to mask his astonishment. The *leader* of the Terak Kutan, no, *Kirillian*, he amended in confusion.

'Kira's spoken of you,' the Feailner said, his gaze still on Kira.

'King Adris awaits,' said Caledon after a little, and the Feailner's eyes finally came to Tresen's.

Their gold was extraordinary against his darker skin and his gaze both powerful and appraising. 'We will speak again, Tresen of Kashclan,' he said.

Irdodun squatted on the ground next to the fire and gently flexed his throbbing foot. One of the stinking Northerner's horses had trodden on it in the muddy darkness. He scowled. His own spear had felled a Northerner's horse and all Arkendrin had to do was kill the rider and take the creature, but the Northerner had wounded Irdodun's blood-tie Irstonin instead. Irdodun had carried him on his back, despite his injured foot, but the Sky Chief's had called Irstonin home.

Arkendrin had offered no aid to Irstonin *or* to him. All he had done was curse the Northerners and the creature, and muttered about Orbdargan and Yrshin whose attacks had prompted the Northerners' flight. But Irdodun had started to wonder just who was cursed.

Arkendrin said the Sky Chiefs would punish the Weshargh and Soushargh for their dishonor and yet it was *they* who suffered. Orbdargan and Yrshin's men traversed the lands close to the Sky Chiefs' domain *and* traded their feet for those of beasts and yet it was Urgundin, Urpalin, Orthaken, Ermashin and now Irstonin, as well as a host of lesser blood-ties, who now dwelt with the Sky Chiefs.

The possibility that it was *Arkendrin* who bequeathed them ill fortune was unsettling and Irdodun pulled his jacket close. The Sky Chiefs' realm might always be sunny, but he was not in any hurry to visit it.

26

Caledon sat drinking with Adris long after the Northern Feailner had been escorted to his rooms. The meeting between the two young leaders had gone more smoothly than Caledon had dared hope possible. Adris had been uncharacteristically restrained and the Feailner wary but courteous, and most importantly, they had both been willing to mend the long silence between their peoples *without* apportioning blame. They would meet again on the morrow to formally plan for what was to come.

Once the Northern Feailner had gone, Adris had produced a jug of ale and Caledon had described the state of affairs in Sarnia and his dealings with the Feailner in Sarnia and on the journey south. 'He's a highly skilled fighter, for all his Kessomi upbringing,' he said, 'and the Terak, and their Kir and Illian kin have lost none of the battle prowess that marked the Terak in the past.'

'We're going to need every bit of it,' said Adris grimly.

'The Feailner's spent the three years of his Feailnership bringing his men behind him and has their loyalty, but I believe there's still some difficulty with his uncle's former advisors in Sarnia.'

'He has my sympathy,' muttered Adris.

'The old dislike giving way to the young, and the young dislike taking advice from the old,' said Caledon diplomatically.

'Things have turned better than I dared hope a moon ago,' said Adris, wearily rubbing his face. 'The Alliance has been renewed and we have Tremen to aid us who, you've assured me, *can* fight.' He paused. 'And you have Kira back.'

Caledon shook his head. 'The Terak Feailner has Kira—at this moment.'

'I noticed their resemblance, of course,' said Adris cautiously.

'Yes,' said Caledon, refilling his mug. 'The seed of Terak meets the seed of Kasheron: a man and a woman united by a bitter history and by gold eyes. The stars' patterns are rarely so perfect.'

Adris said nothing and Caledon glanced sideways at him. 'You wonder whether I accept the stars' design or would undo it? You wonder whether I'll relinquish Kira to the Terak Feailner without so much as a murmur?' He emptied his mug and set it down. 'There's more to love than a sharing of flesh, Adris; there's trust and acceptance. The Terak Feailner gives Kira only his body and I don't believe that, in the end, it will be enough for her.' He paused. 'And what the *stars* intend is still unknown.'

It was dark when Kira woke and for a moment she had no idea where she was. A figure rose from beside the pallet and held a cup to her lips, and Kira savored the cool slide of water down her throat. The dregs of sickleseed were thick in her mouth, and her head so heavy with it she did not know whether it was near dawn or near dusk.

It was too dark to see who tended her but she knew the sense of him. 'Tresen,' she said in wonder. 'I thought I had dreamed you.'

His warm hand tightened on hers. 'It's so good to see you again clanmate and to know you're safe.'

231

'Have Tierken and Caledon and the rest of the men arrived?'

'Tierken?'

'The Terak Feailner.'

'They are here, but I don't know about the rest of the men, except for those who brought you.' He pushed the shutters open to let silvery light spill in.

'Is it near morning or night?' she asked.

'Near morning. You've slept an entire day.'

'An entire day,' said Kira in dismay. 'You shouldn't have given me sickleseed.'

'You have cracked ribs, Kira. We both know there must be sleep to heal.' He settled beside her again and took her hand.

'I don't have time to sleep,' she muttered. 'Tierken's only granted me three days before I have to go north again.'

'You let the leader of the Terak Kutan dictate where you can come and go?' asked Tresen in astonishment. 'What right has he?'

'They're the Terak *Kirillian*. *Kutan* is an insult they don't take kindly to.'

'Whatever they call themselves, they have no rights over the *Tremen* leader!'

'Tierken wanted me to stay safely in Sarnia so I pledged to spend no more than three days here,' said Kira thickly, struggling with the residual effects of sickleseed. 'Breaking my pledges isn't going to help us fight together.'

'So, Caledon was wrong?'

'Wrong?'

'He said the Terak Ku—*Kirillian* wouldn't accept the kin-link.'

'No, he wasn't wrong. The Terak Kirillian claim Kasheron and his followers went north over the seas.'

'So, this . . . this *Northerner* calls us liars, does he?'

'He calls our histories lies.'

'Same thing.' There was a short silence. 'He came here, you know, with Caledon, while you slept. Caledon led us to believe he was to bond with you but it looked more like the Northerner was.' Kira said nothing and Tresen leaned across the pallet. 'Well?'

'Well what?' she asked, struggling to focus. Curse the slow-headedness of sickleseed.

'*Did* Caledon lie to us? Did he pretend love for you to convince us to send men? Or in Caledon's absence, did you turn to the leader of the Northern swordsmen?'

'It's not as simple as that.'

'Whether you bow before a man who denies our very existence *is* simple, Kira!'

'He refused to bond if that's any comfort,' she mumbled.

Tresen stared at her aghast. 'You *wanted* to bond with that man? Stinking heartrot! You're the Tremen *leader*, Kira. To stay with him would mean to leave Allogrenia, *to leave us,* forever! Does Allogrenia mean so little to you that you would give it all away for the scion of the brute Kasheron fled?'

Tierken flicked back the curtain and Tresen froze, then strode past him out of the alcove. 'So, *would* you give Allogrenia away *for the scion of the brute Kasheron fled*?'

'Tresen thinks like I once did. Our tales lie about you as yours lie about us,' said Kira.

'You haven't answered the question.'

'I traded Allogrenia away for just three days here, remember, and I've already wasted one in sleep.' Even keeping her eyes open was an effort and she let them close.

'For three days here but not for me?'

'It was you who refused the bonding, Tierken,' she whispered, as she started to drift.

'I didn't understand what it meant,' he murmured. 'I still don't.' He bent and kissed her, but she was asleep.

Caledon watched the Terak Feailner closely. He was more closed than in the first meeting with Adris and Caledon wondered whether the presence of Soltin, Borzan and Tharoul undermined the tenuous trust of the previous night or whether something else was at play. Beris's advisors had insisted on joining the meeting and it was difficult for Adris to refuse. They sat together on one side of the Crown Room's large meeting table, while he, Adris, and the Northern Feailner sat on the other. It set up an unfortunate *confrontational* configuration but the advisors had arrived first.

'We should summon the Commander of the Tremen fighters, if we're to discuss strategies,' said Borzan, his immense brows bristling.

'I've spoken with their physick,' said Tharoul. 'He seems the only Tremen who knows Onespeak. He tells me the female physick who was here before commands the Tremen.' He peered at Adris. 'Is that true?'

Adris nodded. 'She is the Tremen Leader.'

'A female physick commanding men,' said Soltin, his voice heavy with disapproval. 'Why isn't she here now?'

'The Terak Alliance is with the Tain, not with the Tremen,' said the Northern Feailner shortly.

'That's true, but if we're to fight as three peoples, we must plan together,' persisted Soltin.

'Certainly, how the *third* peoples, the Tremen, are to fight with you must be resolved,' broke in Caledon smoothly, 'however not at this meeting. The Westlans burn and the Cashgar Shargh, Weshargh and Soushargh have joined. They ride Ashmiri horses and cross the Azurcades. But,' he paused, and let his gaze sweep those seated, 'evil sometimes seeds good. The long tradition of friendship between the Tain and the Terak Kirillian, has been rekindled. Our task today is to decide how this friendship is to be made the tool of the Shargh's destruction. What are your troopsmen's latest reports, King Adris?'

Adris outlined the most recent Shargh sightings and attacks, the responses of his men, and the strategies he had in place to protect woodcutters and herders. The tension in the room eased and after a little, Adris and the Northern Feailner discussed how and where their fighters could be deployed.

There were times when Caledon intervened to ease moments of difficulty or smooth over interjections by the old king's advisors, but these occasions became fewer as the morning drew on and by the time they paused to take their midday meal, Caledon felt confident enough to excuse himself from the meeting.

He made his way through the wintry sunshine down King's Way to the Sanctum, intending to see Kira and speak with Tresen, and then to seek out Pekrash, but Kira slept. Tresen did too in the chair beside her and Caledon was reminded of the closeness he had heard tell of in Allogrenia. *Kira and Kandor and Tresen*. He was glad Tresen had come north, despite the risks. The more people that gave Kira reason to live, the better.

He turned his feet back up King's Way, glancing down the side streets as he went. Despite the short time Adris had been king and the strength he must expend to fend off Shargh attacks, the city looked different. There was

235

evidence of gutters being repaired and more wagons at the gate with timber cut ready for building.

There was a long way to go before Maraschin matched Sarnia's grandeur but it would in the end. Caledon smiled dryly. Presuming, of course, the stars intended *them* to be victorious in the fighting and not the Shargh.

27

Kira slowly made her way up King's Way, Tresen's grip on her arm to steady her. Every step sent pain through her ribs but pain was easier to deal with than what lay ahead. She was the Tremen leader on her way to meet with the Tremen who had answered her call to reject everything Kasheron had fought for.

What was she to say to them? *Forget everything good you ever believed about Kasheron; it was his brother Terak we should have followed? You'll find more trust amongst the Tain who are strangers, than amongst the Terak who are kin? Thank you for coming to die?*

'You're tense,' said Tresen.

'Yes.'

'There's no need to be. The men are look forwarding to seeing you. You'll be greeted only with joy.'

'I can't bear the thought of them fighting out on the plain, away from the forest's Shelter, of killing and being killed,' she said hoarsely. 'And I can't even stay here with them to heal. I must return north.'

'You don't have to do *anything* the Northern Feailner says!'

'They have no Haelen, Tresen. I'm going north to make one.'

'And afterwards? Are you coming home or staying there?'

'I don't know.' Tresen had yet to realize none of them might survive the fighting. Spears and daggers were lethal, but taking pain had a price too and Sinarki and her daughter Tesrina had died young.

The Tremen were assembled next to the King's Hall stables, Pekrash at their head but Kira was dismayed to see Adris, Caledon and Tierken there too, *and* the King's Guard *and* Terak patrolmen lined up to either side. She had planned to speak to the Tremen alone but it seemed there were to be many witnesses.

Tresen gave her elbow a final squeeze, bowed briefly to Adris as Adris came forward, and joined the Protectors. Adris looked different, despite being dressed the same as she had last seen him. There was an air of confidence about him and contentment. He had what he had long wanted, she realized.

Kira bowed as low as her ribs allowed, and Adris raised her, and kissed her on each cheek.

'The Tain people welcome back Tremen Leader Feailner Kiraon of Kashclan and rejoice in her safe return.'

'I thank you for your welcome,' said Kira, struggling to meet his black eyes. 'The Tremen offer you our best wishes for a long and wise kingship,' she added, hoping the spirit of her words was acceptable, if not their form.

Adris nodded graciously. 'I know you are keen to speak with your people, but after you've done so, I invite you and Commander Pekrash to join myself, the Terak Feailner and Lord Caledon in celebration of your safe return.'

'I thank you,' said Kira.

Adris nodded again and Kira turned to where the Tremen waited. She kept her attention on them, ignoring Caledon who stood with the King's Guard, and Tierken who waited with the Terak patrolmen.

She came to a stop, took the ring of rulership from around her neck, and held it aloft. 'I, Kiraon of Kashclan, daughter of Maxen and Fasarini, sister of Merek, Lern and Kandor, Leader of the Tremen by virtue of healing, thank you for offering your service in the protection of Allogrenia, the healing place that Kasheron, his followers and their descendants established, countless seasons past.'

A mutter broke out amongst the Terak patrolmen and she sensed Tierken's sharp gesture to silence it.

'We have lived always by healing, by the strength of the green and growing, by the ways of life and of living,' she continued. 'These ways have served us well; *Kasheron's* ways have served us well!'

Tresen's eyes burned into hers but she forced herself to look at *all* the Tremen. 'Healing gives life, mends bones, eases the old on their final journey, but Healing can't turn aside the sword; only metal can defeat metal. If we are to have Shelter again, to reclaim Allogrenia, to live without fear for those we love and for ourselves, we must use the weapons of those who seek to destroy us. We must either fight for Allogrenia, *for what Kasheron built*, or surrender it.

'This is a bitter realization, I know, and one I've struggled with. But we are not alone. The hatred of those who would destroy us, is directed at others as well. We do not fight just for ourselves but for them, and they fight for us.

'You have been welcomed to the Tain lands by King Adris, whose people suffer as we do, and will fight alongside the Tain troopsmen. The Tain have a long treaty of friendship and aid with the Terak *Kirillian*. The Terak *Kirillian*, whose lands lie to the north, will also fight.

'I was rescued from the Shargh by the *Terak* Feailner's men and the Terak *Kirillian* city of Sarnia has offered me generous hospitality since. The *Terak* Feailner and his men have now given me safe escort south to meet with you.'

A wave of speech erupted among the Tremen and those who had not noticed Tierken now stared at him openly. The Tremen were unskilled in hiding their feelings and their faces showed astonishment at his likeness to her, anger, and distrust.

Kira paused for the hubbub to subside. 'Shortly, the *Terak* Feailner, King Adris, Lord Caledon, whose wisdom has guided our path so far, Commander Pekrash and I, will discuss what is to come. Then I will return north, for the northern city has need of a Haelen to heal those who will suffer injury in the coming fighting.'

Kira looked at each Tremen face in turn to imprint them on her memory. Before this was over, *all* of them might be dead. 'I thank Commander Pekrash for leading you out of the Southern Forests, and I thank him for his part in what is to come,' she said thickly. 'May the alwaysgreen Shelter you and guide your way; may its shadow bring you home again, lest . . .'

Kira faltered. How could the alwaysgreen protect them against swords?

She blinked hard and heard Pekrash shout orders and feet scuff the paving as they moved off. The King's Guard and Terak patrolmen dispersed too, Marin's gruff voice issuing curt instructions, as Tresen came to her side. 'I'll go back to the Sanctum and relieve Arlen,' he said. 'The Tain Guard who came south with you isn't any better.'

'Remas?' asked Kira, appalled she had neglected him. 'I should have—'

'Taken his pain? You've got enough of your own.'

'But—'

240

Tresen raised his hand. 'You don't need to do *everything*, Kira, as I've said before.' He glanced beyond her shoulder. 'The Tain King is waiting for you. You spoke well,' he added softly, and kissed her cheek.

Despite Adris's suggestion the meal was to celebrate Kira's return, the conversation concentrated on the attacks, the movement of Shargh, and how their own men would be deployed and supplied. Pekrash was better informed and more skilled in all the areas discussed, and Kira's thoughts turned to Remas. Sitting was painful too, and when the empty platters were finally replaced with the fruit and ale that marked the end of a Tain meal, she stood carefully, and bowed in Adris's direction.

'I thank you for the honor you've accorded me, King Adris, and beg leave to return to the Sanctum to tend Guard Leader Remas and others who were injured on the journey south.'

Adris inclined his head. 'By all means.'

'Please excuse me for a moment also,' said Tierken. 'I require speech with the Tremen Leader.' Tierken followed her out, the room silent as he pulled the door closed behind them. She could already see he was annoyed. 'I've not authorized the building of a Haelen in Sarnia, Kira, and nor will I.'

'I'm not *building* one, Feailner. I'll convert the abandoned stable near the gate.'

'Sarnia has no need of healing nor welcomes it.'

Kira stilled. There it was in a nutshell, the gulf between Terak and Kasheron, but she bit back a retort. She fought for healing now, not for victory in her on-going squabble with Tierken. 'Where are you going to send the wounded?'

she asked instead. 'Kessom? How's a bearer to traverse the Tiar Lookround?'

'The fighting will stay on the southern Sarsalin and the wounded be brought here.'

'That's not what Caledon believes.'

'Caledon e Saridon e Talliel doesn't know everything!'

'Neither do you. If *he's* wrong, you're going to have a very clean stable. If *you're* wrong, your men will die. Which would you prefer?'

'The Terak won't accept a Haelen on top of the news that—'

Her anger fired, despite her best intentions. 'I *won't* watch people die and do nothing!' she said and strode off.

'Kira!' She forced herself to stop and winced as her ribs throbbed. He came level and lowered his voice. 'We need time to speak *properly* but there never seems to be any,' he said. His closeness woke her need of him and she wanted to be in his arms, to have the wonder of his Shelter, but his gaze was on the men at the stables. 'I must return to the meeting. In the meantime, don't do anything to worsen your ribs,' he said, and turned back to the Crown Rooms.

Kira glanced across at the stables too. Some of the Terak horses were saddled and patrolmen wore their packs as they clipped waterskins to their harness. She made her way over to where Marin supervised. 'I'm pleased to see you from your bed, Lady,' he said.

'Are you going on scout?'

'We return to Sarnia.'

'Sarnia? The Feailner's going too?' asked Kira in confusion.

'The Feailner remains here. We return to Sarnia to send patrols south.'

'Then I must go with you!'

'We travel fast with just half a patrol. I doubt your ribs will take it, Lady.'

'I have herbs to dull the pain,' said Kira, knowing she could not take sickleseed *and* sit a horse. 'You're aware of the Feailner's orders that I return to the north within three days?' Marin nodded. 'Today is the third. Will you bring my mare to the gate?' Marin still looked at her doubtfully and she rushed on. 'It will be *quicker* as I must visit the Sanctum first and I don't want to anger the Feailner by *disobeying* his orders or *delaying* you.'

Marin nodded. 'Be swift. My orders are to leave immediately.'

Kira went down King's Way as quickly as her ribs allowed, collected her pack, and went on through the Sanctum to the Garden Room. Every pallet was occupied, but eerily quiet, the groans of the injured quelled by unconsciousness.

Aranz stitched a wounded man and nodded as she went past and she found Tresen in the alcove nearest the end. At first Kira thought he tended an elderly man, but it was Remas, as hollow as a stickspider shell and beyond anything she could offer. 'He's not in pain,' said Tresen. 'We've given him a good death. And the other wounded will recover, thanks to the fireweed and the knowing you've passed onto the physicks.' Then he noticed her pack. 'What—'

'I'm going north, Tresen. I've come to say goodbye.'

'You can't ride with those ribs!'

'They're feeling better and it's the end of my third day.'

'Stinking heartrot, Kira! You don't need to do *anything* that man says!'

'I made an agreement, Tresen. Would you have the Terak Feailner call the Tremen Feailner faithless?'

'He denies *us* and he denies *you*!' He took her by the shoulders. 'Free yourself from him, Kira!'

'He has Kandor's face.'

'But not his heart!'

'I love him, Tresen.' It was the first time she had admitted it and she made an unsuccessful attempt to smile. 'And even if I didn't, the north *must* have a Haelen. Healing *will* win, despite the sword!' She managed to steady and kissed him on the cheek. 'Farewell Tresen and stay safe.'

Tresen shook his head. 'I thought no parting could be harder than the last, but I was wrong. And we've had no time together.' He took a deep breath. 'May the alwaysgreen Shelter you and guide your way; may its shadow bring you home again, lest you stray.' Then he hugged her, careful not to touch her chest. 'Stay safe, clanmate,' he whispered.

Marin cursed silently as he stared at the impassive face of the blue-clad Guard. He was the third Marin had spoken to and he was still no closer to knowing the Feailner's whereabouts. *King Adris, the Lord Caledon, Commander Pekrash and the Terak Feailner are no longer in the Crown Rooms*, the Guard said. Knowing where they *weren't*, was hardly helpful, thought Marin sourly. Time slipped away and he glanced over at the stables, to where his increasingly restless men waited. The fact that the Lady Kira's mare had been taken to the gates, and that she might be beyond them, weighed on him too.

He should have conferred with the Feailner *before* he'd had the mare prepared, but even as the thought crossed his mind, he realized *his* Feailner did not have authority over the *Tremen* Feailner. Her speech had made her status plain and the understanding helped him reach a decision.

His orders, at least, were clear, and he could delay no longer in carrying them out. He returned to his men, vaulted on to his horse, and led them down to the gate, as fast as the crowded streets allowed.

Kira kept her mare at an easy canter, far enough from the wall not to tempt Marin to return her to Maraschin, but not so far his patrol would not catch her before dusk. The mare's gait was just bearable, unlike when she trotted; which was excruciating. At a canter, the bruise-ease and bindings reduced the pain of her ribs to a constant throb, and she had a good supply of bruise-ease to apply as they journeyed. She just hoped it would dull the pain enough for her to reach Sarnia.

Arkendrin stood at the edge of the trees, his warriors silent behind him. The massive wooden gate of the Tain wall was made small by distance, but not so small he could not see who came and went. A single rider had come out, and sometime later, a group of filthy Northern horsemen had followed. Even had it been night, he would have known the rider was the creature of the Telling. The Sky Chiefs' had gifted him the ability to sense its foul presence *and* to predict its movements.

It went north, using the legs of a beast, but it would not escape him. Soon his warriors would come together with

Orbdargan and Yrshin's warriors, who now tested their strength as wolves did, in small, swiftly moving packs. United they would sweep the stinking Northern robbers from the lands, then the creature would be his, and the highest sorcha on the Grounds, and all else he desired.

His eyes glittered as he palmed skywards, thanking the Sky Chiefs for their beneficence. Then he beckoned his warriors and turned north.

End of The Kira Chronicles series: Book 4
The Thunder of Hoofs

Continue Kira's story in Book 5 The Crying of Birds or enjoy the whole series in a single book: The Kira Chronicles – Complete 6 Book Series

Take a peek at Book 5

The door was flung open and Laryia and the Keeper appeared. Niria glanced at them, bowed, and left.

Laryia came forward and caught Kira's hands, her eyes huge in her pale face. 'Kira, I'm sorry, I'm so sorry.'

Kira's gaze jerked between her and the Keeper, and a macabre bargain started in her head. If the Terak gods granted her a single life, whose would she choose: Tierken, Caledon or Tresen's? 'Who?' she whispered.

'Healer Tresen,' said the Keeper.

The room swayed and the Keeper lowered her onto a chair. Laryia crouched in front, still gripping her hands. 'He's at the Haelen, Kira.'

Kira stared at her in astonishment. 'He's *here*?'

'He's terribly wounded Kira. He can't be saved.'

Kira threw herself from the chair and fled. She took

the steps two at a time, sprinted across the square and down the dark, rain-slicked Domain path. Sleet sliced her face and her ribs screamed as she reached the Haelen and slewed to a stop. Tresen lay motionless on a pallet, his face the color of wax.

'I'm sorry, Lady,' said Jonred, muddy and hollow-eyed. 'We traveled fast and without rest. The Feailner gave men to bring him. We've done what we could.'

Tresen had no pulse but Kira tore open his shirt and laid her hands on the cold skin of his chest. She expected empty blackness but found a torrent of fire instead. He was already engulfed in it, and she fought her way in after him. Kandor was lost to her but she refused to lose Tresen too.

Either we're together in life, Tresen, or we're together in death. He turned, but there was no peace in his face and no beauty, just agony as the fire devoured him. His eyes met hers and then she was burning too.

I hope you enjoyed *The Thunder of Hoofs Book 4 in The Kira Chronicles Series.* **Authors need reviews!** It is how our readers find us. I would love you to leave me an honest review on Amazon, Goodreads, or another of your favourite reader sites. Read on to discover my other books.

Works by K S Nikakis
Available on Amazon KDP and a range of digital platforms.

Non Fiction

Journey: Seeking the Sacred, Spirit and Soul in the Australian Wilderness

When we set out into the wilderness, what is it we really seek?

Do we seek new sights or do we seek new selves? And are we really on one journey or on two?

Journeying fifteen thousand kilometres into Australia's blood-red heart, Nikakis discovers that every journey is perilous, for travellers risk carrying the clutter of their outer lives with them; a clutter that blinds them to the other journey they crave; that of the inner soul-journey into a deeper understanding of self.

To enter Australia's vast Outback wilderness, is to enter a place of endless horizons; a place doused with brilliant gold dawns and dazzling sunsets; a place silvered by star-encrusted night skies and, most importantly, a place of hidden sacred places in whose deep stillness our inner journeys can at last unfold.

In the spirit of travellers like Robert Macfarlane and Scott Stillman, Nikakis asks what it is we really see, feel and understand when we follow in the steps of those who have gone before us deep into the wilderness.

Drawing on her Ph.D. in Joseph Campbell's hero myth, and using original poetry and novel extracts, Nikakis takes us on this second journey; a journey of the sacred, spirit and soul, where our inner selves finally have the time and space to gift us richer and more fully-realised lives.

Fantasy Novel Series

Angel Caste 5 Book Series – available complete in one book or as five individual books: Angel Blood, Angel Breath, Angel Bone, Angel Bound, Angel Blessed.

Angel Caste – Complete 5 Book Series - *A modern female hero on a timeless quest*

A troubled half-angel, a beautiful angel guide, a binding promise . . .

Viv is on day release from jail to attend the funeral of the thug she thinks is her father, when she comes face to face with her real father, the powerful angel Archae Kald. If finding out she's a half-angel isn't shocking enough, Viv discovers her mother isn't dead after all but lost somewhere in the tangle of worlds called the Rynth.

Determined to find the only person who has ever truly loved her, Viv goes to Kald's angel world where he appoints the beautiful Thris as her guide. Thris is kind and caring, unlike the males Viv has known before, but after living on the streets, Viv finds it almost impossible to trust.

Friendship grows as Thris trains her to travel the rifts, but the Rynth is a dark and dangerous place, even for angels and, as Thris grows increasingly tempted by Viv's emerging angel traits, disaster strikes.

Viv journeys on alone and stumbles into a war zone where she finds a lost child. She pledges to take the child to safety but, as the war rages on, deciding who is friend and who is enemy becomes a deadly game of chance.

Bound by his promise to guide Viv to her mother, Thris embarks on a desperate search for her, but a greater threat confronts them both and, in the end, they must fight not just for their own lives, but for the lives of those they love.

The Kira Chronicles - 6 Book Series – available complete in one book or as six individual books: The Whisper of Leaves, The Silence of Stone, The Secrets of Stars, The Thunder of Hoofs, The Crying of Birds, The Music of Home.

The Kira Chronicles – Complete 6 Book Series – *traditional fantasy with deep forests and high stakes*

A gold-eyed Healer, a prophecy, two brothers at war.

In seasons long past, twin gold-eyed princes sundered a kingdom. Rejecting his brother Terak's warrior ways, Kasheron led his people deep into the great southern forests and established the healing settlement of Allogrenia. The Tremen flourished, upholding Kasheron's legacy of peace and healing, and protected by the vast, trackless trees.

All Tremen delight in the healing arts, but Kira is the greatest Healer of them all.

To the north of Allogrenia, drought ravages the Shargh's land, and as their suffering escalates, the chief's younger brother seizes on an ancient prophecy to snatch the chiefship for himself. The prophecy links the Shargh's doom to a gold-eyed Healer, and Kira has gold eyes.

The Shargh attack with devastating consequences and Kira must fight to save the wounded, but the Shargh wounds rot, no matter her skill, and Kira finds herself in a deadly race against time. As the slaughter continues, she makes the horrifying discovery that the Shargh hunt her. To halt the attacks and save her people, she sets off for the North to seek aid from her long sundered warrior kin.

But the dangers beyond the forests exceed even the Shargh attacks. The Tremen detest their warrior kin but Terak's descendants have inflicted a worse fate on the Tremen. Kira's new-found love is torn apart by ancient hostilities and when trust turns to betrayal, it risks everything she fought for.

As the battles rage on, Kira becomes increasingly sickened by the bloodshed. Desperate to end the suffering once and for all, she sets out on a quest that could cost her everything and everyone she loves.

Fantasy Novels

The Emerald Serpent – *the Celtic Fae in a fight for survival*

Book trailer: https://www.youtube.com/watch?v=bGpKxnpCEMg

Betrayal, torture, death: Etaine lives on only to destroy those who robbed her of everything she loved.

Seven years before, Etaine met fellow Ranger Cormac, the he-Eadar she believed was her longed-for true-mate. Emerald-eyed, white-skinned, and black-haired, the Eadar had formed into Ranger bands to fight the Fada, invading religious zealots determined to replace the Eadar's Serpent Goddess with their own gods of stone.

The pure blood of the ancient Eadar runs strong in Etaine and Cormac's veins, and their joining had the potential to open the Emerald and Serpent Ways to them, old worlds only true Eadar can enter. But their love affair goes tragically amiss, with catastrophic consequences.

Etaine flees and as the years pass, slowly rebuilds her life, but the Fada's attacks grow more ferocious, and the Eadar are forced to fight for their very existence. When the Fada mass to commit yet more bloody slaughter, and the bands join in a final, desperate effort to defeat them, Etaine comes under Cormac's command, the very last Eadar she ever wants to see again.

Together they have a weapon that can destroy the Fada, but to use it, Etaine must learn to trust again and Cormac to Remember. And time runs short: the Serpent rises.

Heart Hunter – *a female hunter on an impossible quest*

Fleet is a young Sceadu hunter: skilled, strong, and fast. She hunts deep into the icy mountains, seeking meat for her people, for the rains have failed and plunged the Sceaudu into hunger.

Her hunts are hard, but she has much to look forward to. Soon she will be gifted her air-name by the Sceadu's shaman, and then she will be a full adult, and free to marry the man she loves.

But while Fleet is on hunt, the old shaman dies, and the new shaman visions a very different future for her: cross the frozen, ice-locked mountains and complete a perilous quest or lose the man she loves forever.

In a moment of anger and frustration, Fleet commits a terrible wrong and sets out into the frigid mountains to atone with her life. In a journey that takes her deep into the earth's darkest places, into strange new worlds, and even into Death itself, she discovers that only she can save her people. To survive, she must draw on every shred of her hunter strength, and doing the impossible, it turns out, is just the beginning.

The Third Moon – *Science fantasy with a very human quest*

Where does the past end and the future begin?

Haunted by inherited memories of his people's dispossession and theft of their children, Warrain is just twelve years old when the nightmare repeats. But Warrain isn't living on Earth in the 21st Century, he is living on the planet Imago in the far flung future.

Five years before, Station One's Mech's got high on the opioid arrash, and in the bloodshed that followed, Warrain's scientific community were expelled from the Station, his father murdered, and his mother and unborn sibling lost to him.

The scientists carve out a rudimentary Station high in Imago's ranges, and Warrain's friends get on with their lives. Not Warrain; he climbs the Tors to stare down at Station One, dream of his mother and sibling, and plot revenge.

And then one day, everything changes. A third moon appears in the sky, one of Imago's life-forms calls him by name, and disease breaks out at Station One.

When the Mechs visit to seek help for their ill, Warrain seizes the opportunity to deal them a blow they will never forget. But the third moon brings changes that threaten them all and, to aid the life-form whose kind is being dispossessed and slaughtered, he must turn his back on the hate that has long sustained him and find another way to live.

Messenger – *a dystopic future filled with hope*

In a world made deaf by hatred, who will hear the messenger?

Severine's world ends the day her family is murdered. Being raised in the loving community of gay Travelers always marked her as an outsider, but being female puts her in mortal danger. Women are scarce, precious, and hunted.

When chance brings Severine face to face with the father she has never known, he assigns the son of his murdered best friend to guard her. They soon clash. Severine believes all men are violent brutes and Jeph resents his freedoms being curtailed.

An uneasy understanding grows but Jeph is glad to deliver her to the Enclaves, a sanctuary her father has carved out in the mountains for his women and children. But there is no safety in a world broken by war and sickness and when violence follows her, Severine flees to the northern city of Andhaka in search of a home amongst her mother's people. Jeph follows, bound by loyalty to her father, but the north holds terrible dangers for him.

It's been years since Andhaka has welcomed outsiders with anything but bullets, and to survive and to protect Jeph, Severine must learn to use her enemies' weapons against them. As the stakes rise, she comes to understand the horror of her mother's loss, and what drove her father north seventeen years before. His quest becomes her quest, but she hasn't counted on the savage legacy that war and sickness have left behind, or on falling in love.

I Heard the Wolf Call My Name – *gender-fluid shifters in search of home*

Finalist Best YA Novel – 2019 Aurealis Awards

Jax is just twelve years old and in bird-form high above his island home, when it explodes, killing everyone on it. He believes he is the only survivor until ten years later, he comes face to face with his boyhood friend, Matiu.

Matiu is military and the military need shifters for a crucial mission, but Jax refuses. Having spent ten long years burying his bizarre shifter past, he isn't about to resurrect it. But Matiu rouses other feelings too that Jax finds harder to ignore.

As the military ramps up pressure to force Jax's cooperation, he shifts to bird-form and flees to the last remaining island where he crash lands in the middle of Anahera's vision-quest. She searches for her skin-spirit animal to transform her into a protector of her people, and dreams of finding the white-wolf, but finds Jax instead. To save him she must abandon her quest but her kindness only adds to Jax's turmoil.

To decide who he truly is and where he really belongs, he must first confront his painful past, but that isn't the worst of his problems. The forces that blew Jax's island out of existence now threaten Anahera's as well, and he might just be the only shifter who can save it.

And time is running out.

Fantasy Short Stories

The Gift – A Deep Fantasy Short Story #1 – free on my website at www.ksnikakis.com

Excerpt:

Thariel sat for a long time, surveying all around her, as if she ate the world that would soon be memory. Then she took the harness from the mare, and with soft words, thanked her and bade her farewell. Her own feet turned towards the forest, tossing her face-plate aside as she went, so that her hair fell loose to her waist, then she discarded her chest-armour, the sword and dagger, her bow and quiver.

The trees closed in and she came at last to the lake Men call Menios and stood for a while on its shore. An owl cried and a mouse shrieked, and all around her the souls of the newly dead jostled in their journey to the void. She stepped into the water and the new life inside her quivered.

'Fear not, little one,' she whispered, in her own tongue. 'We are going home.'

260

The Tale of Prince Anura – A Deep Fantasy Short Story
#2 – free on my website at www.ksnikakis.com

Excerpt:

I should have been happy, for she was beautiful. Dark rivers of curls, skin as white as moonlight on water, breasts softer than spawn, and she loved me well. But her chamber was small, no matter the comfort of her bed, and the old feelings of entrapment rose, as persistent as gas that bubbles from rot below still waters.

I sat at the casement and listened, as I had once loitered near the watery skin of the second world and waited. The moon grew large and small many times, but it came at last, as I knew it would. The soft lament on the night-time air, the song of a soul as confined as mine. It took me a journey of many days through the depths of a massive forest to find her tower.

Stone it was and sheer, and as remote as the third world's glimmer had once been. I sang to her and she answered with sweet melodies of her own and we made love as frogs do, with our voices. And when trust had built, she let down her shining ladder of golden hair.

Glass-Heart – A Deep Fantasy Short Story #3

Finalist Best YA Short Story, Aurealis Awards, 2019

Excerpt:

Geth moved amongst his band, exchanging quiet words while they waited. Some he had fought with since the Tallon's foul ships had first found their shores while others had come later, when the burn of cot and kin had sent them from their valleys.

Hate drove them but hate was no shield against arrow and knife. It was fighting skills that kept them hale, and Geth ensured they had them aplenty. He needed them living, not just for their own sakes and his, but for what would come later. When the Tallon's stain had been scoured away, the destroyed must be rebuilt.

Kyth sat alone and he went to her and gazed about. 'The glass-heart's fled, has it?'

'I sent her to a place of safety. She will come to me when it is over.'

'Safety was what I wanted for you!'

'And what I wanted for Nyar.' Her eyes caught the star-sheen as she looked up at him. 'But you can't always have what you want, can you, Ceannasai?'

Dragon Sprite – A Deep Fantasy Short Story #4

Excerpt:

Genn rocketed straight upwards, not just because she enjoyed seeing the limitless blue sky before her, but because a Waiwin's wing shape made vertical flight harder for them. Orin didn't try to catch her but swept in circles around her, gaining height in an ever-narrowing spiral. It was a clever tactic and one Genn didn't believe he had thought of in the instant she had cleared the trees. He had obviously studied her strategies and developed a plan to counter them or so he thought.

Genn waited until the spiral narrowed to axeel, the minimum distance a Waiwin must keep from a Velven unless she accepted him, then swerved towards him, narrowing the distance between them. Orin's eyes flashed to black, shocked she had accepted him, but before he could act, she folded her wings and dropped.

The strength that had driven Orin's pursuit had surged to his wing-tendrils in anticipation of locking them with hers and he would struggle even to stay airborne until it flowed back.